ADVANCE

"Gigi Little just gave noir mouth-to-mouth. *Who Killed One the Gun?* resuscitates what was last best about old school radio noir with a spectacular post-genre kick. Characters are numbers, numbers lose their linearity, and time itself is laid bare as an echo chamber. What is staged on the page is a storytelling field that reminds us that we are all always already out of time, and that recreating stories is what saves us. As intellectually stunning as it is creatively playful. A genre and gender-bending brilliant beat of a book."

—Lidia Yuknavitch, author of *Reading the Waves*

"A witty, whimsical, time-bending adventure that hums with hilarity and heart."
—Mo Daviau, author of *Epic and Lovely* and *Every Anxious Wave*

"You turn the page like opening the door in a fun house. You never know what's on the other side, but you know it was not what you expected. *Who Killed One the Gun?* manages to be fun yet mysterious. Gritty and yet, somehow, spiritual."

—Mark Russell, award-winning comic book writer and author of *Grimm and Grimmer*

"Someone died at the Dive and a private dick has to deal with déjà vu while looking for the one who did it in Gigi Little's daring and delightful debut. A super fun noir to lose yourself in, with a cast of characters that form an off-kilter mosaic of suspense."

—Kevin Sampsell, author of *This is Between Us*

"*Who Killed One the Gun?* is all at once a daring piece of speculative fiction, a hard-boiled noir, and a linguistic marvel. It effortlessly combines these genres while never detracting or ebbing from the suspense as our title character attempts to solve his own murder. While One the Gun is a man out of time, the novel has a lot to say about both our contemporary world and the nature of guilt."
—Brian S. Ellis, author of *Against Common Sense* and *Pretty Much the Last Hardcore Kid in This Town*

"If you love noir and parody and magical realism but can't imagine how you might find them all in one place, your search is over. In *Who Killed One the Gun?*, Gigi Little has created a whip-smart pastiche perfect for fans of Raymond Chandler, Franz Kafka, and Monty Python. I can't think of a time when I read anything quite as original. How did she do it? Strap yourselves in, guys and dolls. What a ride!"
—Liz Scott, author of *This Never Happened*

"Gigi Little's prose 'melts like honey on a hot biscuit.' One the Gun, with all his quirky wit, makes you turn the page as you attempt to solve his unique quandary. Told in a charming style all its own, this debut novel was an absolute joy to read."
—Bradley K. Rosen, author of *Bunkie Spills*

"Gigi Little has written a boozy love letter to a bygone era of noir detective radio plays. It's Perry Mason meets *Groundhog Day*. A slick ticking time machine of a whodunit. You can't help but root for the brooding antihero, a tragically flawed gumshoe chasing a cold killer and an ocean-eyed dame. *Who Killed One the Gun?* pops off its pages like a sizzling band of hard-boiled bullets chasing a runaway jazz train."
—David Ciminello, author of *The Queen of Steeplechase Park*

"Gigi Little's *Who Killed One the Gun?* puts the conventions of detective noir to far more playful and adventurous uses than we normally see. Combining a conceit that fuses the best aspects of *Groundhog Day* and *Casablanca* with spry, vivid prose, Little creates nothing short of a literary centaur, an experimental novel that will leave you guessing at the fates of One, Two, and the rest of her shadowy, endearingly numerical crew until you turn that final page."
—Kurt Baumeister, author of *Twilight of the Gods*

"*Who Killed One the Gun?* has all my favorite things: crackling prose, mysteries upon mysteries within time loops, a cast of shady characters who are more than the archetypes they appear to be, and a thrilling adventure with a genuinely satisfying and surprising ending. Like all the best mysteries, the pieces that fall into place reveal different facets to the story so far, while stretching the confines of what a detective story can be. The story is so sharp and the writing so masterful, Gigi Little's debut novel will leave you clamoring for more."
—Michelle Carroll, bookseller, Powell's Books Inc.

"A snappy noir with a *Groundhog Day* twist. Good fun—and a very intriguing book club choice!"
—Tegan Tigani bookseller, Queen Anne Book Company LLC

"Both a hard-boiled detective story and a whimsical, existential meditation on destiny, self-determination, and forgiveness. *Who Killed One the Gun?* rises above its hard-boiled formula to become a heartfelt rumination on how to live life to the fullest."
—Ho Lin, *Foreword Reviews*

WHO KILLED
ONE THE GUN?

WHO KILLED ONE THE GUN?

GIGI LITTLE

FOREST AVENUE PRESS
Portland, Oregon

© 2025 by Gigi Little

All rights reserved. No portion of this publication may be reproduced in any form, with the exception of reviewers quoting short passages, without the written permission of the publisher.

Library of Congress Cataloging-in-Publication Data

Names: Little, Gigi, 1969- author aut
  http://id.loc.gov/vocabulary/relators/aut
  http://id.loc.gov/authorities/names/n2016044216
  http://id.loc.gov/rwo/agents/n2016044216
Title: Who killed one the gun? / Gigi Little.
Description: Portland, Oregon : Forest Avenue Press, 2025.
Identifiers: LCCN 2025019660 (print) | LCCN 2025019661 (ebook) | ISBN
  9781942436683 epub | ISBN 9781942436676 paperback | ISBN 9781942436676paperback | ISBN 9781942436683epub
Subjects: | LCGFT: Noir fiction lcgft
  http://id.loc.gov/authorities/genreForms/gf20140 | Cozy mysteries lcgft
  http://id.loc.gov/authorities/genreForms/gf20190 | Novels lcgft
  http://id.loc.gov/authorities/genreForms/gf20150
Classification: LCC PS3612.I87556 (ebook) | LCC PS3612.I87556 W46 2025
  (print) | DDC 813/.6 23/eng/20250--dc02
LC record available at https://lccn.loc.gov/2025019660

Distributed by Publishers Group West
Printed in the U.S.

Forest Avenue Press LLC
P.O. Box 80134
Portland, OR 97280
forestavenuepress.com

1 2 3 4 5 6 7 8 9

For Tom Spanbauer

"Get this and get it straight! Crime is a sucker's road and those who travel it wind up in the gutter, the prison, or the grave."
—Introduction to *The Adventures of Philip Marlowe*
radio series airing 1948–1951

"When I got around to her eyes, they were the kind that make you think about hard-working geysers: deep and warm and you knew you could count on some fast action when they came to a boil. The smile was familiar, and her lips were red and moist like a souped-up rose waiting for a bee."
—*Pat Novak, for Hire*
"Georgie Lampson"
original radio air date: June 12, 1949

PROLOGUE

At twelve midnight on the eleventh of the month as the tower bells chime and the moon reflects ten thousand moons in the ten thousand windows of the city, chasing shadows across nine dark storefronts along the square, some certain moonbeam banks an eight-point ricochet and snaps a seven-second beeline to the six-story building on Fifth Street, where it shoots through a four-by-three-foot ground-level window of two-layer glass, straight to the basement floor where one wide circle of blood is spreading out around the body of one man.

One the Gun.

He has one minute to live.

ONE

THE BELLS ARE STILL CHIMING as he opens his eyes.

But now he is standing.

This is strange.

Strange enough that the walls to his left and right grab his ears and give a twist, trying to throw him back down onto the floor.

One the Gun shuts his eyes and tries to steady himself. Listens to another strike of the bell. Opens his eyes. The room stops spinning.

She's standing in front of him. This is strange, too, as she certainly wasn't here a moment ago. Such a look on her face. Eyes the color and size of oceans.

Two the True Blue.

He doesn't understand the light in the room. It's bright as day even as the midnight bells ring.

He doesn't understand the room. This is not the basement.

The troubled look on his assistant's face: She looks the way he feels. He sputters out the only thing he can think to say, "Miss Blue?"

"You looked so odd just now," she says. "Are you alright?"

"Of course!" he says, to shrug it off like a man—but actually, yes, truly, really, he's alright. He's not dead. Wasn't he just dead? About to be dead?

Two the True Blue has this radio show she listens to every Friday night and talks about constantly called *Who Is the Villain?*, a trite piece of schlock where the detective—one of those fakey radio detectives with nothing but brawn and clever quips—solves a different overblown case each week. The narrator's always saying ridiculous stuff like "the dame had the kind of eyes that made you want to melt like honey on a hot biscuit." And the victim's always coming to in a hospital bed asking, "Where am I? Where am I?" One the Gun tries to know where he is so that he doesn't have to ask this. He's not in the basement. He's in a room full of light.

Blank white walls and a couple windows. The open blinds shred the sunshine and leave it in stripes on the floor. A couch and chair, a beat-up old filing cabinet in the corner. Bookcase and desk. He's in his office.

One the Gun shakes his head. "I just got a little dizzy all of a sudden. I'm fine."

He needs to sit down.

"I think I'll just sit down."

One the Gun sits down.

He takes the couch where clients generally sit when they come to him to solve their very ordinary and unradiolike cases like *is my wife cheating on me?*, or *is my clerk siphoning twenty bucks a week from the company till?* Sometimes he gets more interesting assignments, yes, sometimes even a murder. One the Gun is on a murder case right now—no, not his own murder, that's a different case altogether. In fact it's not a case at all, in fact it didn't happen at all, he's pretty sure it didn't happen at all.

"Sir?" Two the True Blue's giving him the big blue eyes again.

He kicks out a laugh to show her he's fine and not at all hallucinating his own death in the middle of the night—day—in the middle of the day. "Don't mind me. It's just been . . ." He thinks about it. "A long morning."

She smiles. "Shall I continue?"

He doesn't know with what. He says, "Of course."

She takes a seat opposite him in the chair, looks down at the notepad he didn't notice before in her hand. "Well, the coroner's office confirms that the victim was killed with poison. It's a hard one to pronounce, but here goes."

She's telling him things he already knows, things she reported on yesterday, but he doesn't care. He settles back against the couch, happy to be here and not . . . wherever he . . . probably wasn't before.

"Police say that specific poison was also found in the storeroom in the form of rat poison. I have a box of it for you on the desk. The storeroom was unlocked at the time, but this poison is also not uncommon and could have been brought in by someone from the outside."

She shifts and crosses her legs under her pale peach cotton skirt. Two the True Blue has a heart-shaped face and the kind of beautiful innocence that would make any altar boy give up his ticket to heaven just to steal her lollipop. It's not just her innocence that's beautiful either. She's all-over beautiful. Just look at her there, smiling that smile that melts you like honey on a hot biscuit.

"The poison usually takes about twenty minutes to activate in the body. Once it went to work on the victim, it would have been quick," she says. "A few shocking moments of agony followed by violent convulsions, followed by unconsciousness, and finally death."

He can tell she's enjoying this. Delivering the fiendish details of this murder case. Maybe that's why she's going on about things she already told him yesterday. It probably makes her feel like the sidekick in that radio show she laps up every Friday night like honey on a hot biscuit. One the Gun wonders if he ate breakfast this morning. He remembers nothing of the morning. Did he have some sort of stroke? Temporary insanity? Did he go out last night and get tight and pass out, and was the whole death thing nothing but a booze dream?

He stands and starts pacing. His shoes hitting the worn wood floor say this isn't a dream. So does this very real office, dinky as a broom closet in a fleabag motel, with only space enough for one desk, which he and Miss Blue have to share. It's barely enough room for adequate pacing, but he can't sit still.

Two the True Blue glances from her notes, eyebrows up, but Gun's eyebrows and smile indicate that he would simply like to pace a bit while listening to her very interesting reporting and could she please continue.

"I've made appointments for you to talk to the witnesses and suspects," she says. Little punch of relish in her voice when she says *suspects*. "The doorman of the place, the bartender, that priest. I haven't reached out to the widow yet because I thought you might want to play a little more casual with her."

"Good choice," he says.

Two the True Blue always makes good choices. She's the best assistant a third-rate gumshoe could have. She comes into the office every day at eight when he's still at home sleeping, types up any notes he's recited into the dictation machine the night before—notes that generally come with instructions for her and research to do, which she does—and by the time he arrives at the office, usually around noon, she has all the information he needs, all his notes prepared, and his appointments made for the day. She's indispensable. Not to mention pretty as a stuffed pigeon on a fancy hat. Sophisticated like.

She stands and crosses to his desk in the corner. "I've jotted your appointments on the calendar. Want to have a look?"

He joins her, standing over the desk looking down. Her finger with a clean, filed nail points at a notation on the page. One o'clock time slot. *Meet with doorman at café.*

"I hope this works," she says. "He's on duty at the Dive Inn starting at three, and I wanted to give you a chance to really talk. He's an important witness. He was the one who discovered the body."

It's déjà vu. That's all this is. He didn't really experience this whole conversation yesterday, he's just feeling like he did. Maybe this déjà vu feeling is an aftereffect of the weird nightmare he had last night: the office . . . the power going out . . . him in the basement with the flashlight . . . the gunshot . . .

"Of course," he says, "that sounds perfect." The words coming out of his mouth feel like words he already said.

"Good. And then you'll want to go over to the church," she says. "The victim will be there in an open casket if you want to view him. And I've made an appointment for you to speak with the priest at two thirty. He was one of the last remaining patrons that night at the Dive Inn. Later this evening you'll go over to the Dive where you can speak to the bartender who was also on the scene at the time."

She's standing so close her shoulder brushes his. She smells like jasmine.

"Miss Blue?"

"Sir?" she asks.

"You ever get the feeling you're having déjà vu?"

"Mmm, every twice in a while," she says. "Oh, and don't forget to break for dinner. You know how you get on task. Now this poison." She turns to the bookcase beside the desk. With one hand on a shelf, she rises on tiptoe, lifting off one foot and using the ball of the other to raise herself even further and reach for the thick volume of *The Compleat Illustrated Pharmacopeia* on the high shelf. Sliding the book out and grabbing hold of it, she drops back onto both feet, teeters. Not truly like she's going to fall, but One the Gun, right behind her, catches her in a way that makes her tip back into his arms.

For just a moment she's in his arms.

Then the office door opens and a man walks in. He's annoyingly dashing with his gray tailored coat, homburg, and neatly trimmed whiskers.

Three the Goatee.

"Sweetie!" Two the True Blue steps out of One the Gun's grip, passing him the book. It's heavy in his hand. "We can continue talking about the poison later," she tells him, then turns back to her beau. "Lunch?"

Three the Goatee is shooting a suspicious single eyebrow, as carefully groomed as his whiskers, at One the Gun.

Watching the two of them is like watching a movie Gun has already seen.

"Oh, now." Miss Blue waves the incident away with the back of her hand. "I slipped pulling down a book. He caught me from falling." And then again: "Lunch?"

A hug, a peck on the mouth, Three the Goatee's shoulders relax, and he smiles. "Lunch!"

As Two the True Blue turns to snag a light jacket and pocketbook from the hook on the wall by the door, Three the Goatee angles his eyes back to One the Gun. He snaps a courteous, if chilly, nod of recognition. "Gun."

A short, formal nod back. "Professor."

Then Two the True Blue beams warmth on them both. "Sir, I'll be back in the office within the hour. Give a call with whatever you need." And the couple is off, leaving One the Gun alone at the start of a very strange day.

IT'S A SHORT WALK DOWN the square to the café where he meets his first witness on the case.

And again it's like he experienced this all before: This booth, that zigzag rip in the red-and-white checked tablecloth, the bustle of the place, clatter and chatter, but even that chatter feels familiar, like he already heard it. And this witness. Six and a half feet tall if he's a day, a moose of a man who's built more like a bouncer than a doorman.

Four the Door.

Even sitting down he's a towering hulk, all chest and shoulders, but something in his face, some puppy-dog slant in the way he looks at you, makes it seem like he doesn't at all notice his advantage. He's sipping from a glass of milk and picking at a plate of chicken. One the Gun works on a hamburger and a cup of coffee. Something in him thinks if he acts normal all of this very-not-normal will go away.

"I don't get it," the moose is saying. "I told all this stuff to the cops. Why I got to tell you too?"

"I like to get it in your own voice."

Four the Door rolls his half-full glass of milk between his palms like he's molding a flowerpot out of clay. "Well, how you want me to start?"

"How about with your relationship to the victim. He was your boss?"

"Best boss I ever had. Best job. Never was a doorman before him. You know, folks call it the Dive, but it's the Dive Inn." He taps the table to punctuate those two syllables, *Dive Inn*. "It's not a dive. It's a classy joint."

One the Gun has been to this classy joint.

It's a dive.

"How long have you worked there?" he asks.

The moose thinks about it. "Five years. Maybe eight."

"And you're basically a bouncer?"

The guy's shoulders rise up around his ears, offended. "Doorman, I told you, the doorman."

"Sorry, doorman."

Four the Door talks double-time, like a buffalo who grew up in a house of hyenas, and his mouth is full of more slang than teeth. "Listen, I didn't take this gig 'cause it's a soft buck, alright? I *mean* something. Like an ambassador. In a uniform with buttons. Make things ritzy-like. Sure, yeah, if some lout's got to start in on some beef and the boss gives me the eyes, I take care of it—I take care of it but good—but that's all part of being a doorman, get me?"

"And you were on duty the night your boss was killed?"

"Yeah. Three to close. All the regulars was there, the banker and his wife, them wino office jockeys, the lonely hearts, that preacher that's always scurrying around. Boss's wife was there, all the regular boys in the back room who's always—"

A pause. His eyes bounce around. He slurps at his milk.

"It's okay," One the Gun says, "I know there's gambling that goes on."

"No, Dive's a legit joint, a square deal, classy. No one's tossing jacks."

"Listen," One the Gun says, "if I'm to get the information I need, I've got to believe you're telling the truth. Now I've been to the Dive, I know what goes on in the back room. I'm not worried about it."

"Dive Inn," the moose corrects.

"Inn, yes."

Four the Door makes flowerpots of his milk again, looking down into the sloshing white. "I'm a good doorman. In a uniform with buttons. Classy."

One the Gun leans forward. "You know what? No matter what goes on in the back room, whether your boss ran an upscale supper club or some roach-infested crumb hole, that doesn't make a difference in how good you are at your job."

A grin spreads across the moose's face like . . . like what? Gun can't think of a metaphor. A waitress with doe eyes and big teeth steps up to their table and asks if they need anything, and One the Gun orders a hot biscuit and some honey.

"You sure eat a lot," the moose says.

At times it's as if this day is carrying One the Gun along rather than One the Gun moving through it. And there he'll be, letting one moment lead to the next and to the next like he's half watching, half participating in a movie of his own life—but then something will pull him out of the spell and he'll feel, again, that all of this happened before.

"So you're at the door all night?" One the Gun asks.

"Yeah, yeah, 'less I take a break."

"When was the last time you saw your boss alive?"

"About closing time," the moose says. "He tags by me at the door like always, says he's closing up. I ask who's still in. He says just his wife and the preacher. I don't get why that preacher's got to always be around so late. Don't he have to get up early and say his catechisms?"

"What was his mood when you saw him last?"

"Like a pussycat in a parakeet cage," Four the Door says, matter of fact.

One the Gun doesn't know if this means happy (lots of parakeets to eat) or sad (not a lot of space in a parakeet cage for a cat). He waits for more.

"Not like sick, if that's what you mean," Four the Door says. "Not like he was getting ready to pitch the big snooze."

Didn't Two the True Blue say this particular poison started working on the victim within twenty minutes of ingestion? Yes, and she also said it yesterday. He asks the guy, "You ever get the feeling you're having déjà vu?"

"Nuh-uh," the moose says. "But anyway, then the boss goes off to his office to count the take like always. I stick and let out the last of them, then lock up, go to the bar, fix myself a short one. I'm sagged, I mean, my egg is fried. You try standing all night on these cat sticks."

One the Gun doesn't know from cat sticks.

Four the Door says, "You getting all this, shamus?"

"Well, it's just you're a little hard to—"

"Listen," the moose says, "if you just took the hedgehogs out of your head holes, you could quit tossing horseshoes with your dear old auntie's flapjacks."

"Um," One the Gun says. "So then what happened?"

"I wait for the boss. I always pitch him good night last of all. He doesn't come out. Finally I go to the office door, knock. Nothing. Open the door and there he is."

The moose's smile is gone. He stares into his milk. "Best boss I ever had."

One the Gun gives him a moment. Breaks off a piece of biscuit, chews. Then: "The last folks in the place, in what order did they leave?"

Four the Door thinks. "Our bartender, he left first. Not long after I gabbed with the boss. Then pretty soon the preacher makes with the wings."

"The widow was the last to leave?" One the Gun asks.

"Don't say that with that look on your face."

"What look?"

"You guys always want to make out like someone's a murderer. She's not a murderer."

One the Gun thinks the moose doth protest too much. "Did I say anyone was a murderer?"

"You're a shamus, yeah? Why you scratching around if you're not snooping for a plugger?"

"Well, I've been employed by the insurance company to look into the—"

"Murder, yeah, I know. Well, she didn't do it. That I can tell you."

The most likely suspect, actually, is not the last person to leave. A smart killer would do the deed and get gone, let those left behind take the rap. The most likely suspect, if One the Gun is thinking off the top of his head, is this bartender. He pours the drinks. He could easily drop some poison into a glass with no one the wiser.

"The preacher," Four the Door says.

"Hmm?"

"If anyone dusted anyone, it's the preacher."

IT'S A SHORT WALK DOWN the square to Our Lady of Immaculate Numbers, a big gray stone fortress complete with steeple and stained-glass windows. At one end is the small funeral chapel. The place is as colorless as a snowman's long underwear: white walls, white stone floors, white pillars in every corner holding up white marble urns.

The casket—white—is set up on a pedestal in the center of the room. The man inside is wearing what looks like a ship captain's uniform. Brass buttons and striped epaulettes. On closer look you might notice those epaulettes are made of sequins and beads. A costume. He's wearing a white captain's hat with a black brim and gold braid. Because he's lying down, the hat is hiked up in front and showing some of his mostly bald head. Eyes closed and face appropriately peaceful.

Five the No Longer Alive.

A woman in black with strong square shoulders and more curves than a mountain switchback stands gazing down at the dead man. She's somewhere in her thirties, red lipstick and pearl-drop earrings, black gloves, no hat or veil. She has the kind of beauty that could melt the butter on your baked potato. Pert nose, pouty lips—although when you get to the eyes, there's something in them that's seen enough of the world to turn their twinkle into something more like the dull shine of a tarnished teakettle. One the Gun knows her from a picture in his assistant's gathered files as the wife of the victim.

Six the Kicks.

She looks up at One the Gun with no expression. She doesn't appear to have been crying, but then again, widows don't cry every second of the day. Then again, the guy's right there on ice in front of her.

One the Gun is standing across the casket from her, a few paces back, hands in his pockets. For a moment she looks him up and down like she's trying to work out whether she knows him, and then she drops her gaze to the casket again.

Now a man steps in through a back doorway. He's tall and so thin he looks stretched, arms long and willowy like a rubber skeleton in holy vestments. The priest duds are the standard fare: the long black coat hanging almost to the floor, the collar with the little square of white peeking out at the throat. He goes to the woman and puts a hand on her shoulder. They make the kind of solemn head-bob exchange that seems to say they know each other, and then he circles round to One the Gun.

"May I help you?" The preacher puts out a long-fingered hand to shake. "Seven the Heaven."

When One the Gun introduces himself, the woman's head snaps up. "Another cop?" Her face finally loses the blank look and jumps from hurt to offended, closing in on indignant, her eyes squinting and her brow furrowed, a little curl in her lip. "Please tell me you're not here to question me in the presence of my dead husband."

One the Gun starts, "Well, ma'am, I—"

"You have no right to suspect me." Sticking her chin out at him.

"Why do you think I suspect you?"

"You don't fool me. You know he wasn't the only man in my life. You know I like to get my kicks."

Like she's so glamorous or entrancing that her personal life must be public knowledge.

"But kicks," she says, "don't kill husbands."

They do if you kick hard enough, he says.

Not out loud.

"Yeah, I was there that night," Six the Kicks goes on. "I'm there lots of nights. I like to have a drink or two, hang out with the fellas. Sure, I flirt, but it's just kicks. I'd never hurt my husband."

One the Gun bows a little nod at her. "Well, I'm glad to know that." He turns to the preacher. "Do you have somewhere we could talk?"

"Oh, yes," the preacher says.

The widow blinks back at them both but says nothing.

Seven the Heaven tells her to take all the time she needs and then puts his hand out, palm up, indicating the back doorway with the tips of his fingers. He and Gun head off together, leaving the deceased and his widow behind.

Down corridors lined with framed paintings of shepherds and sheep and fishers of men, their twin sets of footsteps clack along hardwood, then echo against stone as the corridor opens out into the wide sanctuary. Over rows of pews shafts of amber and magenta light angle down through pictures of stained glass.

As he passes the raised dish with the holy water One the Gun on impulse puts his hand into it, but he doesn't make the sign of the cross. He walks on, letting the wetness sit there on his fingerprints.

It feels like it felt yesterday—no, it didn't happen yesterday, it's just that déjà vu thing. One the Gun thought he knew what déjà vu was—some momentary feeling, a wispy thing—but he figures he never actually experienced real déjà vu before. This must be what real déjà vu is. Something so vivid it makes you think you truly did live it already when how could you have? Weird how he can just let himself get swept along in the day, like it's not unusual at all, like time is a stream he's caught in— and then, *blink*, something pulls him out of it, like he's waking from a time dream, to clock the déjà vu yet again.

They come to a door just off the back corner of the sanctuary. It's wood with a small square inset of stained glass—a gold-colored cross against a blue background—and above that a tiny number painted in black.

VII

Inside the place is as cramped and empty as a coffin before the tenant moves in. There's a desk, a cot, a single bookcase, and nothing on the walls but one wooden cross without even a dying savior to fancy it up. A small fireplace's flicker seems the only source of light and heat in the room.

It seems both too little and too much. This asceticism. Like it's all for show.

The preacher sweeps his eyes round his quarters like he's making sure One the Gun is properly taking it all in. The lids are low on the preacher's eyes, somber, his neck bobbing below the surface of the cross of his shoulders. Gun's pretty sure a Catholic priest isn't technically called a preacher, but let's face it, that's what they do, preach. He scans the bookcase, the small chest at the foot of the cot, the religious-looking clay figures decorating the short mantel above the fireplace.

The preacher does that hand-out, palm-up gesture again to indicate a straight-backed chair sitting just opposite his desk. "Have a seat, my son."

After the earful Gun got from the moose about this preacher and his less-than-priestly ways, Gun isn't buying any of this *my son* stuff. "Come off it. If you're a man of God, I'm a millionaire playboy with a yacht and a pony."

The preacher's eyebrows jump, then settle again. "Pardon?"

"I've got it on good authority that you spend your nights in the back room at the Dive playing card sharp to add to your own personal collection plate."

Seven the Heaven takes a seat behind his desk, casual. Leans forward, puts his elbows on the desk, brings his hands together, steeples his fingers, and rests his chin on their tips. Smiling, he asks, "Who told you that?"

"Witnesses."

The preacher's voice is smooth, powdery, sliding up and down the scale in an extravagance of sincerity. "I play a little cards, yes, but that's my way in. I have to commune with the flock if I want to bring them into the fold."

"Sounds like you win a lot."

The charm on the preacher's face could grow sunflowers through a load of asphalt. "Well, between you and me, you have to gain their respect if you're to save their souls. But you're not here to talk about card games."

"True, I'm not." One the Gun finally takes a seat.

"I was saddened to hear what happened on Wednesday night," the preacher says, "and am happy to tell you all I know."

On the pinky of Seven the Heaven's left hand is a ring with what looks like a sizeable gem in it. Like an emerald. Is that what he does with the money he siphons off those poor suckers down at the Dive? Buys jewelry? Under his black robes is he draped with piles of gold necklaces?

"How long were you at the Dive Wednesday night?" Gun says.

Seven the Heaven settles back in his chair, crosses his arms over his chest as if to think about it. The emerald winks. "Oh, from maybe eight to close."

"That's late for a priest to be at a bar, don't you think?" One the Gun says. "Don't you have to get up early and say your . . ." He can't remember the word the moose used. Cataclysms?

Seven the Heaven raises his eyes to the ceiling like God is up there. He recites, "'When I applied my heart to know wisdom, and to see the business that is done upon the earth (for also there is that neither day nor night seeth sleep with his eyes).' Ecclesiastes 8:16."

One the Gun wonders if what the preacher just said was a complete sentence. "Okay, fine. And so that whole time on Wednesday night you were in the back room saving souls?"

Behind the preacher on the bookcase is a huge Bible, five inches thick, black, with *Holy Bible* written in gold and loads of scrollwork up and down. Next to that one is a small book, red, that also says *Holy Bible*. One the Gun tries to see if all the books in the bookcase say *Holy Bible*.

"I played a few rounds, yes," the preacher says.

"That how you come up with stuff like that green sparkler, there?" One the Gun says. "Playing a few rounds?"

"This ring? Not at all. It was a gift from a parishioner."

"Looks expensive."

The preacher puts his hands in his lap, out of Gun's sight line. "It's glass. A trinket. I wear it in her memory. She left it in the church donation box not long before her death. She said it was the only thing she had. Her graciousness warmed my heart."

"Doesn't it technically belong to the church?"

"Have you ever heard the parable of the rich fool?" the preacher says. He turns and reaches with his bare right hand past the big ornate Bible to the smaller red one just next to it. Pulls it out. He's starting to flip through pages, but One the Gun is tired of the stall.

"Did you interact with the victim on the night of his death?"

Seven the Heaven looks up from the book, pauses, then shuts it. The charm that pours back into his face is like honey on—ah, skip it. "Yes, yes, I did. He was in and out of the back room where we were playing a few rounds. He was always a very gracious host."

"You talk to him directly?"

"Well, here and there. You know, to say thank you for being a gracious host."

Sometimes, of course, Gun thinks maybe it's not déjà vu at all, maybe he's gone crazy. Okay, no, what about this? He's turned psychic. That's why he knows what the guy's going to say. Nothing shameful about being psychic. It's like a gift from God.

But Gun doesn't think there's a God, and he's pretty sure clairvoyance is just as phony. He says, "You were one of the last people in the place that night."

"Was I?"

"Did you go to his office?"

The preacher looks up to the ceiling like he's trying to remember. "No, I don't believe I did."

"Say, around the time he was counting the cash register?"

"No, I don't believe I did."

One the Gun says, "You ever get the feeling you're having déjà vu?"

The preacher comes out with his reciting-the-Bible voice again: "'That which hath been is that which shall be; and that which hath been done is that which shall be done: and there is no new thing under the sun. Is there a thing whereof it may be said, See, this is new? It—'"

"Alright, alright," One the Gun says. "Never mind."

AFTER HIS INTERVIEW WITH SEVEN the Heaven, One the Gun goes to the phone booth just inside the nearby drugstore and slides the door shut. Tosses some silver in the slot, calls his office. Two the True Blue picks up and says hello in her clear, bell-like voice.

"Checking in," he says. "Got anything new for me?"

He knows what's she's going to say. She's going to tell him that the police have reported back that traces of the poison were indeed found on the glass that was discovered on the desk in the office following the victim's death, but that the glass contained no fingerprints, not even partials. She's going to tell him her beau was a little perturbed at catching them in what looked like a clinch this afternoon, and she knows he didn't mean anything by it, but could they please keep it to business as usual. To that he's going to want to be professional and say, "Oh, of course, of course."

And she does, and she does, and he does.

That lack of incriminating evidence thing. You'd think that would be a problem, but if there were fingerprints, the police would have their suspect. No incriminating evidence is why the insurance company hired Gun to look into the case before handing any money over to any beneficiaries. No incriminating evidence means Gun has a job.

After he gets off the phone he strolls down the block to the newspaper office to have a look in their morgue, where past issues and reference materials are archived. He reads that Five the No Longer Alive used to be Five the Dive. Which makes sense. He reads that Six the Kicks used to be Six the Tricks. As in magic. As in getting put in a box and cut in half. He reads that Seven the Heaven has a twin brother.

Eleven.

In the café when he's having dinner they're playing Two the True Blue's favorite program, *Who Is the Villain?*, on the small radio on the shelf above the cash register. They play it every Friday night at seven o'clock because the owner of the café is as big a nut for it as Two the True Blue is.

One the Gun does not at all eat here every Friday night at seven because he wants to listen to this program, because it is beloved by Two the True Blue.

He likes their hamburgers, that's all.

Tonight he's polishing one off with a biscuit and honey on the side. And he's doing his best to pretend not to notice all the weirdness of this déjà vu day, but that's far easier to do when you're on the job than when you're sitting, quietly listening to a radio show you're sure you've heard before.

The waitress with the doe eyes and the big teeth stands at the drink station lost in space, notepad in hand, rapt by the detective story.

"Who could it be?" the radio announcer asks. "The upstanding businessman with larceny in his eyes? The goldfish-eyed gunsel with mitts like waffle irons? The curvaceous dame with the striped dress and the checkered past?" A burst of organ music to punctuate the drama of the always-expected query: "Who! Is! The Villain?"

Suspects with no names at all, just descriptions tossed around with as many colorful metaphors as possible. It all seems very gimmicky to One the Gun.

OUTSIDE THE CAFÉ ONE THE Gun heads up the sidewalk. The sun's turned tail, and the streetlamps fight the night to leave some light on the pavement. In the recessed doorway of a dress shop a cat with a black coat and one white ear sits licking one paw and dragging it up over its head. Now that he's on the move again Gun does what any sane person would when faced with eight hours straight of déjà vu: ignores it. He has a job to do: get in some last interviews, maybe have a few drinks, then hit the office and recite his notes into the dictation machine for Miss Blue to type up in the morning.

The neon sign for the Dive Inn is shaped like the hull of a ship with a big anchor and the words *Dive Inn* across it in glowing blue. Underneath, the windows leading to the door are round like portholes. Standing inside the entryway in all his gold-button ritzy-like finery is Four the Door. He's wearing a suit not unlike the one his boss was wearing in the casket this afternoon (and undoubtedly still is): shipshape whites with hat and epaulettes. His has fewer stripes than his boss, and he wears a simple sailor's hat instead of a captain's, but the whole getup is just as twinkly with sequins and braid.

He snaps a salute when One the Gun steps in, says what he always says: "Welcome aboard!"

The Dive Inn isn't as impressive inside as its ship-hull neon sign would have you believe, of course. No polished teak on the bar or ocean liner chandeliers hanging overhead, but the walls are lined with thick fishing nets studded with fake sea stars, and the dance floor where people walk but rarely dance is painted with an elaborate, if foot-worn, nautical compass.

One the Gun steps off to the side and lingers to have a quick word with the moose.

"Business good tonight?" he asks.

"Sure, sure," Four the Door says, "folks been coming by to make with the respects. Look at all them flowers there in the corner."

"Very nice," One the Gun says.

"Prettier than pink ballerinas!" Four the Door says. "We're letting them pile up there because the cops said we've got to keep the bizbox locked up."

"The office?"

"Yeah, yeah, the meat bucket, the clubhouse."

"Can I ask a question?" One the Gun says. "You said this afternoon your boss had a drink every night when he counted the money."

"Yeah, yeah, and that I don't know who brought it to him."

"Any chance he could have poured it for himself?"

"Yeah, yeah, no," the moose says. "I told you, the bartender. Every night he pours the boss a whiskey, puts it neat on one of them little napkins, leaves it on the bar."

"And then goes home," One the Gun says.

"It's an agreement they have. When he spills his last slug, he's done. Every night. He pours the boss a short one, then he heaves ho. That's how he always puts it, 'heaves ho.' He's the one with the boat fix."

"The bartender?" One the Gun asks.

"Yeah, yeah, he talks kind of funny. He's back at the bar if you want to have a, you know, a palaver."

One the Gun has to reach up to give the doorman a pat on the back. "I think I'll do that."

He moves off into the club. The floor under his shoes is sticky. The place smells like the ghosts of a thousand drained glasses.

The Dive's inside is like someone shoved an entire nightclub into the bowels of a ship: low ceilings and too many tables, everything a little too close together except for the empty dance floor. The light from small sea-green ceiling lamps is murky, making it feel like the whole place is underwater. Half the tables have people at them, slurping drinks.

At one of those tables, by himself, sits a cocked eyebrow in a dinner jacket. Three the Goatee with martini glass in hand and pinky all a-perch. How can Miss Blue be so head over heels for this heel? The joker's pupils slide to Gun's, and that one cocked eyebrow lifts even higher. He snaps a courteous, if chilly, nod of recognition. "Gun."

A short, formal nod back. "Professor."

Three the Goatee knocks his high-and-mighty hooch to the back of his throat, leaves the glass on the table, shoots the pig eye at Gun once more, and dusts.

Gun turns away with a shrug. Starts across the place again, continuing his survey of the two-day-old murder scene. Fish painted on the tabletops, two oars crossed like an X on one wall. A cocktail waitress in a sailor dress handing a drink to a patron. At one end of the dance floor a chick in a blue dress is putting in the hard sell on an upright piano. Cross to the other side and you're at the bar, a long counter draped with more fishing net decorated with papier-mâché shells and sea stars.

And look. At the leftmost edge of the bar, nursing a glass of something red, is the widow. Six the Kicks dressed to some sort of nines, still in mourning black, but this particular black, with its slink and sparkle, is doing a better job on her curves than her daywear.

And look again. All the way to the right side of the bar. Well, if it isn't the preacher in his holy blacks, making slow communion with some sort of caramel-colored whiskey. Bless us, O

Lord, for these thy gifts. The preacher's sitting sidesaddle on the barstool and watching the room. Watching One the Gun as he crosses the house and bellies up to the counter exactly halfway between Six and Seven.

Behind the counter, running a rag along the shiny silver beer taps, is the bartender. He's in another one of those sailor costumes. Similar to the doorman's with maybe a little more braid and a few more sequins. Maybe a couple more stripes than the doorman's. A couple less than those on the epaulettes of Five the No Longer Alive. He's short and thick with round ruddy cheeks and the kind of moustache that's waxed up into curlicues like he broke a piece of trimming from someone's wrought-iron gate and stuck it suave under his sniffer. Between the three crew members of the Dive Inn, this man seems somehow the most at home in his nautical duds.

Eight the First Mate.

One the Gun asks for a Scotch on the rocks. Eight the First Mate opens his mouth, but the voice Gun hears is a woman's voice, just behind his left ear: "Put it on my tab."

Six the Kicks. She's left her spot at the end of the bar and is standing behind him. Her perfume wraps round him like the chocolate on a frozen banana.

"Don't be stingy with that Scotch," she tells the bartender, "and pour me another glass of wine."

One the Gun turns to face her. "Good evening."

"Inspector."

He gives her his hand. "May I offer my condolences?"

"I apologize for my rudeness earlier," she says. "I haven't been myself. I'd like to make it up to you."

When the bartender sets their drinks down Six the Kicks takes both, one in each hand, her tiny black beaded handbag dangling from her wrist. "I'm ready to be interviewed."

She leads One the Gun across the sticky floor, weaving between tables, to a booth on the other side of the room in the corner with all the flowers. They slide in—she on one side, he on the other—and she pushes his drink across the table. "I want to do all I can to help find the person who did this to my husband."

"I appreciate that." He takes a sip. The Scotch is just as he likes it—fresh and medicinal, like the scent of the swab before the needle. "So, if I may, I'd like to start with the moment just before your husband went into the office at the end of the night."

She looks down into her wineglass. "Alright."

"Can you tell me about that?"

Eyes to Gun again, she lets out a little huff of a sigh that bounces her shoulders. "Well, it was just like always. He went to the front, told Four the Door he was closing up, then came back to the bar. I remember he said, 'What a Wednesday, my friends! What a Wednesday!'"

"What did he mean by that?"

"Oh, I don't know," she says, "I guess business was pretty good."

"And then?"

"He took the cash drawer from the register and went off to the office. I was at the bar chatting with Father Heaven. First Mate finished cleaning up and poured my husband his drink. Three fingers of the good stuff and a squirt of soda. Set it on the bar to mellow. My husband likes . . . liked . . . to let it mellow."

They've sat themselves too close to the woman playing the piano. She's playing some chunky, jaunty tune just a step past a little too loud.

Six the Kicks leans over the tabletop, but her eyes tick to the side, off toward Eight the First Mate behind the bar. "He's always been jealous."

"The bartender?"

"Let me give you a little information," she says. "This whole place? Used to belong to the bartender."

"Oh?"

"Couldn't make a go of it," she says. "He was running it into the ground. No planning. All he did was think up ways to play ship captain. Pretend he was on a boat. Throw fishing nets all over the place. But he couldn't keep it afloat."

Her eyebrows bounce like she notices the pun.

"Anyway, my husband came along and bankrolled the club," she says. "Saved this place from ruin. And what thanks does he get? I think you know."

She's nodding at One the Gun like she thinks he knows.

"Yes?" he asks.

One the Gun thinks he knows. At least what she's implying. But he doesn't want to tip off the suspect.

"First Mate thinks my husband turned his sweet little restaurant into a dive," she says. "He always resented it. And he wanted it back. And he knew if my husband was out of the way, it would come right back to him."

Across the club Eight the First Mate is mixing up a drink in one of those silver shakers. Is what the widow's saying the truth? Did Five the No Longer Alive will this place to its former owner? One the Gun knows that, in an investigation, clues are all well and good, but the most important consideration of all is *cui bono*—something he heard on a detective radio show once. It means *who benefits?*

"And"—Six the Kicks sits back in her seat—"the cop told me he was poisoned."

"True," One the Gun says, "whether willfully or by accident." A third scenario, of course, is always suicide, but he doesn't bring this up to the widow.

"He said it probably came from the storeroom," Six the Kicks says. "The poison used to kill rats. Who do you think uses poison in this place to kill rats? The bartender. And who better to know all about poisons than someone who mixes drinks for a living?"

One the Gun doesn't know why this last thing should follow. He says, "You said you saw the bartender pour the drink. You didn't mention seeing him put anything in it. And if you did see that but didn't question it, you may be complicit."

"Well, no," she says, "but he could have. I wasn't watching him with an eagle eye."

"You said, 'Three fingers of the good stuff and a squirt of soda,'" Gun says. "That's pretty specific."

"That's my husband's drink," she says. "And anything could have happened to it between the bar and the office."

"Doesn't the bartender generally pour the drink and then take off?" One the Gun asks. "Doesn't someone else, maybe even you, generally take that drink to the office?"

She makes the same face she did at the church when she thought he was a cop—a suspicious squint in her eyes. "Generally. Doesn't mean he didn't take it on Wednesday."

"You saw this?"

She blinks and her eyes shift to the side. "Well, no. Doesn't mean he didn't."

One the Gun glances at her hand on her wineglass. Black satin gloves to match her dress. She wore gloves this afternoon as well. If they're a regular accessory to her attire, it'd be awfully convenient for delivering poison and not leaving a trace.

"I thought you were right there at the bar," he says. "You didn't see who took it?"

"After he poured it I went to the ladies' room to powder my nose."

"And you didn't take it yourself?"

Her eyes narrow. "I went to the ladies' room to powder my nose."

The piano is louder, clanking in his ears. The player hits a particularly brisk series of chords that makes the widow wince.

"The preacher—" he says.

"Preacher?"

"Well, priest. You said he was sitting with you at the bar. So he'll corroborate your statement that you went to the ladies' room?"

"Sure, I'm sure he will, yes." Six the Kicks is up, grabbing her handbag. Leaving her wineglass. "I can't concentrate in here. I'll come to your office if you have any more questions."

One the Gun rises too. He thinks he's gotten plenty out of this little interview. He reaches into the inside pocket of his jacket, pulls out his wallet, fishes out a card. "How about you call my office in the morning. If we feel we need more information, my assistant can set up a time."

She shakes his hand, the black glove satiny smooth against his fingers. He leaves her there and steps past the woman giving a shellacking to the piano, heading back to the bar.

As before the barstools are mostly empty, just Seven the Heaven down at the far end, although now he's chatting and quietly laughing with some seedy-looking goon who's standing just beyond. One the Gun steps up to the bar, sets his half-drunk drink on the counter, and leans in toward the bartender. Eight the First Mate smiles curled moustaches at him, but as One the Gun opens his mouth to speak, the guy raises a tray with four drinks, then steps through a break in the bar and goes to deliver an order to a table.

And Seven the Heaven is standing behind One the Gun. Gun knows this before he turns to see him there. Gun's getting a little tired of having to pretend to himself that nothing is seriously wrong with this whole déjà vu thing, that he's not completely cracked up. The preacher is alone. Who knows where the seedy guy got off to. He's smiling all sweet sermon on the mount, whiskey in hand. "A gracious good evening to you, my brother."

This guy gives One the Gun a pain. "Come off it, if you're a man of God, I'm a cowboy with a ranch and a golden lasso."

Seven the Heaven chuckles, turning his rude remark into a charming joke. "I want you to know that I'm here and available if you have any more questions."

One the Gun rests his wrists on the bar top with his glass between both hands. "Well, I do have a question. A moment you didn't bring up in our meeting."

"Oh?"

"At the end of the night," Gun says, "when the deceased went into the office to count the till. You were here at the bar."

The preacher slants his head at One the Gun. "I didn't go in the office, I told you."

"Yes," One the Gun says, "but just before. Essentially the last time you saw him alive, if what you've told me is true."

The bartender is back behind the bar, and One the Gun isn't thrilled the guy'll be able to overhear the preacher's account of that moment—but no, Gun knows the guy's going to pour a beer and leave again, and look, there he goes.

"Well, let's see," the preacher is saying, "it was just like always. He went to the front to tell the doorman he was going to be closing up, and then he came back to the bar. I remember he said, 'What a Wednesday, my friends!' Then he pulled out the money drawer from the cash register and headed to the office."

"And then?" One the Gun asks.

"Oh," he says, "the bartender poured him his usual drink. A whiskey and soda. Set it on the bar."

"And then?" One the Gun prompts again.

A little shoulder bounce from the preacher. "That's it. That's all I saw. I went to the back room. I'd left my Bible in there."

"You bring a Bible to card games?"

"It's my lucky Bible," Seven the Heaven says. "I went and got it and then headed out for the night."

"Was the widow still at the bar when you left to go to the back room?" One the Gun asks.

"I believe so."

"She didn't go to the bathroom to powder her nose?"

"I don't know. I suppose she could have done that when I left."

Seven the Heaven's eyes bounce around at spots behind One the Gun's head in a way that might be trying to remember and might be calculating.

"No, I can't say I recall her doing that. If you're wondering if she took the drink to the office, she may have. Or the bartender may have. It's possible the doorman did too. I didn't see if the drink was still there before I headed out for the night."

One the Gun turns away from the counter, leans back with his elbows on it. Across the wide room Four the Door is bidding a snappy salute to a woman on her way into the club: the waitress with the doe eyes and the big teeth from the nearby café. Six the Kicks is over in the corner past the piano, alone, picking up bouquets of flowers and smelling them one at a time. Swaying to the piano music that curiously seems like the same song from before. Light glitters on her dress.

"You seem to know the deceased's widow," One the Gun says. "Does she always dress that way?"

"In black? She's in mourning."

"But all fancy in like a thousand beads?"

The preacher shifts slightly on his feet, looks over toward her. "That's Six, always. Beaded gowns, jewelry, gloves, the whole nine yards."

"But in a dive?"

The preacher makes a flip of the hand. "Oh, yes, always. That, to Six, is class. She's the reason the Dive's sailor costumes are full of beads and sequins." His chin nods toward the moose at his station at the front of the house. "She got the doorman to wear gloves, too, told him it would make him look ritzy—and believe me, he'd do anything to appear ritzy to her."

"Oh? Are you saying he's sweet on her?"

This possibility is not a new one to One the Gun, not after seeing how insistent the moose was, in their interview, that she couldn't possibly be a murderer.

The preacher raises his glass in a toast: "'There hath no temptation taken you but such as man can bear: but God is faithful, who will not suffer you to be tempted above that ye are able.' First Corinthians 10:13."

The winsomeness in the preacher's eyes turns to sharpness. One the Gun follows his gaze, and there at a table not far beyond are three shady-looking guys, one of whom is the goon from before. He's holding up a deck of cards and giving it a little shake. A grin spreads across the preacher's face. He downs his drink, leaves the glass on the counter, reaches into some hidden pocket in his long black robes, pulls out a tiny red Bible, makes a single nod back at One the Gun, and steps off.

One the Gun's glass is empty. Piano music is a rollicking roll in his ears: Up and down, up and down, and always a crash of notes at the end of the measure like waves against a bow. A crazy sea shanty in double time. One the Gun is almost certain the piano player has been cranking out the same song since he got here. There are a few couples on the dance floor now, as if they don't notice this or don't care. That same song over and over, and he feels, again, like he's experienced this all before, like déjà vu on top of déjà vu. The bartender comes over. Smiles his shipshape smile, moustache curled perfectly, and nods at Gun's empty glass. "Can I get you another?"

"Thanks. Scotch on the rocks."

"You're that detective, aren't you?" Eight the First Mate pulls a bottle from the back wall.

He's wearing a black armband over his nautical whites. If he's so in mourning, what is he doing here like business as usual? Hey sailor boy, did you poison your boss so you can be the captain again and quit pushing drinks for cheap hoods and scooping stray coins off whiskey-sticky tables?

One the Gun says, "I believe my assistant contacted you about an interview."

The bartender slides the new drink to him. "We can talk here if you don't mind an occasional interruption."

"Thanks, yes."

"Looks like we've got time now." He puts the empty glass upside down in a bin on the opposite counter. "What do you want to know?"

Gun takes a seat on the barstool. "I'm told this used to be your place."

"Yeah. Yes, it did." Eight the First Mate's eyes look into the middle distance. He has a small smile that pushes his cheeks round. "It was just a sweet little restaurant back in the day. Fish and chips with a nautical theme. I'm not much of a businessman, but I've loved the sea since I was eight."

"What happened?"

"Well, as I said, I'm not much of a businessman." Eight the First Mate starts wiping the counter, looking down at the rag in his hand. "After Five took over it changed. He knocked out the kitchen to make the place bigger. It became a place for booze, not dinner. Then the games started up. Card games every night. Clientele changed. It all changed."

Gun looks toward the door to the back room, where those card games usually happen.

Following this, Eight the First Mate says, "Back room's not open tonight. Didn't feel proper, this being the first night open after . . . what happened."

Gun's gaze now goes to the preacher's little foursome all hunched round their cards at their table. The bartender glances, then gives Gun a sheepish little shrug.

He goes back to his wiping. "Not sure what I'll do with that room now," he says. "Maybe make a private room for upscale customers."

Cui bono. Who benefits? The wife who maybe wants to have more than just kicks with the men she meets here? The doorman who maybe wants to have kicks with the wife? Or this guy with so much to gain: a better job, more money.

"He saved this place." Eight the First Mate looks up with a small smile that Gun thinks looks genuine. "He saved my dream."

An old lady carrying a pound of rouge on a face as droopy as a melted candle steps up to the bar and orders a rum punch. She glances at Gun blankly, like she has no idea how familiar she looks to him, how she's part of his déjà vu day. Eight the First Mate fixes the cocktail and then exchanges a bill with some coins, one of which the woman leaves on the bar.

Gun works on his drink. "Can you tell me about the last time you saw the deceased alive?"

Eight the First Mate, returning, crosses his arms and leans against the edge of the opposite counter. "Well, it was just like always. He'd gone to the front to tell Four the Door he was closing up, and then he came back here. All I remember him saying was, 'Ah, friends, what a Wednesday!' Seemed very chipper. He took the cash drawer and went off to the office to count it. I poured him his usual. Three fingers of rye and some soda. Left it on the bar."

Gun says, "You ever get the feeling you're having déjà vu?"

"Oh, all the time!" It's the waitress with the doe eyes and the big teeth. She's behind them on the dance floor. Her partner is twirling her round and round to the repeating music.

"Then I took off," the bartender says, like he didn't hear the question or the answer. "I had nothing else to do. The glasses were all gathered for the morning dishwasher and the tables were all wiped down, so."

A cocktail waitress in a sailor dress hands the bartender a tray with three empty glasses on it. He takes the tray, discards the empties, and hands her the tray back without a word.

"You didn't take the drink to the office?"

One the Gun knows what he's going to say.

"No."

"Did you see who took it?"

One the Gun knows what he's going to say.

"No."

The *no*s are said flatly with no inkling as to their reliability. One the Gun hears himself asking yet another question he feels sure he asked before. "The deceased's widow and the priest were sitting at the bar at the time. She says after you poured the drink, she went to the ladies' room. He says he went to the back room. Can you confirm either of these things?"

One the Gun knows what he's going to say.

"Well, I just grabbed my coat and headed off. I suppose they could have as I was leaving. Sorry, I guess I wasn't paying attention."

One the Gun isn't paying attention either. How can he pay attention to any of this when none of it makes sense? Has he slipped into some otherworldly realm, some fourth dimension?

Is this all just an extension of the bizarre dream of dying in the office basement—and if so, could he wake up, now, please?

The dance floor is full of dancers. As the song comes to a particularly raucous end the dancers cheer and the customers at tables raise their glasses like midnight on New Year's Eve.

"It was his favorite song," Eight the First Mate says. His eyes are wistful over his curled moustache.

He reaches down to something below the counter. Raises it. A fifty-dollar bill. Across the bar the piano lady gives a nod and starts playing the song again.

OUTSIDE, THE SQUARE IS SEWN up tighter than a graveyard. Storefronts dark and the streets vacant. The pavement under One the Gun's feet is mottled shadow and dim streetlamp amber.

It's late. He should have left the Dive when he was done with his interview with the bartender, but he stayed around to have a couple more drinks since he's on an expense account from the insurance company. And to chat up a cute little trick with a turned-up nose—and yes, that, too, felt like he'd done it before, but at least for however many times he did do it, it was pleasant. Now he's tired. What was it the moose said? His egg is fried.

Now there's a sound he's not sure he really hears. Like just the thought of a sound. Footsteps? When this all started the déjà vu was a curiosity, but here, in the dark of night, it feels eerie. Like it's leading him somewhere he doesn't want to go.

That sound of footsteps again. Like he's being followed. He swings a look behind him but sees no one. It's hard to tell in the night's dimness. He keeps walking.

The crazy repeating sea shanty is still in his head. They say sailors at sea for extended periods of time can experience hallucinations brought on by the endless tip and roll of the boat, the unfathomable stretch of the water. Loneliness. One the Gun has read that sailors in heightened states dream about mermaids and sea serpents. Do they ever dream about déjà vu? Could a man alone on an endless sea find the day folding back on itself so that everything he saw, everything he said, everything he heard—

That sound of footsteps again. A thrum of warning creeps along his spine. He should have a gun to match his name. Maybe if he were more than a third-rate gumshoe, he would. He turns back, tries to peer down the block. Dark shapes and shadows. There are too many nooks and crevices along this street, recessed doorways, alleys to duck into.

In a flash under streetlamp gold, the cat with the black coat and the one white ear scurries out from an alley and across the sidewalk, a tiny figure bounding through the empty street and to the other side where it keeps going, off toward the monument of a man on a leaping horse that stands at the very center of the square.

One the Gun comes to his office building. Goes inside. Takes the elevator up to the sixth floor. All down the hallway the office doors are closed, the glass dark. He's always the only one here late at night.

The dictation machine hums. One the Gun sits at his desk and recites all the details of the day, all his passing theories. Everything that comes out of his mouth is something he remembers saying just as he says it. He wonders how many drinks he had at the Dive because he's starting to think he's not having déjà vu anymore, he's starting to think, No, I *did* say all this before. I *did* do all this before. Today is yesterday and yesterday today.

He pulls a half-empty bottle of Scotch from the middle desk

drawer and swigs. He's sure of it now. Everything he's saying right now he said last night.

He tries to say something different into the horn of the dictation machine, something out of the blue, but his mouth won't obey. He just keeps saying the things he said last night. Like the closer he gets to the end of this day, the harder it is to pull away from it.

Now the lights go out.

Thick black before his eyes.

That warning feeling spreads across his shoulders.

He's up, feeling for his flashlight. This damn old building. Moonglow angles down through the window blinds to make stripes on the floor. He fumbles along the worn spines of books on the bookcase behind the desk until his hand finds the cold metal of the flashlight. Switches it on.

A beam of light cuts the dark. He hopes the batteries are new enough for him to make it down to the fuse boxes in the basement. He'll have to take the stairs.

But no. What is he thinking? He took the stairs last night.

He went down into the basement last night.

Stop, this is all wrong. He knows what happened last night.

But his hand twists the doorknob, and he walks out into the black hall. Closes the door behind him.

No.

He can't go to the basement.

The flashlight beam runs shadows up along the dark corridor walls.

He can't go to the basement.

His feet won't stop walking.

He squeezes his eyes shut. He fights to reach down into himself to rip himself away from the forward flow of time.

Stop.

Stop.
Please stop.

THE BELLS ARE CHIMING AS he opens his eyes.

It's bright as day in the room. He's back in his office.

Dizzied by the blast of light, by the sudden halt to his walking, by the impossibility of it all, One the Gun shuts his eyes again. Tries to steady himself. Listens to another strike of the bell. The chiming that seems like it should mean midnight. But these twelve chimes mean noon.

He opens his eyes. The room stops spinning.

Two the True Blue is standing in front of him. Such a look on her face. Eyes the color and size of oceans.

He sputters out the only thing he can think to say: "Miss Blue?"

TWO

STANDING IN FRONT OF ONE the Gun in the office, where just a moment ago he absolutely was not, Two the True Blue absolutely is wearing the same outfit as yesterday. The pale peach cotton skirt, the white blouse with tiny eyelet flowers. Two the True Blue absolutely and unequivocally would never wear the same outfit two days in a row.

Two? Or is it three?

It's three.

This is day three.

No, he's cracked up, it can't be true.

A bubble floats between them. Between and above. He only sees it for a moment and then it bobs off and away. Like it's the old day in there, the one he just lived, encircled, confined, now gone.

He thinks maybe he saw one yesterday at this same time. None of anything makes sense.

Two the True Blue says, "You looked so odd just now. Are you alright?"

He just looks at her. Truth isn't truth unless it truly seems true. Is it?

"Are you sick?" she asks. "Feel alright? Need to sit down?"

He follows her to the client couch, the one he got so that he could use it to sleep it off whenever he worked too late with a bottle. He'd kind of like to sleep it off now, but he just sits down.

Two the True Blue, notepad in hand, smiles that way you do to make someone feel better and takes a seat opposite him in the padded chair. "Well, the coroner's office confirms that the victim was killed with poison. It's a hard one to pronounce, but here goes."

You see? She said all of this yesterday. Absolutely and unequivocally and indisputably, every word of it in exactly the same way. She mispronounced the poison in exactly the same way. One the Gun gets up and crosses the room to the calendar pinned to the end of the bookcase. The little squares of the days are each marked off with a single diagonal slash. All marked off, that is, up until the eleventh of the month. The day that was yesterday but now is today.

He turns to the desk and looks past the sample box of rat poison to the daily paper rolled up on a stack of mail. He flips the paper over. Zeroes in on the date. The eleventh of the month. The day that was yesterday but now is—

"Sir?" asks Two the True Blue, still seated.

All the mail stacked on the desk is the mail that came in yesterday. Two the True Blue never misses bringing in the mail, never misses getting him his paper.

The appointment calendar open on the desk to the left of the stack of mail has the same appointments as yesterday and nothing beyond.

Miss Blue comes up behind him. "Ah, as you can see, I've jotted your appointments here."

It's all true. Time is circling back on itself. And Gun is somehow able to control when it does. At least he did that last night. Reaching down inside himself and somehow—he doesn't really know how—jumping out. Will he be able to do it again? What will happen at the end of today if he can't jump out?

He supposes he'll do what he was going to do the first time around: die.

Miss Blue's going on about who he's to meet and when. He's only half listening since she's said this all before. And also she's standing so close, her shoulder brushing his. She smells like jasmine.

"Later this evening," she says, "you'll go over to the Dive where you can speak to the bartender who was also on the scene at the time. Oh, and don't forget to break for dinner. You know how you get on task." She straightens and turns away from the desk. "Now this poison."

Two the True Blue has this radio show she listens to every Saturday night and talks about constantly called *The Rim of Beyond*. In it a narrator with the voice of a lethargic weasel introduces a new science fiction story each week. There was a story they did once about a man who wakes up in the same day every day, just like One the Gun, and he can't get out of the endless looping of time until he makes some important discovery.

One the Gun tries to remember what the important discovery was.

The blur at the corner of his eye brings him back to the present—his present, anyway: Two the True Blue is balancing on one foot, reaching up to the top of his bookcase, and grabbing the huge volume of *The Compleat Illustrated Pharmacopeia* on the high shelf.

Quickly he positions himself behind her so that—like yesterday, like the day before—as she slides the book out and drops back onto both feet and teeters, not truly like she's going to fall but a little bit unbalanced, her heel trips just so slightly against his shoe in that way that makes her tip back into his arms.

But this time, because why not, because he's pretty sure the day is going to start over anyway, he does the thing he's thought about doing every day since he hired her.

He kisses her.

It's so fast, the softness of her lips.

Her sea-blue eyes surprise up into his.

And then he lets go just as the office door opens and her high-and-mighty, toffee-nosed, whisker-bedizened boyfriend, Three the Goatee, comes in to take her to lunch.

She doesn't say anything about the kiss. She just puts her eyes to the floor, turns away, and shuffles herself and the unsuspecting suitor out the door, not looking at Gun. He can't get a read on what she's feeling. Attraction? Aversion? Plain old shock? She might be highly insulted and want to quit, but would it matter? This won't have happened tomorrow.

OF COURSE HE REALIZES, AS he goes to the café to meet with the moose, the moose might have killed him.

Not *might have* as in *maybe would have* but as in *did*—as in, on the Friday night he experienced the first time, not last night but the night before, that seminal Friday night when he was lying on the basement floor in a pool of blood, the person who absolutely and unequivocally pulled the trigger . . . that might very well have been the moose.

It stands to reason, right? Because One the Gun spent a day interviewing suspects in a murder case. He grilled the moose, the widow, the preacher, the bartender, and anything he said to one of them, or anything one of them admitted to him, might have been the prompt that led to the killer of Five the No Longer Alive deciding to make One the Gun no longer alive as well.

Maybe this is the important discovery he needs to make. Like in Two the True Blue's radio show.

"Best boss I ever had," the moose is saying. He's hunched over the café table, rolling his glass of milk between his hands. "Best job. Never was a doorman before him. You know, folks call it the Dive, but it's the Dive Inn. It's not a dive. It's a classy joint."

"Where were you last night between eleven o'clock and midnight?" One the Gun cuts in, off script for the first time since meeting the moose. That's what it's like, isn't it? Like reciting a script. Like in a radio show. Except that it's not fiction, it's real, and it's coming out of your mouth automatically because you said it before.

Four the Door looks up at him with round, puzzled eyes.

Because, of course, last night for Gun and last night for the moose were entirely different nights. For the moose it was Thursday night. For all Gun knows, last night between eleven o'clock and midnight, the moose was sleeping like a baby and dreaming of his sweet granny. One the Gun clinks his teaspoon against his coffee cup. He can't keep it all straight. For cat's sake, how can he find out who killed him if no one's killed him yet?

He tries to remember where he left off in his questioning. Tries to get back on script. It seems the closer he keeps to the details of the original day, the easier it is for him to adhere to it. But when he veers off course, like he just did, he can feel himself come a little unmoored from the forward flow of time. And it takes repeating a comment or an action from that original day to reanchor himself again.

"Um," he says, trying to remember, "so how long have you worked there?"

The moose thinks about it. "Five years. Maybe eight."

People tend to do what people tend to do, One the Gun thinks. They tend to think and say the same things all the time. That must be why it's so easy for the conversations of today to match up with the conversations of the today that was yesterday and the conversations of the today that was the day before that. Even when Gun once in a while swerves off track.

"And you're basically a bouncer?" Gun asks, sticking to the script.

"Doorman, I told you, the doorman."

"Sorry, doorman."

He lets the moose talk about how he's an ambassador in a uniform with buttons, how he makes things ritzy-like. The moose couldn't be the one who kills him, right? He's got that innocent something in his face, that puppy-dog slant in the way he looks at you. Sure, he's a big guy, powerful, but guys like that, if they wanted to kill you, would they use a gun? Poison? Or would they just pound you down?

The way Gun sees it, the first murder, the murder of Five, was something planned out, sneaky. But the second murder, Gun's own murder, would have been rash. A reckless move, a rookie move, made with a weapon the killer had on hand. Lots of folks have guns these days. The moose could have a gun. But the poison thing. Does this big oaf with his mouth full of shoddy grammar and slang seem like the type to plan out and execute a poisoning right in front of witnesses?

When the waitress with the doe eyes and the big teeth comes up to their table to ask if they need anything, One the Gun orders a hot biscuit and honey.

"I don't get why that preacher's got to always be around so late," Four the Door is saying. "Don't he have to get up early and say his catechisms?"

"What was your boss's mood when you saw him last?"

One the Gun is sick of this script. What can he learn if he hears nothing but what he's already heard? He'd like to get into that office at the Dive. Check out the scene of the crime. But what if it's dangerous to go so far off script? He doesn't know the rules of time. If he does veer too far, if he does become too unmoored, could he just—what? Float away?

The waitress with the doe eyes and the big teeth sets a plate down at the edge of the table next to him. On it, instead of the biscuit, is a pickle spear and a scoop of cottage cheese. She winks at him and steps away.

He stares at the dish he didn't ask for. Normally he'd send back an incorrect order, but this feels like a sign. That he should maybe just dispense with the script. See what happens. He grabs the spoon sitting on the plate and shovels cottage cheese into his mouth. He doesn't float away.

He dispenses with the script. "Say, I've got an idea."

"Yeah?"

"You said down at the Dive that they were keeping the biz-box locked up."

The moose is giving him the puppy-dog face again. "Huh?"

"You know," Gun says, "the meat bucket, the clubhouse. You told me last night no one was allowed in the office but the cops."

"I told you last night?"

"I'm just wondering," Gun says, "I'm essentially a cop. I'd like to get in there and investigate. Do you think you could let me inside?"

Four the Door thinks about it. "You're a cop?"

"Essentially."

"Well, I guess so."

ONE THE GUN WOULD LOVE to go to the Dive right now and get into that office and see what clues the cops might have left behind, but Four the Door says, "I got stuff to do after lunch." And since the moose has been doing most of the talking, the guy still has plenty of chicken to get through. He says come round to the Dive Inn later, in fact come late. Late enough that folks have enough booze in them to put a nice soft edge on things. To put a nice soft edge on, in particular, Six the Kicks, Seven the Heaven, and Eight the First Mate, all of whom are well aware of the fact that, as the moose so eloquently puts it, the cops say nix on making mix with piggy's house of sticks. Which Gun is *pretty sure* means, again, that no one's allowed in the office?

So One the Gun gets back on script, goes on with the day as he's used to it. Trying, the whole time, to notice something he didn't notice yesterday, some clue to who might be wanting, at the end of the day, to kill him.

He walks to the church and looks down on the dead man in his casket.

Looks up into the narrowed eyes of the widow.

"You know he wasn't the only man in my life. You know I like to get my kicks. But kicks don't kill husbands."

He walks through the sanctuary, lets his fingers dip into the holy water. Meets with the priest in his chambers.

"Come off it. If you're a man of God, I'm a millionaire playboy with a yacht and a pony."

Research at the newspaper, dinner at the café, hamburger and coffee and Two the True Blue's Friday-night radio show.

"The upstanding businessman with larceny in his eyes? The goldfish-eyed gunsel with mitts like waffle irons? The curvaceous dame with the striped dress and the checkered past? Who! Is! The Villain?"

But at the Dive, instead of talking to Six the Kicks, then Seven the Heaven, then Eight the First Mate, he has a drink in a booth by himself and waits until Four the Door takes a break, just long enough to unlock the office door and let him in.

The moose leaves him alone with the promise that he'll follow police protocols, not touch anything, and bring back the key when he's finished.

The office is about as classy as a broom closet in a third-rate bookie joint: Torn curtain in the window, rusty filing cabinet, a rickety set of shelves full of ledgers. A dented metal desk with the chair overturned, obviously left where it ended up two nights ago when Five was killed. In one corner, out of place against the rest of the décor, is a blue chaise longue.

Gun takes a slant at the desk. Not much there: an open ledger and fountain pen, a scratch pad, a telephone. The cash drawer was undoubtedly checked for evidence and allowed back onto the floor so business could reopen, and the glass that held the poison and its accompanying cocktail napkin are currently in police custody.

In his investigation One the Gun does not follow police protocols. He does *not* not touch anything. He's positive by now that this day is going to fold back on itself again, so he opens desk drawers, riffles through the filing cabinet and the ledgers stacked on the shelves. With the cops already having swept the place, there's not much for Gun to find, but he does tumble to a couple items of possible interest.

Like Five's bookkeeping. Gun takes probably too long a quick peek at the ledgers, noting that it mostly looks like the bookkeeping of a dive ought to—booze buys and utility bills and nightly takes—but there are also monthly notations of payouts of fifty fish apiece with no memo as to where the money's going. With records as meticulously kept as Five's seem to be, why the blanks in the description column? Could this be hush money for the cops to keep their hands off of his little backroom shenanigans? That's a distinct possibility, but is there something more?

Gun can't peg that floofy chaise in the corner. That thing sticks out like a peacock in a chicken house. There's a blue silk scarf hanging over it all *ooh la la*. Was Five bundling babes into the office for some less-than-businessy business?

That together with the mysterious accounting notations make One the Gun wonder: Was Five keeping some dish on the side, maybe paying for some secret love nest?

It's getting late. The moose is going to be worried. But One the Gun's pockets are full of little envelopes waiting for clues, and he's got nothing but an accounting notation here and there and a blue couch that may or may not be where the boss routinely took naps.

But wait. As he turns to leave something catches his eye. Something tiny, so tiny the police must have overlooked it, almost completely hidden under the desk and sitting against its wooden leg.

A bead.

His immediate thought is Six the Kicks. In fact, who does he see after he leaves the office, goes down the little hall, and steps back into the club to return the key to Four the Door but Six the Kicks, alone in the corner, glittering in all her black-beaded mourning finery, swaying to the piano music as she picks up bouquets of flowers and smells them one at a time.

The beads on her dress are nothing like the bead concealed in the small envelope in his pocket, but didn't Seven the Heaven say that all her dresses are full of beads?

Two the True Blue tracked down addresses and phone numbers for all the suspects and witnesses. One the Gun is going to his office to get that list now. Six the Kicks will be hanging out at the Dive for a good long time. And One the Gun is going to search her home.

***

OUTSIDE THE DIVE IT'S QUIET. The pavement under One the Gun's feet is mottled shadow and dim streetlamp amber.

Gun has never done what he's planning to do. Breaking and entering. As a third-rate gumshoe, he's done plenty of spying, peeking through windows, snapping unauthorized pictures, stuff that would be deemed shady outside his line of work, but he likes to think of himself as a pretty upstanding guy. Not like some of the more sleazy characters in the business. He's got pride. But being in this strange looping of time, where what happens today won't have happened tomorrow, makes busting into someone's digs and riffling through their stuff seem pretty small potatoes.

One the Gun reaches into his jacket pocket to let his fingers find the small envelope containing his precious clue. Removing evidence from the scene of the crime is another thing he's not used to doing. He slips the envelope out to make sure it's still there. He'll need to compare it to what he finds among Six's belongings to be sure he's got the right match.

He feels along the surface of the paper. This is one of the empties. He can't remember how many envelopes he grabbed to prepare for his search. He shoves it back in his pocket and pulls out another. Another empty.

Now he's sure they're all empty. He's sure the bead is gone. It's worked its way out of the envelope and gotten lost. It's somewhere in his pocket. It's fallen out through some hole in his pocket.

He stops on the sidewalk, pulling envelopes out and then shoving them back in.

Empty.

Empty.

No, this one. There it is. He can feel the nugget of a clue under the paper. He lets go of the breath he didn't know he was holding.

He goes to stick the envelope back in his pocket.

The corner of the envelope hits the edge of fabric and slips from his fingers.

The small white square sails through the dim night. Into the street.

The emptiness of his fingers sends a spark across his palm. The envelope lands on the thin metal bars of a sewer grate at the edge of the street. For a moment he doesn't move.

He steps carefully toward it, sure his movement will cause it to fall inside.

There's the smallest of breezes. It touches the envelope and makes it twitch.

One the Gun reaches his hand out.

From just behind him a shape blurs at the edge of his vision, making his hand freeze in place. It's the cat with the black coat and the one white ear. The cat bounds between his reaching hand and the envelope, its black form blotting out the shadowy white square. The breath disappears in the back of Gun's throat.

The cat leaps on through, up onto the curb, its tail a black swish as it goes.

The envelope is still there.

Gun's fingers close around it. He straightens. He breathes again. Gently slides the prize into his pocket.

Double beams of light sweep in from a side street and turn, blasting bright into One the Gun's eyes. The car is coming straight at him.

In the moment before the very different death he didn't expect tonight, One the Gun squeezes his eyes shut. Reaches down into himself to rip himself away from the forward flow of time.

Go back.

Go back.

Go back.

THE BELLS ARE CHIMING AS he opens his eyes.

It's bright as day in the room. He's in his office.

Day four.

Two the True Blue is standing in front of him. Such a look on her face. Eyes the color and size of oceans.

In his joy that he did it, he did it, he did it again, he sputters out the only thing he can think to say, "Miss Blue?"

She's in that outfit again. The pale peach cotton skirt, the white blouse with tiny eyelet flowers. "You looked so odd just now. Are you alright?"

A bubble floats between them. The image that reflects along its surface is not their figures, not her pale peach and white. For a moment the slip and shift of color and shine that shows inside the tiny sphere is two beams of headlights along a road. Then the bubble bobs off and away.

"Say," he cuts in, "you made a list of the phone numbers and home addresses of the witnesses, right? Can you get that for me?"

She's looking at him, perplexed, but then she blinks and steps across the room. "Of course. It's right over here."

And he's going to need some tools. He'll stop at the hardware store, or maybe the building super's got something in the basement.

He reaches into his pocket to retrieve his hard-won clue.

But wait.

He's forgetting what happens when the day turns back on itself.

Nuts.

His pocket is empty.

THREE

THE WINDOW IN THE OFFICE of the Dive Inn opens into an alley just off the square. It's a long, narrow alley filled with the trash bins of various businesses—a bit stinky but also convenient for hiding in the shadows, even in the bright of day, and using a screwdriver to work the hasp off a very rudimentary latch. Which is the only thing keeping a detective from climbing through said window and retrieving a bead from the floor of said office, then slipping out again.

Very convenient. He should have thought of it yesterday. He'll have to keep it in mind for tomorrow. And if need be, tomorrow. And if need be, tomorrow.

IT'S A SHORT WALK DOWN the square to the apartment building where Six the Kicks (and, until recently, also her husband) lives. Gun recognized the address the minute he saw it on the list. It's the same building where Two the True Blue lives. Stepping into the lobby, his shoes tapping along the polished stone floor, he pauses to peek at his assistant's lovely name on the card in the inset of her mailbox. Apartment 2. Not far along is the mailbox belonging to Six.

A flash of black at the corner of his eye. It's the widow. Gun freezes.

She's walking to the front door of the place, not looking in his direction.

Almost before he can even start to panic that she's going to foul up his plan, she's through the entryway and gone. Gun lets out a breath.

A quick trip to the second floor reveals that Six's apartment door is not, in fact, unlocked (couldn't hurt to try), but One the Gun should be able to access the place from the fire escape on the south side of the building. He goes back outside. It's getting on toward two o'clock. Gun doesn't know how long Six the Kicks will be at the funeral chapel, so he'll have to work fast. He'll focus on finding the article of clothing or jewelry that might be missing one particular bead. He can always come back and search the rest of the place on some future today. He has all the time in the world.

One the Gun heads to the fire escape. That's the nice thing about buildings that front on the square like this. Many of the windows you might want to climb into are hidden down an alley. And look: The window that opens onto the living room of Six the Kicks's apartment—you can see it through the slats of the blinds—is directly above the window that opens onto the living room—you can see it if you peek through the yellow curtains with little white daisies—of the abode of Two the True Blue.

Yes, their apartments are stacked one on the other: the home of the maybe femme fatale and the home of the femme *vrai bleu*.

Two the True Blue's living room is tastefully decorated. Powder-blue couch and chair, a small end table with a book on it. He squints, trying to read the title of the book. Maybe after a long day of work for One the Gun she lays her body across this couch and—

Come on, Gun. Concentrate.

The building across the narrow alley from him is all red brick. There are a few windows but none directly opposite. Still, he'll want to get in quick. One the Gun hikes himself up the fire escape and tries the window, but it's locked. He looks, feels around, but there doesn't seem to be any way to pry it open. He's going to have to break it.

He was hoping it wouldn't come to this, but alright. In his pocket along with the screwdriver is a small cross peen hammer and a roll of duck tape. Luckily the panes of the window are small, so he won't have to break much. Working fast, he tears strips of tape and lines the glass of one pane until it's covered completely. That should make this operation as quiet as possible. He'll have to smash the glass, reach through, unlatch the window, climb inside, and hope no neighbor hears him and calls the police.

He pockets the tape and brings out the hammer. He gets in position. This definitely feels more questionable than what he did at the Dive, like it's going to take him down a peg from third-rate gumshoe to fourth. He tells himself this won't have happened tomorrow, but still he feels like he's stepping outside his moral code somehow.

Still. When the hammer hits the taped-up glass, the power in that smash, even through the muffle of the tape, feels pretty darn good.

INSIDE THE PLACE IS LIKE someone tried to shove a penthouse suite into the third room of a back-highway motor lodge. Rummage-sale furniture covered with fancy scarves and knickknacks, gold-painted statues of satyrs and cherubs, huge silver frames with cheap prints of classical art. One the Gun would like to search the whole digs, but he doesn't know when the widow might come back. He opens doors and finds the bedroom: a big king-sized bed with a swirly gold headboard and more fake gold statues.

He stops, listens. If the door of this place starts pounding with the cops, he can jump out of time and start over. He pulls the envelope from his pocket, opens the flap, and drops the bead onto his palm. It's a glass bead, translucent blue, with a tiny symbol on it in red. So tiny he can hardly make it out: a circle superimposed on an eight-pointed asterisk. Four of the arms of the asterisk are more pronounced so that it looks like a cross with thinner rays radiating from it. He sticks the clue back in the envelope and shoves it back in his pocket. Goes to work. In the closet he finds trousers and shirts lined up on one side, dresses on the other.

And on those dresses, and on her hats, and on her handbags, and in her jewelry box are beads and beads. Glass beads and ceramic beads. Metallic beads and painted beads. Cloisonné beads, lampwork beads, carved wooden beads, cheap plastic pony beads. Rhinestones, crystals, costume pearls. Satin finish, matte finish, frosted finish; silver lined, color lined; iridescent, transparent, mosaic, dichroic. Drop beads, twin beads, bugle beads, seed beads, piggy beads—all the beads you could ever want to find in the world.

Except, of course, for the one One the Gun wants to find.

He goes through everything twice. He sits down heavily on the bed. It's just not here.

The preacher was right: She does wear beads all the time. But a lot of good that does this investigation.

Although . . . the preacher.

One the Gun stands.

That symbol looks kind of like a cross. Maybe it's not a bead for fashion at all.

ONE THE GUN IS RIGHT on time for his 2:30 appointment in the chambers of Seven the Heaven.

The preacher's giving him the hand-out, palm-up gesture to indicate the straight-backed chair sitting just opposite his desk ("Have a seat, my son"), and One the Gun is playing along with maybe a little more relish than he should.

"Come off it! If you're a man of God, I'm an oil tycoon with a gold-plated swimming pool."

The preacher's eyebrows jump, then settle again. "Pardon?"

"We've been over this," One the Gun says, although they haven't yet. "I know you spend your nights gambling and taking money off of poor saps down at the Dive, and don't give me that bunk about needing to gain their trust to save their souls."

Seven the Heaven takes a seat behind his desk, casual. Leans forward, puts his elbows on the desk, brings his hands together, steeples his fingers, and rests his chin on their tips. Smiling, he says, "My methods may be unorthodox, but they're pure, my brother."

One the Gun is making a casual mosey around the room. There isn't a bead in sight. "You got any other costumes?" he asks.

The preacher's eyebrows bounce again. "Costumes?"

"Your, you know, holy vestments there. Anything with a little more pizzazz?"

"Pizzazz?" the preacher says.

One the Gun stoops and pulls open the chest at the foot of the cot. The preacher jumps up. "Hey!"

Nothing in there but more black robes.

"You got a rosary?" Gun asks.

The look on Seven the Heaven's face is a funny blankness, his eyes a little too wide, like he's so shocked at what's going on he can't think straight. "Um, of course, I—"

"Give it here." One the Gun puts his hand out at him, walking back over to the desk.

"I don't see why I have to—"

"This is a murder investigation," Gun shouts, "and there is evidence that you may be involved. Now let me see it! Now!"

The preacher fumbles in the pockets of his black priest coat and pulls out a long loop of connected beads.

Gun lets his hand drop. He already knows they aren't what he wants.

They look to be gold, and here and there is a smooth red one, maybe amber. The cross that hangs from the bottom is big and fancy and studded with what might be diamonds.

"Gee, that's some pretty jewelry you've got there," One the Gun sneers.

The preacher looks down at his rosary dumbly.

One the Gun waves it off. "You can put it away."

The preacher pauses a beat, then tucks the rosary back into his robes. "Have you ever heard the parable of the rich fool?" he says. He turns and reaches past the big ornate Bible on the bookshelf to the smaller red one next to it. He starts to flip through pages.

One the Gun pulls the envelope out of his pocket. Drops the bead onto his palm again. Nuts, he was almost sure that tiny icon was something religious. See? Isn't that a cross with rays radiating from it? Isn't the circle that encloses the cross some liturgical representation of unity or purity or some other theological hooey?

Wait.

Truth breaks across the top of his head like someone's cracked a raw egg up there.

He can't believe it.

He knows exactly where this bead came from because he's seen it before.

The symbol? It's not a cross. It's a boat wheel.

ONE THE GUN IS AT the door of the Dive Inn when they open up at three. Four the Door, who did not meet him today at the café because Gun did not bother making that appointment, gives him the same unfocused and chipper look he gives every other anonymous customer. He snaps a salute. "Welcome aboard!"

"Thank you, appreciate it." But One the Gun is staring at the beads hanging from the edges of the striped epaulettes on the doorman's uniform. The translucent blue glass beads with the tiny red boat wheels on them.

There seem to be eight beads on each epaulette. Well, eight on the front of each epaulette and eight, presumably, on the back. Unless the doorman is missing one.

Four the Door is watching his eyes. "Ah, you like my duds?"

"Very classy," Gun says.

"I tell you!" says Four the Door, pleased. "Five dogs couldn't flute that fiddler on a backhanded jipper, get me?"

"Oh, certainly!"

"Not to brag or anything."

"Oh, no, not at all," One the Gun says. "In fact, can you give me a little . . ." He points at the floor and twirls his finger.

Four the Door grins big. He turns round slowly to show off the rest of his duds.

Eight beads on the left, eight beads on the right.

Four the Door turns back to the front, his hands up, palms out in a shy ta-da. His smile pulls his eyes into crescents.

"Very nice," One the Gun says. "I'd say you're the picture of class. Like an ambassador!"

Four the Door's grin flashes more teeth than the gift shop in a shark museum. He bows low. "Thank you, sir, and have a good evening!"

So the bartender, then. One the Gun snaps a nod at the doorman and moves off into the empty club. It's quiet with no crowd noise and no one assaulting the piano. Behind the bar, Eight the First Mate is putting away drink glasses. His thick frame swivels to the tub of freshly washed glasses on the back counter, then forward to stoop and stash a glass below the bar. Back to the tub of freshly washed glasses, forward to stash another glass.

"Good evening," he says as he works.

One the Gun is counting beads.

It's harder to count when the body is moving. One, two, three, four, five, and Eight the First Mate swivels to the tub of freshly washed glasses.

One the Gun tries to count the beads along the back of his left shoulder. One, two, three, four, five, and Eight the First Mate swivels to stash another glass.

"Just let me know what I can get you," Eight the First Mate says. One, two, three, four, five, and he swivels to the tub.

"I'm still trying to decide, thanks." One, two, three, four, five, and he swivels to stash another glass.

One the Gun huffs. Turns. He steps back from the bar, walks a little ways until he comes to the break in the counter.

When he steps through, behind the bar where customers aren't supposed to go, Eight the First Mate doesn't even notice, just keeps swiveling and putting away glasses.

One the Gun steps toward him. He could do anything, really. Knock him down and examine him, tear the jacket off and steal it. What does it matter? It won't have happened tomorrow.

Finally Eight the First Mate hears him and turns. His eyebrows, funny black triangles, jump up on his face. Before the bartender can open his mouth, One the Gun puts on the biggest smile, marches up, and claps his hands on the bartender's shoulders.

"It's you! I knew it! I'd recognize you anywhere!"

"Sir," the bartender says, "you can't be back—"

"How long has it been? Five years? Maybe eight?"

One the Gun looks him up and down like *gee, how you've changed*, but really he's counting beads. Eight on the left, eight on the right.

"Sir, you need to—"

"You didn't used to have that moustache, right?" Gun plows ahead. He tries to turn the bartender, but the bartender doesn't budge. "That's why I didn't recognize you. My sister's going to be thrilled! You know what she thought of you!"

Now there are hands on his own shoulders. Someone behind him. Four the Door, who has appeared from nowhere, silent as a moose. How silent are mooses? Arms come up under his armpits and cross in front. One the Gun is being dragged away. Eight the First Mate turns his back on them both. Four the Door said he's not a bouncer, but One the Gun is getting bounced. Lugged out from behind the bar and across the Dive.

"You shouldn't ought to have done that," Four the Door is murmuring as One the Gun's heels skid across the worn dance floor, then bounce over the threshold of the entryway, and then—fast as all that—he's shoved through the door to land on the sidewalk, butt first, then his shoulder and the back of his head hard against concrete. There's a ringing in his ears. The moose has maybe a rough side Gun didn't notice before.

One the Gun sits there a moment. Late-afternoon sun on the sidewalk pavement. A crumpled page of newsprint in the gutter.

At least he got what he needed. When the bartender turned away, he saw eight on the left and eight on the right.

Which means he's exhausted all his possibilities for the owner of the bead.

Well.

Except one.

THE FUNERAL CHAPEL OF OUR Lady of Immaculate Numbers is as colorless as a snowman's long underwear: white walls, white stone floors, white pillars in every corner holding up white marble urns. And in the white casket in the center of the room—yes, you probably guessed it. Well, Gun didn't, but that's because he's a third-rate gumshoe. But look there in that casket. At our victim in his nautical getup with his captain's hat and his brass buttons and his epaulettes with the little glass beads, translucent blue with tiny red boat wheels on them. Eight on the left, seven on the right.

FIVE O'CLOCK. ONE THE GUN sits in a booth at the café, staring at the menu. It has occurred to him that he spent hours searching, breaking and entering, stalking and manhandling the Dive employees, never stopping to think that there may have been any number of spare uniforms missing beads in, say, the storeroom. It has further occurred to him that he also never stopped to think that a bead found on an office floor may have been sitting there at the edge of the desk for five years.

It's weird to waste a day of your life when you know that day is going to start over anyway. Does it even matter? Do your personal failures even matter?

One thing he's learned for sure. You can unmoor yourself completely from the forward flow of time and you don't just float away. He doesn't know why he thought that might happen in the first place. Maybe because of those strange bubbles he always sees lifting away and disappearing at the start of every new old day.

He should order something different. He always orders hamburgers. Biscuits and honey. He always drinks coffee. If you were given the chance to relive one day over and over, wouldn't you want to try the pork chop?

The waitress with the doe eyes and the big teeth sets a cup of coffee on the table. He hasn't ordered it, but he does like coffee.

"You're here early," she says. "Or is it late?"

"I think I'll have the hamburger," he says.

"Grilled onions?"

"If you were given the chance to relive one day over and over," he says, "what would you do?"

"I'd have the milkshake," she says.

"Every time?"

"It's a really good milkshake."

Something keeps nagging at One the Gun. Something he noticed at some point today that, at the time, felt like a clue to follow, but then disappeared into his obsession with that stupid bead. He can't recall it now. He doesn't know why he got so excited about that bead. Why does he always get obsessed with singular things? That bead probably had nothing to do with the night Five was killed. Sometimes Gun thinks when people want something enough, they sculpt their beliefs to fit the shape of that want. Maybe there's absolutely no clue to follow, no way to know who killed Five, no way to know who killed One the Gun in the basement on the night that hasn't quite happened.

And if there's no way to know, what then? What if the forward flow of time is always inevitably going to lead to the basement? What if being here in this bubble of time, no matter what he does inside it, can't stop what lies ahead?

The waitress with the doe eyes and the big teeth sets a milkshake on the table.

One the Gun doesn't remember ordering it.

He sits quietly in his booth in his bubble of time and drinks his milkshake.

She's right. It's really good.

The milkshake is chocolate. It's in a tall glass. He sucks it through a straw, looking up and across to where the waitress with the doe eyes and the big teeth, behind the counter, has poured the little bit of leftover milkshake into a small water glass for herself. She raises the glass in a toast and drinks.

Odd dame. He can't help but chuckle at the two of them sharing this unexpected treat across the crowded café. The big milkshake and the small milkshake. Might not be proper for a waitress to cop a bit of someone's order, but—

That's it. The big milkshake and the small milkshake.

He knows what's been nagging at him. And he knows what he's going to do about it.

The waitress sets down his hamburger. He eats slowly, savoring every bite. He might just hang out here for a while. Have some more coffee, maybe listen to Two the True Blue's radio show when it comes on at seven. He's going to go back to the church, yes, but he might as well wait a while. He'll want to make sure the preacher's headed away for the night if he's going to break into his chambers.

THE CHURCH IS OPEN AND empty with no one in the corridor just off the back corner of the sanctuary, but the preacher's door is buttoned up tighter than a miser's purse on the day after Christmas. Why do people have to lock things all the time? One the Gun doesn't know a thing about picking locks, and there's no window to the outside, so unless he turns into Santa Claus and comes down the chimney into the guy's fireplace, the only way he's getting in there is by breaking more glass.

The small inset of stained glass in this door, the gold-colored cross against a blue background. It's probably sacrilege to bust a cross, but Gun tapes it up and pulls out his hammer. Gives the works a good whacking. Gun stops, listens. Then he reaches through the hole and unlocks the door.

The preacher's room is cold. In the fireplace a handful of glowing twigs is making a play at a flicker.

One the Gun goes right to the bookcase. To the big Bible next to the small Bible. The big Bible the preacher always passes over whenever he goes to read parables to One the Gun. The big Bible is black and ornate with *Holy Bible* written in gold and loads of scrollwork up and down. Must be five inches thick. Thick enough to hide something inside.

It's a simple ruse. You cut a hollow into the pages, stick the something inside, and when the book's shut, no one's the wiser. You could keep money in there, like a secret safe, but what about a gun? What about *the* gun used to kill One the Gun? After all, the to-be murder weapon has to exist somewhere. Killers often toss the weapon after the crime, but they don't usually toss it *before*.

If he finds the gun that will be used to kill him, if he takes it and leaves and lives the rest of the day, maybe today will turn over into tomorrow.

That thought makes him a little sad. He kind of likes it in this bubble of time now that he's realized he can basically do anything he wants without long-term consequences. But solving murders and skirting your own death is pretty swell too.

He grabs the big Bible along its huge spine and slides it out. Careful to keep the book shut, he carries it across the room with one hand across the spine and the other cradling it underneath. The book is heavy. Is that because there's a weapon hidden inside or because the book is heavy? He lays it on the preacher's desk, face up. He's afraid to open it. He's afraid he might find that all that's hidden inside are words.

One the Gun lifts the front cover open. He takes one finger and runs it along the edge of the stacked pages, but they don't separate.

They're glued together.

A hum of anticipation starts along his ribcage. That must be some sort of sin, gluing a Bible. Worse than busting a stained-glass cross, even. He reaches down along the block of glued pages until he finds the break and pulls it open.

And what's hidden inside?

Words after all.

Letters.

It looks like ten or twelve of them. Each letter is folded in thirds. All of them are stacked and tied together with a piece of twine. No envelopes. One the Gun at first assumes these must be the preacher's own letters, but then he opens one and it addresses someone else.

Darling Nine,

It's a love letter.

Hardly a weapon.

Or so One the Gun at first believes.

I have to see you. I know we shouldn't do this. I don't care. Come to the Dive tonight.

Aha, the Dive.

If you want to see me, carry a red flower. If you want me to back off, blue. I'll understand.

An *illicit* love letter! But from whom to whom? And why does the preacher have them? One the Gun reads the flowery details of eyes meeting across crowded rooms, sweet nothings murmured in secret under the din of the bar. A snippet of poorly written poetry about this woman's "lovely, luscious eyes." At the bottom it's signed . . .

Oh god.

Snookie.

Still. This is a very interesting development. One the Gun folds the note up and slides it back into the tied bundle. Pulls another out.

Darling Nine,

I'll be waiting for you at the Dive tonight. I have a gift for you. I'll slip it to you and you can go into the ladies' room and put it on. Then once everyone has cleared out, we can go to a little place I know of off the square.

More bad poetry, but then this one is signed with something a little closer to a signature. The single letter *V.*

One the Gun knows no one with a *V* name. No one at all that he can think of. Well, there was that cheap hood Fifty the Very Shifty, but he's been in the can for the past eight months.

Gun flips through the stack, hoping for more of a signature, but they're all signed with a single *V* or the less-than-stately sobriquet *Snookie.*

One the Gun stops and listens for sounds outside the door. Nothing.

He should get the hell out of here, but he pulls out another letter and gives it a scan.

Nine mine,

Don't come to the Dive tonight. I think Six suspects something. I think we need to lie low for a while.

Oho.

Recognition starts to prickle across One the Gun's forehead.

It won't be forever, I promise. In the meantime I'll content myself with memories of your eyes in the bar light, your naked body on the chaise, our many forbidden meetings.

And suddenly everything falls into place. Six, the chaise, and the cryptic one-letter signature that, as it turns out, isn't a letter at all.

V.

It's a Roman numeral.

OUTSIDE, THE HEAVY FACADE OF Our Lady of Immaculate Numbers is dark, but the lit-up stained-glass windows blaze bright red, blue, and green. One the Gun heads off, feeling his own glow inside.

Five. He's just discovered a stash of love notes written by Five the No Longer Alive.

Five, playing all fancy with his Roman numerals and his sequined sailor suits. One the Gun remembers the mysterious payouts he saw in Five's bookkeeping ledger in the office. At the time he'd guessed it was hush money Five was paying to the cops. But try this on for size.

Hush money he was paying to the preacher.

Gun walks past the funeral parlor, all closed up and dark, where Five still lies in his casket in his silly captain's hat. Poor Five, it's not Six who had your number. Try six plus one. Yes, it all adds up—the preacher got hold of Five's letters and has been doing a little blackmail. In fact, take that blackmail, put two and two together, and what does it total? Murder.

He touches the bundle of letters through the fabric of his jacket pocket to make it crinkle. They won't be there tomorrow, but he feels exhilarated from stealing them now.

Who is this Nine? And how did the preacher get hold of these letters? Is the woman in on it? Or is he shaking her down too?

And how much, really, does Six know?

Walking down the street through the cool night air, Gun feels tall and wide and invincible. He can do anything.

He has stolen letters in his pocket. He's broken into three different buildings today. He's threatened a priest, been thrown out of a bar, and no one involved will remember tomorrow.

This time thing. It's like magic. A power. And he's going to take full advantage of it while he's got it.

FOUR

DAY FIVE.

When One the Gun steps into the café it's early, a quarter to one. Instead of going to the booth where, on past days, he's sat with Four the Door, he takes a seat at the counter. It's tiled in red and white squares so it looks like the tablecloths. The rest of the counter seats are empty except for a moustache in a blue suit working on a newspaper at the far end. One the Gun picks up a menu and scans it, but he already knows he's going to order the hamburger.

The waitress with the doe eyes and the big teeth steps up in front of him. She's wearing what she, of course, was wearing yesterday and yesterday and yesterday and (he has to stop and think about it) was there another yesterday? A white apron over a dress the color of faded lemonade. Well, the dress is faded, not the lemonade.

She's got her hands behind her back, and she's tying that apron like she just arrived for her shift. Smoothing the apron down, she turns and lifts the coffee carafe from the warming burner, turns back with that and a cup, sets the cup down, and starts pouring.

"You're here a little early," she says.

"You said that yesterday," he says.

She makes a little smile at the pouring coffee. "Did I?"

She's a sly one, this waitress. He realizes she's been dropping hints at him. Remarking that he's here early. The milkshake. That scoop of cottage cheese she served him two todays ago that she wouldn't have served him if she were going along in her nonrepeating Friday like everyone else.

"Your day is repeating too," he says, to show her he's a good detective.

She purses her lips and slides the coffee toward him.

A funny balloon of longing presses up against the bottom of his lungs. He wants to know everything she knows. "Are we the only ones?"

"As far as I've been able to detect."

"Is it the same for you?" he keeps his voice down. "You go along in the day and then you jump out, and it's noon again and you go along and you jump out, and it's noon again?"

"And the bells are chiming," she says.

"The weird thing is," he says, which is kind of a stupid thing to say, "the jumping out part. I have control. I can start the day over on purpose whenever I want. So then how did it happen the first time? I don't think I did it on purpose on that seminal day."

"Seminal day." The waitress grins. "That's a good word."

"Fancy word," Gun says, proud.

"Do we have the same seminal day, I wonder," she muses. "It's day five for me."

He nods. "Day five for me."

"I think I did do it on purpose," she says, "on that seminal day. I just wasn't aware of it yet. Jumping out of time isn't something you know you can do until you've done it." She nods at the menu still in his hand. "Hamburger?"

"With grilled onions," he says.

Taking the menu, she looks over his head toward the door. "When that huge man comes in, do you want to join him, or?"

"Not today."

She bobs a nod at him. She goes away, to send his order to the kitchen, and then she's carrying a plate to a table.

In a little while she's back behind the counter, bending over a notepad, jotting something down, probably tallying someone's bill.

"Okay, the really weird thing is," One the Gun says, quiet, "on the seminal day . . . at the end of that day, someone killed me."

Her eyes bounce up over the notepad and then back down, and she's writing again.

"I'm pretty sure I know who did it," he says. "See, I'm a private investigator. But it's only a theory, and I want some sort of proof, something that says to me, unequivocally, this is the killer."

Her face lights up. "You're a detective on your own case. And you're going to prove who did it. And then comes the capture, and then the trial, and then justice will be served. Did you ever read the book *I, Homicide*?"

One the Gun sips his coffee. "I don't have time for books."

"You have all the time in the world," she says.

Then she's gone with the bill to take to someone's table. One the Gun turns and scans the restaurant. At the front Four the Door walks in, looks around, then goes to a booth. One the Gun makes time with his coffee. He feels a little bad that he's standing the guy up for the second day in a row, but he doesn't feel like going through the rigmarole again.

Next when the waitress comes up she's bringing his hamburger. It smells just as good as yesterday and yesterday and—

"Biscuit and honey?" she asks.

"Not today."

She sets down his napkin and silverware.

"Why do you think this is all happening?" he asks.

"I've been thinking about that," she says. She takes the bill pad out of the pocket of her apron but just stands there with it in one hand and the pen in the other. "Here's my theory. Time is numbers, right? One plus one plus one plus one, do you see what I mean, Mr. . . . I'm sorry, what was your name?"

"Gun."

"Mr. Gun." She stops. "That's a brutal name."

"When I was younger it was Fun."

"So one plus one plus one plus one, but no!" The waitress jounces her eyebrows for dramatic effect and points the pen at him. "It's more complex than that. It's equations! It's more like one plus five minus five over one to the first power plus three fifths of fifteen over nine plus—"

"You're kind of losing me here."

"My theory"—she's pointing at him with the pen again—"is that something went wrong with the equation. There's a number out of place. Maybe two. And it just . . ." She sweeps the pen and pad out in a kind of extravagant shrug. "Screwed up the whole system."

"Do you really know what you're talking about?"

She starts writing something on the pad. Her eyebrows over her downcast eyes are tweaked in annoyance. "It's just a theory."

"And why are you and I the only ones caught up in it? What would we have to do with the equations of time? And if it's all just numbers, then what's with the bubbles? I always see a bubble, like the old day is inside it and just floating away."

She hikes her shoulders up at him. "Maybe it has something to do with pi. That's a very important number. The circle is the most perfect shape in geometry, isn't it? The sphere is just a three-dimensional representation of the circle, and three, again, is a number, so . . . would you like more coffee?"

She doesn't wait for an answer, just brings it over and pours.

"I could give you a trial," she says, watching the coffee.

"A what?"

"A trial," she replaces the pot on the warmer behind her. "Like we were talking about before? So justice can be served?"

He says, "What are you talking about, a trial for my killer?"

The waitress looks around as if to make sure no one's watching. Then she reaches below the counter to where she put his menu before and brings out a huge, heavy-looking book bound in cloth. The cover says *Introductory Theories in Jurisprudence*. She flashes her big teeth at him.

"I'm studying law in my spare time," she says.

She sneaks the book back under the counter.

"I've got a lot to learn," she says. "But I figured I might as well use my extra hours wisely, you know what I mean?"

He's not sure what to say to this, so he nods.

"I have to keep checking the book out from the library every morning," she says, "but at least I don't have to worry about checking it back in. And I've learned a lot! You just let me know when you're ready. I'll give you a trial."

He wonders if time travel can scramble one's brain. "How could you do that? You're just a waitress."

Now she's annoyed again. "Hey, don't knock being a waitress. I'm a smart woman with lots going on, okay?"

"I didn't mean anything by it."

"Here's a piece of advice for you," she says. "Never say to another person, 'You're just.' No one is ever just."

One the Gun rakes his hand across his brow and up under his hat. "Hey, jeez, sorry if you felt like—"

"Alright, here's another piece of advice. Because you seem like someone who needs some advice." She's writing again, scowling at the paper. "Never apologize for someone's feelings. Apologize for what you did."

"Gee, I thought we were just having a conversation here."

"Don't say, 'Sorry you're offended,' say, 'Sorry I offended you.' Do you see the difference?"

"Yes. Yeah, I get it."

She tears the bill from the pad, sticks the pad in her pocket, and kicks a nod and a closed-mouth smile in his direction, satisfied that she taught him something. "Good," she says.

GUN MAKES A PASS AT his lunch but loses interest in the time it takes for the waitress to push some bills and change around in the cash register. He pulls out some money of his own and leaves it on the table, gets up, shoots her a wave as he heads out. Starts down the block. He'd kind of like to stay on script for a while. When he stays on script, when he follows along with the forward flow of time, letting the day be as it was before, as it's supposed to be, it centers him. There's a way he can rest in it. Something he doesn't do much lately, rest—especially since, with the days only existing from noon to midnight at the latest, he doesn't ever sleep.

But he's got things to do and time, such as it is, is wasting.

It's a short walk down the square to the police station, a squat building the color of toilet paper tubes with short, stunty windows and half-dead petunias fainting in their window boxes. At the front counter he asks to see the police detective on the case.

The guy's a hard-nosed cop with a face like a pile of bricks and a hide as tough as a rhino's pajamas.

Cinco the Toss 'Em in the Clinko.

They shake hands and the cop leads him to a dingy little office with a scarred wooden desk and two metal chairs, one (the one One the Gun sits down in) with one leg too short, making the whole works wobble. The walls are painted white and left bare except for some sort of certificate in a little frame.

The cop takes the chair behind the desk and leans over the tabletop, planting his elbows across scattered paperwork and folding his hands. As casual as this posture is, he's a guy who talks in exclamation points, as if periods are too puny for his pertinacious puss. "This case is tanning my hide, Gun! I've got four suspects, all with motive and opportunity! I want answers! You know my reputation. I've got to catch this killer—or killers—and—"

"Toss 'em in the clink?"

"—slap 'em in the slammer!"

"Well, anything I can do to assist," One the Gun says.

"You can give me all you got," the cop says. "This thing is whipping my eggs! I'll take any information you can give me that will help me round up this killer—or killers—and—"

"Toss 'em in the clink?"

"—pack 'em off to the pokey!"

Gun shifts and his chair wobbles again. "Hey, I've got a bone to pick with you. Why did you disclose to one of the suspects that the method of murder was poison?"

"*May have been* poison," the cop says. "Four little words, that's all I said, Gun. And that suspect happens to be the victim's widow, you know."

This is true, and Gun's complaint is uncalled-for, but something about Cinco always makes Gun want to bust his chops. "Yeah, yeah, well, it makes it hard for me to grill the suspects when they know everything already."

"You can't just button up when a woman asks how her husband died, Gun." The cop looks his usual hard-nosed self for a moment, but then the corner of his mouth gets a little leer in it. He straightens away from the desk and leans his chair back on two legs. "Especially a woman like her. In case you hadn't noticed, that dish is as stunning as a billy club to the back of the head! If I weren't so professional, I'd sure like to take her for a tumble, roll her in the hay—"

"Toss her in the clink?"

"You ever catch her act back when she was Six the Tricks?"

Oh, right. When she was in a magic act. One the Gun has somehow forgotten all about that.

"With those curves of hers in those tiny little costumes," the cop says, "and those calendar legs, let me tell you, she could disappear into my basket any day." He sits back up in his chair. "But you didn't come in here just to razz me about the way I do my job, did you, Gun?"

"Actually, I wanted to ask about something that wasn't on the police report. I'm curious if Seven the Heaven has a record."

"That priest?"

Gun knows it sounds ridiculous, but he'd love any extra scrap of ammunition he can get for the grilling he's going to be springing on the preacher a little later today.

"Are you kidding?" the cop says. "Guy's a cheap hood, a lowlife, a no-good! If you ask me, I wouldn't be surprised if that weasel goes down for this job. I have it on good authority that Heaven whiles away his churchy evenings gambling with the mugs in the back room of the Dive—and I'll bet he's fleecing them dry."

"Fantastic," Gun says, "give me all you've got on him."

"Oh," the cop says, "well, he's a corrupt character, I'm sure of it, but he doesn't have a police record."

The bubble of excitement that had been rising inside Gun deflates. "Oh."

"Now don't get me wrong." The cop points at him. "If he's guilty I'll get him but good! I've got a job to do! I've got to catch this killer—or killers—and—"

Gun doesn't bother.

"—haul 'em to the hoosegow. Hey, want to have look at the evidence file?"

The cop pops up in his seat like someone yanked him up by the ears. Without waiting for Gun's answer he takes himself and his exclamation points out of the room. One the Gun waits. Through the open blinds in the window the cat with the black coat and the one white ear is sitting in the window box, sniffing around the half-dead flowers.

When the cop returns he sets down a small box containing the physical evidence of the case. There's not much: a glass, a cocktail napkin, and one small paper envelope. He sits, reaches into his desk, and pulls out a couple pairs of white gloves, handing one over to Gun.

The cop wriggles his fingers into his and then reaches into the box, bringing out the small paper envelope, opening the flap, and shaking the item into his palm.

A bead.

"This was found on the floor not far from the victim," the cop says. "It's not like any kind of bead I'm used to. That symbol. It almost looks religious to me. So that could point to the priest. But Six the Kicks wears loads of beads, so it could have come from one of her dresses or hats or jewelry. Not that that necessarily gives us anything. She was his wife, so she could have been in and out of the office any number of times, and it wasn't necessarily left there on the night of the murder anyway."

"My suggestion?" One the Gun says. "Check the uniforms they wear at the Dive."

"Hey, why didn't I think of that?"

"In fact, don't forget to check the one the victim is wearing in his casket right now."

This isn't the bead One the Gun found. That one is, in this

iteration of today, still sitting under the leg of the desk in the office of the Dive Inn. Which means there's probably at least one more bead missing from Five the No Longer Alive's uniform, which isn't unexpected given the convulsive way he died, at least according to the reporting of Two the True Blue. Of course, to find the spot this second bead is likely missing from, you'd have to pull the dead man out of his casket and inspect the back. But Gun doesn't need to tell the cop that.

The cocktail napkin is white with the circular indentation of the glass centered on it. Small crinkles expand out from the ring. In one corner, embossed, are the words *The Dive Inn* in script over the silhouette of a boat anchor. The glass is a tumbler with no particular identifying characteristics. It looks like all the other tumblers he's seen in the place.

Gun, hand in a white glove, reaches toward it and hesitates.

"Oh, you can pick it up," the cop says. "There aren't any prints or anything you could obscure."

One the Gun reaches in and brings out the glass.

In a flash he has a theory. Something so brilliant that, if it's true, will knock Miss Blue's socks off. "Hey, try this on for size! The glass is a decoy."

The cop sits back in his seat. "Oh, come on, I already told that secretary of yours. Traces of poison were definitely found in that thing."

"Okay, but then why are there no fingerprints from the victim himself?" Gun says. "What if the *real* glass was removed and this one was put in its place to throw us off? What if it wasn't even a glass at all?"

"No soap," the cop says. "Victim was found still wearing the gloves he always wore to count money."

"Ah."

"Nice try, though." Grinning.

WHO KILLED ONE THE GUN? 79

Gun looks close at the glass, tries to squint some evidence onto it.

The object perched on his white-gloved palm makes him think about magicians again. Makes him think about sleight of hand.

"Alright," he says, "try this on for size. It's magic."

The cop is subtle for once, just kicking up a single eyebrow at Gun.

Gun says, "We know the preacher, the widow, and the bartender were all right there when the drink was poured. So how did the poison get in there? How about this? Six the Kicks, alias Six the Tricks, uses her magician skills to drop the poison into the glass right there under the noses of witnesses."

"No soap," the cop says again. "She wasn't a magician. She was a magician's assistant. That's the woman's role. They're cheesecake, just there to hand the magician the props and get cut in half."

"I don't know," Gun says, "maybe she did all sorts of—"

"I've seen her. She was just a body and a pretty face."

"Ah."

"Got any other theories?"

Gun does. It involves a certain preacher and a certain stack of letters hidden in a Bible, but now that they've gotten themselves off the track of Seven the Heaven, Gun is going to keep this one to himself.

INSIDE THE PREACHER'S CHAMBERS THE fire in the fireplace has its dancing shoes on and is dishing out plenty of heat. The preacher's doing his hand-out, palm-up gesture to indicate the straight-backed chair sitting just opposite his desk. He says, "Have a seat, my son."

"Come off it," One the Gun shoots back. "If you're a man of God, I'm an eight-armed octopus with rings on every finger."

At this one the preacher just looks confused.

"Sorry, I've got to try not to be so rude." Gun sits in the chair. "A friend of mine was just complaining about that."

Seven the Heaven takes a seat behind his desk, casual. Leans forward, puts his elbows on the desk, brings his hands together, steeples his fingers, and rests his chin on their tips. Smiling, he says, "Perhaps you've heard that I like to play a game or two at one of the local hangouts. But I assure you, everything I do is in service to the Lord. My methods may be unorthodox, but they're pure, my brother."

"Am I your brother or your son?" Gun asks.

"Pardon?"

"Sorry. Rude again. My fault. It's been a long day."

Seven the Heaven puts concern into his eyes. "Oh, has it been, my brother?"

"Yeah, yeah, feels like about four," Gun cracks back. "So I need you to know I'm here to take you downtown."

Like he's a cop and he can just order a suspect to the police station. But he's mostly here today to lean on the preacher, tell the guy what he knows, what he suspects, and watch for the reaction.

The preacher's face, peaceful over his steepled fingers, doesn't move. "For what?"

One the Gun springs the snapper: "Suspicion of murder."

This time there might be a tiny twitch in one of the preacher's eyes.

One the Gun pulls a folded sheet of paper from his inside jacket pocket. He opens it and flashes it at the preacher. "This is a search warrant."

People don't know what a real search warrant looks like.

He folds it back up and tucks it away. "I expect you to cooperate."

"Well." The preacher smiles, showing his teeth to Gun like they prove something. "Of course you know this is ridiculous."

Gun says, "I happen to know you're in possession of some love letters."

The preacher's smile doesn't change.

"I have reason to believe," Gun says, "those letters were written by one Five the No Longer Alive"—at this the preacher blinks a couple times—"to a Nine the, well, we don't need to go into that, but just know that this is very strong evidence that you were blackmailing the deceased, which is very strong evidence that, ipso facto, you killed poor"—he slips this last detail in just so the preacher is completely assured that he knows what he's talking about—"Snookie."

One the Gun's got to hand it to the preacher. His expression doesn't change no matter what Gun throws at him. He guesses it's one of the talents of a card sharp: having a good poker face. The preacher sits back in his chair, easy, like he's just a little amused by this whole thing. "Now that doesn't quite make sense to me. If I were blackmailing someone, which is preposterous"—at this his eyes tick over, for just a second, to the big Bible—"why would I kill my meal ticket?"

It's not a bad question.

"Because maybe he stopped paying," One the Gun says. "Because maybe he threatened to go to the police."

"And what is this"—the preacher hesitates like he can't quite remember the word—"Snookie?"

"That's how the letters are signed. We think it's some sort of pet name."

We. Like Gun's already been consulting the cops.

"So these supposed letters I supposedly have that

supposedly prove I killed Five," the preacher says, "aren't even signed Five."

"Did I say that?"

"You said they say Snookie."

Gun leans back in his chair and crosses his ankles. "Some," he says. "Some say Snookie."

He's trying to be suave, but it's hard to be suave when you keep having to say *Snookie*.

"You realize," the preacher flips his hand out, blasé, but his smile is looking painted on. "There are plenty of Fives in this town. If all the letters say is Five—"

"Did I say that's all they said?" Gun cuts in. "How would you know that's all they said if you supposedly don't have these supposed letters?"

The preacher tries to laugh, but it comes out sounding like the dying bleat of an ill-used hot-water bottle. "This all sounds like you're chasing your tail, inspector. Not like proof of any murder or even blackmail. If I'm a blackmailer, where's all my money?" Broadcasting a gaze around the humble room.

"That's a nice ring you've got there," One the Gun says. "Emerald?" And then before the preacher can answer: "What's that parable in the Bible about how you should feel all ginger peachy about rooking the collection box? Maybe it applies to blackmail too."

The preacher stands. Something in the way his body hovers over his slightly bent legs makes it look like he might make a dash for the door, but then he swivels to the bookcase, and his voice is just as relaxed as before. "Well, there is a passage that might pertain."

He reaches right for the big Bible. Pulls it out.

"It seems there was a wealthy farmer," he says. He holds the Bible exactly like Gun held it yesterday, one hand on the spine, one underneath. "He had a particularly abundant harvest, and worried that he didn't have room to store all his crops." He lays the Bible face up on his desk. "And then the Lord said—"

The preacher flings open the big Bible, grabs the letters, and throws them in the fire.

One the Gun is on his feet.

The bundle flares up yellow in the flames.

The preacher's eyes flash.

The letters turn to ash.

There's a funny wobble in the corners of the preacher's grinning mouth as he says, "So you see, as I said, you have no proof."

"You just destroyed evidence!"

"It's your word against mine, Gun," the preacher says. "And I'm a man of God. So the only thing you've accomplished here is made it so that the evidence is gone."

The words the preacher says are like he's cool and unaffected, but there's a hoarseness in his voice.

One the Gun stares at the fire. Then he turns his gaze on the preacher.

"It may be gone now, Heaven," he says, "but it won't be gone tomorrow."

The fire crackles.

That line felt pretty smooth when One the Gun said it, but the preacher just looks confused.

"Okay, okay." One the Gun waves it off. "Never mind."

IN SEARCHING THE PREMISES TODAY—the chest, the cot, the preacher's desk—One the Gun did not find anything more of interest. Whatever loot the guy's been nicking in his shakedown, he must be keeping in a good old-fashioned bank.

Inconvenient.

Worse, there was no gun. And it's got to be somewhere, if the preacher is indeed One the Gun's killer.

Gun goes to the phone booth just inside the drugstore and slides the door shut. Tosses some silver in the slot, calls his office. Through the double set of glass—the phone booth and the drugstore window—the cat with the black coat and the one white ear trots by. Two the True Blue picks up and says hello in her clear, bell-like voice.

"Checking in," he says. "Got anything new for me?"

He knows what's she's going to say. She's going to tell him that the police have reported back that traces of the poison were indeed found on the glass that was discovered on the desk in the office following the victim's death, but that the glass contained no fingerprints, not even partials. She's going to tell him her beau was a little perturbed at catching them in what looked like a clinch this afternoon, and she knows he didn't mean anything by it, but could they please keep it to business as usual. To that he's going to want to be professional and say, "Oh, of course, of course."

And she does, and she does, and he does.

But then, for the first time since this all began, One the Gun changes the conversation of this everyday (except yesterday, he didn't bother to call her yesterday) phone call. "Say, I have something new for you. I want you to call the insurance company. Ask them if Five the No Longer Alive made any provisions in any of his insurance policies for someone named Nine."

"Nine the . . . ?"

"Just Nine is all I know," Gun says.

Two the True Blue never shies away from a difficult assignment. "Alright, sir," she says. "I'm on the job."

"Oh, hey. Here's something else I'd like you to check on," he says. Another lead he'd forgotten about. The cop's mention of Six the Kicks in her incarnation as a magician reminded Gun of it. "I read in the newspaper morgue that Seven the Heaven has a twin brother named Eleven. See what you can find out about him. My biggest question is whether they're fraternal or identical."

"Oh?" she asks.

He wags one hand in a sort of shrug. "I mean, maybe Eleven is posing as Seven, or Seven is posing as Eleven, or—"

"And doing what?" she asks.

"Oh, I don't know," he says, "but twins can be sneaky."

"Okay. Eleven the . . .?"

"Just Eleven is all I know," he says. "I suppose it could be Eleven the Heaven, I mean, maybe they're both preachers. It's probably Eleven the Heaven. Start there. I can't think of anything else that rhymes."

AFTER HE GETS OFF THE phone he strolls down the block to the newspaper office to have a look in their morgue. This time he's looking for any clues to the identity of a woman named Nine.

He finds stories about a Nineteen the Quite Clean, a man who launders suits by day and apparently has been cleaning out the safes of local shops by night.

And a Ninety-Nine the I'm Fine I'm Fine, who keeps saying that every time he's almost run over by a bus.

One the Gun calls Two the True Blue back to check on her progress. She says no provisions have been made in Five's insurance policies, nor his will, for anyone named Nine.

"His life insurance policy is in his widow's name," she says, "and the business is half in her name, half in the name of the bartender, Eight the First Mate."

This is interesting. "Oh?"

"Fifty-fifty," she confirms, and he can hear the twinkle of her eyes in her voice. "I hope they get along."

Well, this is definitely not the way things were presented to Gun by Six the Kicks. "Aha," he says. "Did you track down anything about Seven the Heaven's brother?"

"Yes," she says. "They're fraternal twins."

His shoulders drop a little. "Ah. Well, I guess that was a shot in the dark anyway. What did his name turn out to be?"

"Eleven the Leaven. He's a baker."

IN THE CAFÉ WHEN HE'S having dinner they're playing Two the True Blue's favorite program, *Who Is the Villain?*, on the small radio on the shelf above the cash register.

"Who could it be?" the announcer asks. "The upstanding businessman with larceny in his eyes? The goldfish-eyed gunsel with mitts like waffle irons? The curvaceous dame with the striped dress and the checkered past?" A burst of organ music to punctuate the drama of the expected query: "Who! Is! The Villain?"

When the waitress with the doe eyes and the big teeth brings him his check she says, "You and me, we're like in the radio show. You're the hero detective who's right there for the story, but I'm the part that happens after the show ends. After they pack the bad guys off to court."

"Do you even have time to read that lawbook?" One the Gun asks. "You work all day."

She says, "I take breaks."

OUTSIDE THE CAFÉ ONE THE Gun heads up the sidewalk. The sun's turned tail, and the streetlamps fight the night to leave some light on the pavement. Time carries him along again. Carries him to the ship-hull-shaped neon sign of the Dive Inn under which, inside the entryway in all his gold-button ritzy-like finery, stands Four the Door.

The moose snaps a salute when One the Gun steps in, says what he always says: "Welcome aboard!"

It's hard to remember which Four the Door he's talking to: the one who knows him or the one who doesn't. This one is the one who doesn't, since Gun skipped out on their interview today. Furthermore and luckily, this is also not the Four the Door, theoretically speaking, who tossed him to the pavement on the today that was yesterday.

"Business good tonight?" Gun asks.

"Yes, sir," Four the Door says. "You might not have heard, but we had a tragedy on Wednesday. See, the proprietor of this establishment, he went and got himself dusted. Anyway, folks been coming by to make with the respects. Look at all them flowers there in the corner."

"Very nice," One the Gun says.

"Prettier than pink ballerinas!"

Gun moves off into the club. Papier-mâché shells and sea-green lamplight. Half the tables have people at them slurping drinks. At one end of the empty dance floor a chick in a blue dress is putting in the hard sell on an upright piano.

Nuts. Somehow Gun kind of forgot about her.

He points himself toward the bar. As he goes he sees, at a table all alone, Three the Goatee with his martini and his pompous, perky pinky. If the guy had any self-respect at all, he'd be out with Miss Blue, not sitting at a dive, drinking alone.

Three the Goatee's pupils slide to Gun's, and he snaps a courteous, if chilly, nod of recognition. "Gun."

A short, formal nod back. "Professor."

Three the Goatee knocks his high-and-mighty hooch to the back of his throat, shoots the pig eye at Gun once more, and beats it. Gun puts his back to the professor's retreat and walks on.

At the leftmost edge of the bar, nursing a glass of something red, is the widow. Six the Kicks dressed to some sort of nines, still in mourning black, but this particular black, with its slink and sparkle, is doing a better job on her curves than her daywear.

And yes. All the way to the right side of the bar is the preacher. One the Gun wasn't sure he'd see him tonight. You'd think if you went back in time and changed something, something big—like calling out a priest as a blackmailer and a murderer—you'd change the trajectory of his day going forward. But here he is. That probably says something profound about human nature.

Unlike when Gun was in here two tonights ago, though, the preacher isn't sitting and nonchalantly watching the crowd. He's hunched over the bar, head low, hand raising and lowering, rocking his whiskey to sleep like he doesn't notice anything around him. One the Gun crosses the house and bellies up to the counter exactly halfway between Six and Seven. Now the preacher looks up. His eyes on Gun's look faraway for a moment, then spark recognition. Then they grab hold and don't let go.

One the Gun can't tell what's in those eyes. If it's something vicious or desperate.

Unlike when Gun was in here two tonights ago, the preacher's glass is already almost empty.

Behind the counter, running a rag along the shiny silver beer taps is Eight the First Mate. One the Gun leans in and says, "Scotch on the rocks."

Eight the First Mate opens his mouth—and even though Gun knows better, knows the bartender doesn't have any memory of what Gun did yesterday, he almost expects the bartender to tell him to get out, almost expects the moose to come up and grab him from behind. But instead, from behind comes a woman's voice. "Put it on my tab."

Six the Kicks. She's left her spot at the end of the bar and is standing behind him. Her perfume wraps round him like the red on a candy cane.

"Don't be stingy with that Scotch," she tells the bartender, "and pour me another glass of wine."

One the Gun turns to face her. "Good evening."

"Inspector."

He gives her his hand. "May I offer my condolences?"

"I apologize for my rudeness earlier," she says. "I haven't been myself. I'd like to make it up to you."

When the bartender sets their drinks down Six the Kicks takes both, one in each hand, her tiny black beaded handbag dangling from her wrist. "I'm ready to be interviewed."

She starts to lead One the Gun to a booth on the other side of the room in the corner with all the flowers, but One the Gun does not want to sit that close to the piano, so he says, "How about that table over there?" and they change course. They cross to a spot not far from the entryway to the Dive. At the angle they approach they can see out through the door to where the moose is standing outside, just down from the door, taking in some air. The moose glances sidelong back in at them, then steps back inside. He crosses his arms, positioning himself at a three-quarter turn as if to keep an eye on the man who's pulling out a chair for Six the Kicks.

"You don't mind moving over here?" One the Gun turns his back on the moose and takes a seat. "It's just that that piano player gets awfully loud."

"You think so?" Six asks. "I haven't heard her before. She's new. I think she sounds nice."

She sounds like a player piano hooked up to a washing machine.

Six the Kicks pushes Gun's drink across the table. "I want to do all I can to help find the person who did this to my husband."

"I appreciate that." He takes a sip. The Scotch is just as he likes it—fresh and medicinal, like the scent of the swab before the needle. He glances across the room at the preacher. The guy is sitting mostly with his back to them, still stooped over his drink but turned slightly, his head turned more, just enough to be watching them out of the corner of his eye. "What's with the preacher tonight?"

She tweaks her eyebrows at Gun, equal parts puzzled and annoyed. "He's in mourning. We all are."

Right, right. Even this far out, it's still only Friday, still only two days after what happened.

One the Gun says, "Did he know your husband well?"

"Well enough. He was here enough."

"You said on—" One the Gun catches himself almost referencing something she said on a different tonight, and he readjusts. "Uh, I heard that on Wednesday, at the end of the night, when your husband took the cash drawer to the office, you and Seven the Heaven were sitting at the bar."

"Yes."

"He claimed he didn't go to the office. Can you confirm that?"

"My husband?"

"The preacher."

"The preacher didn't go to the office?"

"Correct."

"I'm not sure. Pretty soon after my husband took the cash drawer back, I went to the restroom to powder my nose."

Her saying this on a new tonight, in a slightly different context, makes One the Gun almost believe her.

She tips her head at him. "You don't think Father Heaven killed my husband. I think you're barking up the wrong guy."

"Am I?"

"Let me give you a little information." Six the Kicks ticks her chin in the direction of the bartender across the way, delivering drinks to a table. "This whole place? Used to belong to him."

"The bartender?"

"Couldn't make a go of it," she says. "He was running it into the ground. No planning. All he did was think up ways to play ship captain. Pretend he was on a boat. Throw fishing nets all over the place. But he couldn't keep it afloat."

Her eyebrows bounce like she notices the pun.

"Anyway, my husband came along and bankrolled the club," she says. "Saved this place from ruin. And what thanks does he get? I think you know."

She's nodding at One the Gun like she thinks he knows.

"Yes?" he asks.

One the Gun knows. Because she's said it all before.

"First Mate thinks my husband turned his sweet little restaurant into a dive," she says. "He always resented it. And he wanted it back. And he knew if my husband was out of the way, it would come right back to him."

"That's funny," One the Gun says. "I've checked with the insurance company, and they say this business is now owned 50 percent by Eight the First Mate and"—he pauses to watch her react to the fact that he knows what she knows—"50 percent by you."

The satisfied, knowing look on Six the Kicks's face doesn't change, but she shifts in her seat. She takes a sip of her wine and puts it down.

"I don't know what you're implying," she says.

The piano player is working the keys over like she's going

at them with brass knuckles. Even halfway across the room it's still pounding into Gun's head.

"What were *you* implying just now?" he counters. "Maybe that the bartender wanted to take sole ownership in this place so he killed—"

"Well, *I* didn't kill him!" Indignation flashes the eyelids back from the whites of the widow's eyes. "You know nothing about me."

One the Gun shrugs it off. "Maybe not, but I think I'm hearing you kind of accuse the bartender of murder when—"

"Alright." She flaps her hand at the inference like it's a mosquito. "I might have forgotten to tell you that the Dive is now half mine, but that doesn't change the fact that First Mate wanted it back and would do anything he could to get it." Her lip curls away from her teeth. "He just didn't expect that if he succeeded, his big prize would go half to me."

"Ah, sure, yeah," Gun says in a voice that's rolling its eyes. He's been in a mood ever since the jabs the waitress took at him at lunch. "So you were hoping he'd get convicted of murder because you'd like it to go *entirely* to you."

Her eyes flash again. Then she settles and sips her wine. "Well, a girl can dream, can't she?"

One the Gun opens his mouth, closes it. It's not doing him any good to bully the woman. He tries to get back on track. "I suppose she can." He smiles at her. "I wonder if I can ask you about your husband."

She uncrosses and recrosses her legs. "Of course."

Over at the bar Eight the First Mate sets another drink down in front of the preacher. The preacher isn't paying attention to the drink. The preacher is sitting sidesaddle on his stool and staring across the Dive at One the Gun.

Irritation zips up the back of Gun's neck. What is with this guy? Is he trying to be threatening?

"You say you like to get your kicks," he says to the widow. "But isn't it true that your husband liked to get his kicks too?"

Her eyes narrow. "What is that supposed to mean?"

"Did you or did you not know that your husband was carrying on with a woman behind your back?"

Six the Kicks is on her feet. "That is inappropriate."

"You are correct," he says, "and I'm just wondering if you knew about it, and if so, what you—"

She reaches for her glass to throw it in his face. Her black-gloved hand hovers over the glass, then diverts to his glass, then back to hers.

Now One the Gun is grabbed from behind.

If he could, he would say to her, Do you ever get the feeling you're having déjà vu? Because this feels exactly like it did when he was being thrown out of here before: two arms under his armpits and locking across his chest. He's dragged to his feet. The moose, of course. Gun shouldn't have chosen a table so close to the front door.

"My husband never had a dalliance in his life," the widow is announcing, like she has a right to be indignant about getting one's kicks, but something in her eyes—at least the glimpse he catches of them before he's dragged sidelong from the booth—makes him think she believes what she says.

"Come along," Four the Door says. As if One the Gun has a choice in the matter.

Gun's feet skid across the floor. He fights to get them back underneath him. The moose pauses, sets him to standing, then grabs him by one arm and continues lugging him along. Gun thinks they're heading for the entrance, but then the moose drags him past it, all the way to the far wall and to another, more nondescript door. He opens it, and they're both shoving out into the alley. Cool air and the sounds of the street somewhere beyond. Dark gloom after the brightness of the club.

One the Gun expects to be left here, but Four the Door swings him round, grabs hold of his coat and shirt—one fistful at the top, making the collar choke around his neck, and one fistful below—and slams him up against the alley wall. His head hits brick. Wisps of white flicker across his vision.

The look in the moose's eyes is different than Gun has ever seen in them. Fury.

"I better never catch you disrespecting the lady again, get me?"

The whites are showing all the way around Four's irises. His pupils are shrunk to points.

One the Gun, somehow more stunned by the expression on the man's face than the empty air below his feet, bobs his head at the moose.

The moose lets him down. Gives him the eyes for one moment longer. Turns. Goes back in and wallops the door shut behind him.

Quiet in the alley. The moldy-bread reek of trash bins. One the Gun rubs at his throat, catching his breath.

For cat's sake. It's like Four the Door turned into someone completely different.

One the Gun straightens his coat and heads down the alley past a flattened cardboard box leaning up against the brick wall. A crumple of paper blows by his feet. At the mouth of the passage he turns and deliberately walks past the entrance to the club, shoulders high, trying to look tall. The door is open, pouring music, but the moose isn't there.

One the Gun passes by.

As he steps away the quiet of the square draws around him like a fog. Hazy moonlight sags in the branches of sidewalk trees. There's a strange quality to the light along the street, an extra glow hovering around storefront windows. Maybe it's the knock to the head. Now there's a sound he's not sure he really hears. Like just the thought of a sound. Behind him or inside him. Footsteps?

Someone's following him again. Maybe. He turns back, tries to peer down the block. Dark shapes and shadows. There are too many nooks and crevices along this street, recessed doorways, alleys to duck into.

Who cares, Gun? Why are you getting itchy around the edges? You know the future. All you have to do to play it safe is not go down to the basement.

One the Gun walks on. A car passes on the street, pouring light ahead of it, and turns at the end of the block.

A thrum of warning creeps along his spine. He should have a gun to match his name. Why doesn't he have a gun to match his name? On impulse he steps into the street to cross to the other side, get a different vantage point from which to scope out his surroundings.

The thing is, tonight isn't last night, isn't the night before, isn't the night before that. It isn't even the same time of night as when he's walked to the office before. Even if the person who may or may not be following him is the same person who followed him on that first night and eventually killed him in the basement, even if that person is, say, the preacher, he's a different preacher now. This preacher stood in his chambers and listened to Gun accuse him of murder. This preacher destroyed evidence in front of Gun. This preacher may be desperate.

A sound breaks open the air.

Short and sharp.

A gunshot.

He pounds asphalt to the other side of the street.

His shoe clips the curb and he almost goes down, stumbles, rights himself, keeps going.

Up ahead in the center of the square is a towering bronze statue of a soldier on a leaping horse. Moonlight through the horse and rider paint long, crooked shadows across the murk of the manicured grass.

It's possible the sound was a car backfiring.

He tries to remember if he heard a car backfire on any of these other nights. At this time he's usually in the Dive. He tries to remember how to jump out of time. He can't think.

The only thing that's jumping out of time is his heart against his ribcage. He's brought himself to the most wide-open spot on the square. This stupid statue and yards and yards of nothing all around.

He makes a dive for the shadows behind the horse and rider. What's he going to do, hide between the horse's skinny legs?

He squeezes his eyes shut. And the last thing he thinks before he reaches down into himself to try to rip himself away from the forward flow of time is Two the True Blue. That kiss he slipped her two todays ago. That he took a flyer on because he was in this place where you can do whatever you want because it won't have happened tomorrow. That kiss was so puny. He should have really gone for it while he had the chance.

FIVE

THE BELLS ARE CHIMING AS he opens his eyes.

It's bright as day in the room. He's in his office.

Day six.

Dizzied by the blast of light, by the fact that once again he's not dead, One the Gun shuts his eyes again. Listens to another strike of the bell. Opens his eyes. Waits for the room to stop spinning.

Two the True Blue is standing in front of him. Such a look on her face. Eyes the color and size of oceans.

Two the True Blue with her heart-shaped face and her clean, filed nails and her aura of classiness and purity. Always looking impeccable, always ready to take care of business competently and without complaint. This woman who seems to Gun like the ideal woman, the kind of woman who, if you're with her, makes you an ideal man.

He sputters out the only thing he can think to say, "Miss Blue?"

"You looked so odd just now," she says. "Are you alright?"

Yesterday's bubble floats off and away.

"I am great!" He shakes his fists like triumph, which makes the eyebrows push together, confused, on her pretty brow.

But then she smiles, and the day moves forward. Like it always does. She reads him her notes on the case and tells him about the poison. She mispronounces its name. She tells him the victim probably suffered a few shocking moments of agony followed by violent convulsions, followed by unconsciousness, and finally death. She details his appointments for the day, her finger pointing at a notation on the calendar open on his desk. One o'clock time slot. *Meet with doorman at café.*

But when she reaches to the high shelf of his bookcase, standing on one foot, to work out the huge volume of *The Compleat Illustrated Pharmacopeia*, when she grabs hold and drops back on both feet, teeters, and he, right behind her, tucks his shoe against the back of her heel and trips her in that way that always makes her tip back into his arms, the day moving forward stops.

For a moment he just holds her. Gun above, Miss Blue below, her eyes surprise up into his. The book flattened between them.

Then he kisses her long and soft and hot enough to melt the honey on any biscuit on any plate in any café in the world.

When he pulls back, her sea-blue eyes are big on his.

Those eyes could mean stunned or enticed or appalled or bedeviled or torn or dismayed or offended or swept away.

He's going to go with swept away.

Now there's sudden movement at his periphery. It's the blur of Three the Goatee who, having just entered, is barreling across the room at them. Gun doesn't let go, just looks up from Two the True Blue's still swept-away face. The goateed goose's eyes are wide and wild.

Miss Blue pushes away. "Sir, please!" she says under her breath. The book clutched against her chest.

And fast as all that Three the Goatee is nearly nose to nose with him. "Gun, I'm not an idiot. I see all your little plays for her. I'm sick of it. You keep your hands off!"

Three the Goatee, a good six inches shorter than Gun, puffs out his chest like he thinks it looks manly. Gun would like to shove himself right back at the self-important ass, but Two the True Blue likes men to be gentlemen. So he takes a step back and puts his hands up at the professor like *who, me?* "Sorry, friend."

"I'm *not* your friend."

Gun turns to Miss Blue. "I'm sorry. I don't know why that happened. But when you tripped I—"

Three the Goatee grabs her arm. "We're getting out of here, and you're not coming back."

Her eyebrows press together, annoyed. "Sweetie, this is my job, and I think I have the right to decide—"

"The man's a pig." His eyelids are cranked back from the whites of his eyes.

"Miss Blue, let me just say," Gun is saying as the professor pulls her across the room. But before anything else can be said, they're gone, and the door is slamming shut behind them.

For a moment One the Gun stares after them. He feels . . .

Great!

Like a first-rate romancer. A first-rate man. Look at the way she refused to be told she wasn't ever coming back. She was swept away for sure. And do you know what he's going to do? He's going to solve this case. And do you know what happens when the detective solves the case? He wins the girl.

A LITTLE EARLY FOR HIS lunchtime appointment today One the Gun sees the doorman standing at the newsstand just down from the café. The guy's so tall the scallops of the newsstand's awning drape his head like the flaps of an aviator hat as he stands looking down at the stacks of papers.

Instantly when he sees him, Gun's fingers itch to grab the oversized ape and find some alley wall to slam him up against. But he walks over, nonchalantly putting his hand out to shake.

"Four the Door, I believe? I'm One the Gun. We have an appointment to go over the circumstances of your boss's death."

The moose is looking at him with that innocent puppy-dog slant. So different from the wide-eyed fury Gun saw on him last.

Gun would like to wipe that innocent look right off his face. Sure, now that the day's started over, that assault in the alley hasn't actually happened for the moose. But it happened for Gun—you can't take away the fact that when today was yesterday, the moose did what he did.

They shake hands.

"Happy to make with the acquaintance," the moose says.

"Say," One the Gun says, "instead of the café, what do you say we go on over to the Dive?"

He calls it *the Dive* because he knows it irks the moose.

"I'd like to look at the layout," Gun says, "and have you point out the positions of a few people for me."

The moose rubs the back of his neck. "Well, place is closed up."

"You have a key, don't you?" Gun says. "You were the one who let in the cops after hours, I believe?"

"Well, I can't go letting in just any—"

"Listen," Gun cuts in, "this is police business."

"You're a cop? I thought you were a detective."

"What do you think a cop is?" Gun says and gives the truth a little twist. "A detective sergeant in the police force. That's what I am. I'm a plainclothesman."

"Oh. Well, I guess it would be okay."

***

THE LIGHTS ARE OFF WHEN they go inside, and the joint feels gloomy and cold. Faint smell of booze on the air. And it's quiet. None of the usual oppressive pomp of dive-bombing piano chords. The moose closes the door behind them and snaps on some overhead lights.

The quiet makes Gun think of something. "Say, was there music playing the night your boss died?"

"Radio was going."

They walk across the empty dance floor to the bar.

"See, I'm wondering why no one heard anything," Gun says. "The poison that killed your boss was particularly . . . well, he might have cried out or something."

"Well, place gets pretty loud," Four the Door says. "And the boss likes the tunes fit to beat the house down. Puts a muffle on the ruckuses in the back room."

"Ah."

"This what you want to look at?" the moose asks. They've come to the end of the bar.

"I wanted to ask about the end of the night," Gun says, "just after your boss told you he was shutting things down and came back here and took the cash drawer and went off to count the till."

"Yeah?" the moose says.

"From where you stand at the door," Gun says, "you have the perfect vantage point to see pretty much everything in the club. Now both the preacher and"—he almost calls her *the widow* but doesn't think the moose would like it—"Six the Kicks were sitting at the bar."

Four the Door's face grows dark anyway. "What's your investigation got to do with her?"

"Routine," Gun says. "We've got to trace the last moments to see what we can learn."

"You cops are always looking for people to be murderers," the moose says. "She's a lady, she's no murderer."

"We've got to get all the facts," One the Gun says, "so we can clear her name. Don't you want to clear her name?"

Four the Door has his head tipped back, showing his chin to Gun, a suspicious squint in his eyes. "What you want to know?"

"Where was she sitting?"

The moose puts his hands on a barstool.

This surprises Gun. It's the last seat in the row, where he always sees Seven sit. Granted, the alwayses are always a single day, so just because the preacher's always there doesn't mean it's his usual seat.

"Okay," One the Gun says, "and the preacher?"

Past the stool where the widow sat, there's one more stool stationed at the cap of the bar, perpendicular to the rest. Four the Door puts his hands on this seat.

Interesting. Behind whoever sits here and across the way, yes, is the back room, where Seven the Heaven claims he went to retrieve his lucky Bible just after the bartender poured the fatal drink. Behind him and to the left is the piano, which doesn't matter, but behind him and to the right, not too far, is the open doorway that leads to the short hallway and the boss's office.

"Mm-hmm," One the Gun says. "And the bartender?"

"Bartender's always all over everywhere," the moose says.

"I'm talking about the moment he poured your boss's drink and set it down."

"Oh. Would have been there."

It's a spot on the back side of the bar, making a close little triangle of the three of them, Six, Seven, and Eight.

"Mm-hmm," Gun says again. "And the ladies' room?"

The moose points.

Gun scopes it out, and it's true. A direct line behind where the preacher sat leads to the back room. In a direct line behind where the widow sat, angled to chat with the preacher, is the ladies' room. And directly behind where the bartender would have stood is the hook where he supposedly grabbed his coat before heading out. Which means if all three turned away the moment the drink was set down, each would have headed in a completely different direction and wouldn't have seen what the others were doing.

"Does that clear her name?" the moose asks.

"Here's another question. Do you know exactly where Eight the First Mate set the drink down?"

The moose taps a spot at the corner of bar equidistant between where Six and Seven sat.

"You saw him set it down?"

"This is where he always puts it, shamus." Four the Door taps the counter again. "That's all."

"So you didn't see him pour the drink and put it down?"

Four the Door opens his mouth, almost closes it, opens it again. "Who cares if I saw him do it, he always does it. Every night. The same way."

"So you didn't see it."

The moose is getting steamed under the collar again. "Are you calling me a greased-up mackerel, is that what you're doing? You're telling me I'm making sandcastles with a nickel-plated tuba?"

"I'm not accusing you of anything." Gun puts his hands up at the moose. "I'm just trying to establish whether you looked or not and what you saw."

"Yeah, no," the moose says. "Yeah, I didn't see him do it."

"Or what happened after he set the drink down?"

"End of the night I like to stand outside as folks is leaving," the moose says. "Catch me some air."

"But you did actually see that the preacher was sitting here and the w—" He stops himself. "Six the Kicks was sitting here."

"Oh, yeah, I saw that, yeah."

"Alright." One the Gun wishes he could sleep sometime. He also wishes they'd caught some lunch at the café before coming over here. "You got any . . . does this place serve crackers or anything?"

"There's some pickled eggs under the counter."

"No, thanks."

"You want a drink? There's plenty of booze."

One the Gun takes the stool where the preacher usually sits, where the widow sat on the night in question. "You know the clientele of this place. You know anyone named Nine?"

The moose turns away. Walks along the line of barstools until he comes to the break in the bar, steps through, then comes back to stand opposite Gun, probably where Eight the First Mate stood to pour the fatal drink. The moose bends down, pulls up a jar from below the counter, and twists it open. Slides the jar across the counter to One the Gun. "We were talking about Six, Seven, and Eight," he says. "Why you want to talk about a Nine?"

Pickled eggs. Who eats pickled eggs?

"I have reason to believe," Gun says, "your boss might have been having an affair with a woman named Nine."

"It's not true." Red starts across Four the Door's face. His eyes dart from Gun to a place over his head, then back to Gun. "My boss was a gentleman. He'd never disrespect his wife like that."

"I'm wondering about that blue chaise in his office."

"See, sounds like you're accusing her again," the moose cuts in. "Boss goes out two-timing and she goes gunning for paybacks, that it? You listen to too many radio shows, shamus. He didn't have no side mouse, and she's no murderer. I don't think I got to talk to you anymore."

"Hey, it's not my job to accuse." Gun puts his hands up at the moose like *simmer down*. "It's my job to ask questions."

"Well, stick to the ones that don't disrespect the lady." The moose turns away and strides back down along the back side of the bar, heading for the break in the bar again.

Gun stares at the jar. He's not getting anywhere with this line of questioning.

The pickled eggs bob around in the juice like eyeballs.

The moose comes back out from behind the bar and is heading Gun's way. Maybe when he reaches Gun the guy'll hustle him out the door, and the interview will be over. Gun stands and tries to look official again. "So you said the preacher sat here and Six sat here."

Almost to him now. "I already told you that."

"And then you went outside and caught some air," Gun says, "and then said goodbye as folks left the Dive."

"Dive Inn."

"Dive Inn," Gun says. "Can you tell me about that? The bartender left first?"

Putting the focus back on the bartender seems to be bringing the moose back around. He takes a seat on one of the stools. Even seated he's about eye to eye with Gun. "Yeah, yeah, he left first."

"And it was just you few left? No other waitstaff?"

"Not at the end of the night," the moose says. "It's me, the bartender, and the boss. This ain't no hoity-toity steak joint, shamus."

Gun takes the stool next to him. "Did the bartender chat with you on the way out?"

"No, but he pitched me good night when he tagged by me the second time."

Wait.

"What do you mean second time?" Gun asks.

"Well, when he piled out of the Dive, I mean the Inn, he had a sack of garbage, and he went around down the alley to axe it. Then in a little bit he comes back and pops me good night and heads home."

No one has mentioned taking the garbage out in Gun's questioning before. Was it a deliberate omission or just a detail no one thinks about?

Gun is up off the stool again. "And where does the garbage go?"

What if a bartender, having dispensed with the contents of a vial of poison, simply takes the evidence out with the trash?

"Sure, I can show you," the moose says.

They cross the nightclub, skirting empty tables, heading for the front door. As they go, Gun glances across to the side door through which, yesterday, the moose very roughly threw Gun out of the Dive. Gun knows the garbage cans are in the alley through that side door. He says, "Wait, so the bartender went through the front door and all the way around to the alley to toss the trash instead of going out that way?" Pointing.

"End of the night the side door's locked," the moose says. He swings the keyring round his finger and makes it chime. "Anyway, he likes to cop a survey of the digs when he leaves. Make sure them tables is all clean and shipshape. That's how he always puts it, 'shipshape.' He's the one with the boat fix."

The moose snaps off the lights and locks up as they leave.

"How long was the bartender in the alley before he came back out?" Gun asks.

"Not long, five minutes."

"As long as five minutes?"

"How long is five minutes?"

"Well," Gun says, "I guess it's longer than people think it is."

"I don't know from time. I just know he went down there and then in a little while he came out."

They head along the sidewalk in front of the place.

"He did tell me there was a cat in the alley," the moose says. "He tried to catch it and take it home. How long does it take to try to catch a cat?"

They go into the alley and walk past the side door. A ways down is the window to the office, and just past that is another door. Nondescript. Gray paint cracking.

"Where does that lead?" Gun asks.

"Used to be the kitchen door before they busted things up to make the joint bigger. Now it just goes to a storeroom."

"And the storeroom's next door to the office?" Gun says.

"Yeah, yeah."

In the time it takes to try to catch a cat, could you sneak through a door and kill a man?

Just past the door are the trash cans: silver and dented with lids on top, like shabby treasure chests.

It might not have been a vial at all. What if it was an almost-empty bottle of rye with just enough for the boss's drink? A whiskey-and-contaminant cocktail, preprepared. All that bartender would need to do is pour it, right there in front of everyone, and then toss the bottle in the trash.

One the Gun starts pulling lids off garbage cans.

They're all empty.

ONE THE GUN GOES TO the phone booth just inside the drugstore and slides the door shut. Tosses some silver in the slot, calls his office. He grits his teeth: What if she's not there?

But then Two the True Blue picks up and says hello in her clear, bell-like voice.

"Say, listen." He jumps right to it. "I want to apologize again. I don't know what came over me. I was just so surprised when you fell into my arms, and there you were, and there I was, and it just . . . happened."

What Gun wants to do is ask her to dinner. Stand up and be suave. Not simper like he's doing now with his apologies but go for what he wants. He broke the ice with the kiss. He shouldn't turn back now. But you can't just kiss your secretary without at least doing the gentlemanly thing.

"Well, I appreciate that, sir," Two the True Blue says.

"I wouldn't want you to think," he says, "that anything could come between you and me and our professional partnership. You're truly an outstanding assistant. Practically a detective in your own right."

"Oh!" she says. "Well, thank you, sir."

Take her to dinner. Then back to her place, which is close by, for drinks, to discuss the case. Pour on the charm and business talk will lead to other things.

"I appreciate you being candid with me," she says, "and professional. Now you just let me know what detective work I can do for you this afternoon."

"Oh, well, yeah," he remembers. "Actually I'd like you to track down anything you can find out about a woman named Nine."

"Nine the . . . ?"

"Just Nine is all I know," Gun says. "And don't bother checking with the insurance company, you already did that—or *I* already did that. But see what else you can find out. Check with the police to see if they have any records, check the phone book, check . . . well, you're resourceful."

"Exciting!" she says. "Sounds like you're making progress. I'll get right on that. Good luck with your interviews. Call in later and I'll give you an update."

And he tries to take a breath to say something else, but she's gone.

ONE THE GUN KNOWS WHAT he needs to do. Wining and dining is all well and good, but first he needs to impress Miss Blue. That high-and-mighty mephitic weasel of a boyfriend of hers might be a college professor, but what Miss Blue really goes for is detectives. Look at the way she moons over that radio show. Thing is, Gun's plenty good at taking snapshots of cheating spouses, but he doesn't have a great track record when it comes to flashy stuff like murders. He's had one or two murder cases before, but . . . alright, he's never actually solved one.

He's got to solve this one.

Still hungry after his nonlunch with the moose, he heads to the café. Inside and working the tables is a different waitress altogether, a tall woman with black hair piled up about a mile high. Gun swings his gaze and finds the waitress with the doe eyes and the big teeth sitting alone in a booth. She's not wearing the lemonade dress or the white apron. She's in a sweater set in dusty blue with black buttons. She's poring over an open book with a stack of other books beside it.

One the Gun slides in the booth opposite her without saying anything. When she looks up a grin turns the high beams up on her face.

"What are you doing?" he asks.

"I have so much to learn," she says. "I took the day off! I don't know why I'm always so steadfast about this job."

"Yeah, that's kind of weird," he says.

"Well, I was kind of enjoying seeing how fast I could guess and deliver orders," she says. "Yesterday was great. I just started announcing what people wanted before they could even open their mouths and—" She stops and gives her body a little shake. "Anyway! I just woke up this morning and decided—well, I guess I didn't wake up, and I didn't really have a morning, but you know what I mean—I decided to get my shift covered!"

"And you still came here?" he asks.

She's got a half-drunk milkshake next to the open lawbook. Each slab of pages on either side of the huge book looks three inches thick. "I didn't know how else to meet you." She folds her arms across the book and leans in over it. "So what have you learned? I'm dying to know!"

"Well, I've got some very intriguing leads," he says.

The stand-in waitress with the mile-high hair comes over to the booth with a menu, but the waitress with the doe eyes and the big teeth smiles up at her and says, "He'll have a hamburger with grilled onions. And coffee." And to him: "Biscuit?"

"Sure."

"With honey," she tells the stand-in waitress. And to Gun again as the other woman moves off: "Tell me all about it. I'm all ears and my ears are all open."

He's never told her about the case. It takes a while to detail all the suspects—the preacher, the widow, the bartender, the doorman—to tell the story about the bead that ended up meaning doodly-squat, to lay out the different possible motives, how the widow and the bartender now own the Dive in equal parts, how the Dive used to belong to the bartender, how the widow likes to get her kicks, how the doorman would obviously like to get his kicks with the widow and gets a little bit insanely enraged when you hint at disrespecting her.

"Can I ask, so, you're saying they pretty much all have motives?"

"Seems so to me."

The waitress is sitting in rapt concentration, doe eyes big and excited on his, although the way she keeps interrupting to ask questions is getting annoying. "Can I ask, so, if they found either the widow or the bartender guilty of murder, would ownership of the Dive go to the other one, lock, stock, and barrel?"

"I don't know. You're the one with the lawbooks."

The stand-in waitress with the mile-high hair has forgotten the grilled onions for Gun's hamburger, but he doesn't feel like sending it back. He's doing too much talking to eat much anyway, and he's getting to the juicy stuff now. He's starting in on the confrontation with the preacher over the letters hidden in his Bible.

"How did the suspect react when you brought up the name Snookie?" the waitress puts in. "I assume you brought up the name Snookie."

"Hey, I'm telling the story." He waves his burger at her. "Why do you keep stopping me to ask questions?"

"Just think of yourself as the expert witness on the stand," she says, "and I'm the prosecuting attorney. Like when I give you your trial." She raises the thick lawbook at a slant so he can see the green of its cover and then lets it thump back onto the table as if to prove her abilities as an attorney.

"That isn't helpful," he says.

"It is to me."

He huffs. "Well, so I say to him, 'These letters are very strong evidence that you were blackmailing the deceased, which is very strong evidence that, ipso facto, you killed poor Snookie.' I threw that in there to get his reaction. He didn't even blink. The preacher's got a hell of a poker face."

"Can you describe for me," she starts to ask, "a moment in your interview when—"

"Come on," he cracks, "I'm not on the witness stand, and you're not an attorney."

"I object!" she says. And looks like she does.

"But listen, this is getting good," he says. "So I keep putting the pressure on. He tries to make some play like I have no proof because all the letters say is Five, and I tell him, 'How would you know how the letters are signed if you don't have these letters?' And suddenly he grabs the Bible, opens it, pulls out the letters, and throws them in the fire."

"Wow!"

"Destroys them."

"Wow!" again.

"Yeah," he says. "Too bad he didn't know he wouldn't destroy them for good."

The waitress sinks back into her chair with a wide-eyed grin. "What a tale," she says. "That could easily have been an episode of *Who Is the Villain?*"

"That's what I thought too!" Gun says. "Also I just came from the Dive, where I found out from the doorman that the bartender took out the trash at the end of the night. I'm thinking, What if that trash contained the bottle of poison used to spike the drink? The garbagemen had already come, so I couldn't get any bottles or vials for analysis, but I think it's a very interesting development."

The waitress nods slowly in a thinking way. They sit in silence, and he works on his hamburger, she her milkshake.

"So I'm interested in this doorman," the waitress says. "You say he has a temper?"

"Weren't you listening to me?" Gun says. "The bartender never said anything about taking out the trash. And the preacher's a slimy blackmailer who destroyed evidence; I saw it with my own eyes."

"So he's a blackmailer," she says. "Why would he kill his meal ticket?"

"Because maybe Five stopped paying," Gun says. "Because maybe Five threatened to go to the police."

"I don't know," she says. "I suppose it's possible, but those seem like pretty flimsy motives for murder. And where's this gun he's going to shoot you with? I thought you said you searched his room."

"Well, what about the bartender?" he says. "He could easily have had a nearly empty bottle of rye with the poison already in it, poured the drink right in front of everyone, and then tossed the evidence."

"I guess," she says.

"You guess? Of course he could."

"Alright, sure," she says, "both of these are possibilities. But from the standpoint of a trial, possibilities don't count. What you need is proof."

ONE THE GUN GOES TO the phone booth just inside the drugstore and slides the door shut. Tosses some silver in the slot, calls the sanitation department. From the bored dame on the other end he learns that the trash was picked up along the east side of the square yesterday at six in the morning. And no, there's no way to track down a specific trash bag from a specific establishment, are you kidding?

He walks to the church. He's still calling the preacher his number one suspect—that guy is as corrupt as they come—but the waitress is right: Where's the gun? If he could just find the gun.

There's a long wooden bench along the wall just outside the door to the preacher's chambers. The base of that bench opens, but all he finds inside are hymnals. He wanders through the empty-for-the-moment sanctuary. At the pulpit he discovers a drawer built into its back-facing side, but all that's in there are the requisite Bible, a notepad and pencil, a brass chalice, and whatever you call that plate they put the communion wafers on.

Behind the altar is the statue of the crucifixion, the figure huge, his eyes painted bright blue, a plaster drape of white artfully arranged across his plaster midsection to hide his godly goods from the congregation. Between the figure and its wooden mounting are some open spaces that might make for hiding spots: behind the crossed ankles, at the small of the back.

When a nun passing through gives Gun the squint eye for feeling around the crevices of her savior, Gun quickly makes the sign of the cross and gets the hell out of there.

Damn it, what does it take to solve a murder in this town? After spending another fruitless hour searching for Nines in the newspaper morgue, One the Gun goes to the phone booth just inside the drugstore and slides the door shut. Tosses some silver in the slot, calls his office. As he waits he runs the kiss over in his head, the feeling of Miss Blue's lips on his lips. That pretty face of hers all chaste and pure, but if he could get her alone, get a little booze into her—

She picks up and says hello in her clear, bell-like voice.

"Checking in," he says. "Got anything new for me?"

"Well, I spoke with the police," she says, "and there's no criminal record for any woman named Nine. Hospital has a Nine the Quinine listed as a resident nurse, but she's been overseas for the last year working on malarial cases. I spent some time on the phone with the Hall of Records, and here's what I was able to pull up."

She tells him about a Nine the Byline who works for the newspaper, but he's male. A Nine the Asinine. Male. A Nine the Valentine. Female. But dead.

"You mean like maybe very recently dead," Gun asks, "or—"

"Nine years."

Well, nuts.

And even with all these dead ends Two the True Blue's detective work has obviously been more proficient than Gun's ineffectual meanderings today.

"I went through the phone book like you suggested," Miss Blue says, "but that netted me nothing too. It's like this woman doesn't exist."

Just ask her to dinner. Maybe the story about the preacher throwing the letters in the fire would be enough to impress her. Or would she shoot down his theories like the waitress?

"Say, sir," Two the True Blue says. "I'm going to head out for the evening if that's alright. I've got a date with my beau."

SEVEN O'CLOCK. ONE THE GUN sits at a table in the café alone. The waitress with the doe eyes and the big teeth must have taken her stack of books home so she can keep studying to become a genius lawyer, so she can keep busting his theories in this case that he's never going to solve anyway, so who the hell cares.

Gun is in a mood. He sits and drinks beer because they don't serve anything stronger and listens to Two the True Blue's Friday-night radio show and broods. He supposes he should get a hamburger. He hardly touched the one he ordered this afternoon. Bah, he's not hungry.

Miss Blue's probably out at some swanky night spot with her boob boyfriend.

How can it be possible that he can't sniff out this Nine? How can she not even be in the phone book?

Gun swigs his beer. It tastes like sweaty socks, but at least it goes down fast. The lukewarm reception he got from the waitress for his theories is still stuck in his craw. She could have given him a little encouragement.

He raises his empty glass to signal to the waitress with the mile-high hair for another. He sits back and lets the dialogue from the radio show wash over him.

"Light up, golden boy, I'm sick of being left in the dark. And don't reach for that gun or I'll tune your glockenspiel."

At the Dive he gives the moose a hello and his usual query.

"Sure, sure," Four the Door says, "folks been coming by to make with the respects. Look at all them flowers there in the corner."

"Yeah."

"Prettier than pink ballerinas!" Four the Door says.

Having to make small talk is getting on Gun's nerves. "I'm not much for ballerinas."

"My sister was a ballerina when she was little," Four the Door says. "Dressed all in pink."

"You've got a sister?" She's probably a moose too.

"Sure. Ain't you got a sister, shamus?"

Gun moves off into the club. He's got an itch to ditch the Dive and go over to Miss Blue's apartment and see where more kisses might land him—but she has a date.

Say, wait a minute. She's never had a date on any other tonights. In fact, Gun looks around, and yes, there he is as always. Three the Goatee, sitting alone, having his little pinky party with his martini at the usual table.

So Miss Blue only pretended to have a date. She lied.

As Gun steps closer Three the Goatee glances up at him.

It just doesn't figure, her being so true blue to this whiskered wombat. Gun looks down and snaps a short, formal nod. "Professor."

But Three the Goatee is on his feet. He shoves his face in Gun's, rage twitching his moustache. His pinky isn't up now. He grips the stem of his glass with his fist. "Gun! You get the hell away from me."

One the Gun puts his hands up at the professor like *hey, pal, cool your kettle*. "I understand you're—"

"You," the professor is sputtering, "you. You're a pig."

The word bites more when he says it this time, and Gun wonders for a half second whether the guy's going to hit him.

Three the Goatee whips his fist and booze hits Gun's face.

It stings his eyes and runs down his neck, soaking his collar. The shock of it leaves Gun frozen for a moment. Before he can blink out of it the professor turns, leaving the glass on the table, and stalks off toward the Dive's front door.

One the Gun clears his throat. Well. He might have kind of deserved that.

Martini is seeping into Gun's shirt, cold and clammy. He looks around and there are eyes looking back at him.

He swipes one hand across his wet face. Drags his sorry pig hide over to the bar and bellies up halfway between Six and Seven at their usual spots at each end. Across the counter Eight the First Mate, with maybe the tiniest hint of mirth in the round of his cheeks, hands Gun a couple of those little bar napkins without a word. Gun tosses a short nod back and mops his face.

Six the Kicks hasn't met Gun on this today, so she doesn't come up from behind and offer to buy him a drink and say she's ready to be interviewed. Gun orders a Scotch and sits down alone. He's sick of interviewing the widow. He came here to grill the preacher some more. But he needs a little time to focus. Have a drink and calm down and focus. Have a drink and calm down and dry off and focus. He couldn't think in the café with that radio show playing in his ear. That radio show kept making him think about Miss Blue. He'll get Miss Blue if he can solve this case, and to solve this case he'll have to stop obsessing about Miss Blue.

What he'd like his interview with the preacher to consist of is, "Hey, God-man, you thought you'd destroyed the evidence when you threw the letters in the fire, but all you did was make me that much more sure that you're the killer." But the preacher threw the letters in the fire on a different today. Sometimes time magic can be very inconvenient.

After a few drinks, when the preacher gets up from his spot at the end of the bar and heads to the restroom, One the Gun steals his seat. He hopes this will anger the preacher when the guy comes back. He wants to pick a fight with someone. He'd like it to be the preacher.

The piano lady is pounding his skull with her stupid breakneck sea shanty. Maybe her name's Nine, did he ever think of that? Maybe she killed the boss and hid the vial inside the piano, did he ever think of that? No, because it's stupid and she wasn't even here two nights ago. It's the preacher, he's the killer, Gun can feel it. Who is this Nine? Why can't he find this Nine?

Now there's a voice somewhere halfway down the line of barstools: "Let me have a bourbon, my brother."

One the Gun's head snaps up. It's the preacher, back from the restroom, standing dead center at the bar, talking to the bartender.

Gun's eyes shoot bullets at the preacher. The preacher, who hasn't met Gun in this today, glances back blankly, then looks away. Smiles and watches the bartender pour his drink.

Anger simmers at the bottom of Gun's stomach. Seven the Heaven and his stupid, self-important face. Calling people his brother.

Murderer. Gun knows he's a murderer.

Gun gets off the barstool. The floor under his feet is on casters. He's drunker than he thought he was. He moves across the empty dance floor to a table where a couple is sitting. The woman has blond hair in a twist like a huge cinnamon bun on her head and eyes so mascaraed it's like two fat centipedes fell asleep over her baby blues. Those eyes blink surprise up at him as he pushes his chin over the table toward her.

"Hey, doll," he says, "what's your name?"

The man with her takes a pointed survey of Gun's booze-wrinkled shirt stuck to his chest and says, "I beg your pardon!"

"Are you Nine?" Gun asks. "I'm looking for someone named Nine."

"No, and kindly get your breath out of my buttermilk," she says.

He moves off. Crosses to another table. It's a redhead sitting all by herself. Face like the kind of pug dog people slap a bonnet on and stick in a baby buggy. He sits in the chair opposite her. "Hey, doll, what's your name?"

"Thirty-four the Give Me Give Me More More More," she says. "Buy me a drink?"

He stands quickly and moves on.

There at another table is the cute little trick with the turned-up nose who he'd chatted up at the end of that seminal night and then again on day one. He never did ask her name, did he?

What's your name, doll?

What's your name, doll?

At the door across the room the moose has his eye on him, so Gun stops accosting the customers and goes back to the bar.

This time he arrows in right upside the preacher. So fast it makes the preacher twitch.

"I know what you did," he tells him.

The preacher stares at Gun with a kind of small-rodent vacant shock on his face.

The piano player is giving the ivories a working over like a schoolyard bully with an empty pocket for lunch money.

"I know you killed him," Gun says. "Yeah, I know all about it."

The preacher's beady eyes. His two front teeth showing between his parted lips.

"What are you going to do," Gun says. "Kill me? Again?"

Someone is at Gun's right elbow. The moose, come to bounce him. No: a woman.

One the Gun swings his gaze her way. It's the waitress with the doe eyes and the big teeth. First she glances down, perplexed, at his rumpled, booze-stiffened shirt, and then she's giving him more teeth than ever. "Hey, handsome! Dance with me!"

She's pulling him away from the preacher and onto the dance floor. She's swinging him round and round to the repeating music.

"What the hell are you doing?" she asks him.

"He's a murderer."

"You've proven this since I saw you last?" she asks.

"I just know is all."

"Gun," she says. "You can't pass sentence if you haven't proven guilt."

The room spinning round them is blurring into flabby streaks of color. "Oh, he's guilty."

"Yes, we know the priest dupes those guys in the back room, and yes, we know he was probably blackmailing Five—"

"Probably?" Indignant.

She says, "But unless you're holding out on me, we don't have proof he killed him."

"I'm going to catch him in the act," One the Gun blurts. A plan that's just occurred to him. "Tonight."

She blinks at him. "Catch him trying to kill you?"

"I'm going to lie in wait for him."

"You're stewed to the eyeballs, Gun," she says.

"Then why do you keep turning me like you don't think I might puke at any second?"

She stops turning him. "Listen. If you try this tonight, you will fail."

"You don't know that."

She puts her hands on each of his shoulders and gives his eyes the kind of stare down he maybe should have gotten from his mother once or twice. "You will fail," she says, "and he will kill you."

The room is still turning even though they're not.

"And this will all be over," she says.

He rakes his hand across his face. "Okay, alright. I'll wait until tomorrow."

Her mother eyes don't believe him. "Do you promise?"

"Yes."

"Do you really promise?"

"Okay, yes."

SIX

DAY SEVEN.

The sign above the door says *Square Pawnshop*. One the Gun has walked by this place over and over but never gone in. A little bell dings when he steps inside. The place seems stuffed full of evening even though it's the middle of the day. The walls, ceiling, and display cases are all gray.

The guy behind the counter is all gray, too, from his shabby shirt to his big tufts of eyebrows, but not all the way up to his hair because he has none.

"Help you?"

"Good morning," Gun says.

"Afternoon," the guy corrects him.

True, although afternoon always feels like morning these days. One the Gun leans his elbows on the counter. It's a glass display case. Inside it are watches, bracelets, rings. Guns. He says, "I need to know all the people who've purchased firearms from you in the last"—oh, just for good measure—"seven days."

The gray guy behind the counter says, "I can't hand out that information."

One the Gun's ready for that. He pulls a badge from his pocket. Flashes it at the guy. "This is police business, mister." Puts the badge back in his pocket. People don't know what a real police badge looks like.

"What? You're not dressed like a policeman."

One the Gun raises his voice. "I'm a plainclothesman, a detective. I need you to cooperate."

"Okay, okay, I didn't know, sorry." Hands up at Gun like he's already being arrested. "If you want, you can look through my record book."

The guy quickly turns to a short gray table behind him and grabs an open ledger. Turns back and slides it across the counter to One the Gun. "Let's see, seven days ago starts here. I don't record the names for all purchases, of course, but I do write down my repeat customers, folks who sell me stuff, things like that. And, for security purposes, I get names when people buy weapons."

One the Gun bends over it. At first he can't make out what he's seeing. Just names and numbers and prices, that's all. And prices are numbers and names are mostly numbers, so it's basically a pile of numbers. Some of them must be item numbers. No way to know what's a weapon and what's not.

Gun scans through pages. He doesn't see the name. Damn it, he doesn't see it.

Then finally, on the very last page, "Here it is!" He points at the name. "Steven!"

"What?"

"I mean Seven," Gun says. "Huh. What the hell kind of name is Steven?"

"You done with that yet?"

"Listen," Gun says, "I'm looking for a Seven the Heaven who might have bought a weapon from you."

The guy leans in over the ledger. Light gleams on the top of his head. "That says Seventy-Seven. And she bought a flowerpot."

Gun huffs. "Alright, skip it. You can put this away. I'd like to buy this one right here." Pointing down into the display case.

The guy blinks his little gray eyes up at him. "What's a cop need to buy a gun for?"

"Just get it for me, alright?"

Night. One the Gun stands in the shadows under the staircase that leads up from the lobby of his office building. All he has to do is lean out from this nook, look sidelong, and he's got a beeline sight line to the front door where anyone who plans to kill him is going to have to enter. He waits. Flashlight in one jacket pocket, the newly purchased pistol in the other.

Usually this lobby is bright, its stone floor and white tiled walls lit by the two fancy sconces flanking the entryway, but a quick twist on each bulb made One the Gun much less conspicuous in his spot under the stairs. The smaller lamp at the back of the lobby has left the place dusky—just enough light for his stakeout. He's ready with the flashlight in case he has to wait all the way to when the power goes out, but he hopes he won't have to.

He leans out just enough from his hiding spot and watches the door. Waiting is weird when you're stuck in a time loop. You shouldn't care about the fact that time's wasting when you know time will start over anyway. Why hate waiting when you have all the time in the world?

A car goes by on the street outside, its headlights a dim streak through the glass of the windows to the left and right of the entryway. Whir of the retreating engine and then the kick of a backfire.

He keeps his hand on the handgun in his pocket. His body feels weird, slightly disconnected. It's the pull of time. It wants him to be at the Dive. His hand on the gun wants to be around a glass of Scotch. He notices that pull of time during the day, a faint otherworldly quality about his movements, but he really feels it the later each day gets. The closer, maybe, that he gets to the death hour. Time wants to claim him.

He tries to think about something else. The feeling of Miss Blue's lips on his lips. Maybe if this stakeout doesn't take all night, he'll go over to her place and—

A shadow on the window to the right of the door. His fingers tense around the handle of the gun. He shifts back into the shadows under the staircase.

The door opens. The shape of a man is outlined in a rectangle of moonlight. One the Gun moves farther back, listens for the footsteps on the stone floor to tell him whether the man is going to take the stairs or pass by him to the elevator. Click of the door closing. A pause. The footsteps head his way. He slides the gun from his pocket.

The footsteps are strange, halting. Almost shuffling.

A figure passes in front of his alcove. One the Gun steps out behind him.

He tries for shock: "I know what you did, and I know what you're planning."

But he can see as the words come out of his mouth that this is not Seven the Heaven.

The man freezes, his back to Gun. He blurts, "The door was wide open. I didn't take anything, I swear!"

The voice slurs. The man is drunk. One the Gun slides the pistol, unseen, back in his pocket. He sighs. He says, "Relax."

The man turns round. He's a small, wiry guy with the map of nowheresville written all over his face, and his eyes are so rheumy with the booze they might float clean out of his head. Shabby slacks and a stained work shirt. He's the building superintendent.

"Let me guess," Gun says. "That door you said was wide open? It was one of the offices upstairs. And that money you didn't take was enough for a night on the town."

Gun makes a mental note to keep his office door locked.

"What were you doing under there in the dark?" the guy asks.

"Waiting for someone. And I'm still waiting, so if you wouldn't mind moving along..."

"I've got to change those light bulbs by the door," the super says, and he ducks in under the stairs, going to a short wooden chest in the shadows.

Gun swings his gaze to the door, then back to the super. "Listen, the lights are fine. I switched them off, alright? I need to be inconspicuous." He tries the ruse he's been using lately. "This is police business."

The super straightens. "You're that detective on the sixth floor, aren't you?"

Gun steps back into his alcove, trying to watch the door and the super at the same time. Eyes front, eyes back, eyes front. "This is a stakeout."

"Let's have a snort!" the super pulls a half-empty bottle from his pocket.

Gun doesn't want to flash the pistol at the guy, but he will if he has to. "Pull a fade, alright? Buzz off, beat it."

The super twists the cap off the bottle and seats himself on the little wooden chest under the stairs. He cops a long slug.

"Say," Gun says, his eyes back on the door, "let me ask you something. If the electricity went out in this building, what would be the cause?"

"Well, sometimes a circuit trips in one of the boxes in the

basement." His booze mouth makes it sound like *bosses in the bassmem*.

"No, I mean if the whole works went out at once," One the Gun says. "Could that be on purpose?"

"What's your name, detective? Mine's Fifty the Nifty. That's because I'm nifty!"

"Could just anyone flip a switch somewhere to trip the whole building, or would they have to, you know, climb up some power pole outside and cut some wire?"

"You're looking at it," the super says, and he sucks down another belt.

"What?"

The super hiccups, points with the bottle toward something Gun can't see in the shadows of the alcove under the hang of the lowest steps. "Main electrical panel's under there. But you need a key."

"Could someone break it open if they wanted to?"

"You want to, detective?" The super wipes his forehead with the back of his bottle hand. "Hey, what's your name, detective? Mine's Fifty the Nifty. That's because I'm—"

"Name's Gun," Gun says.

"Well, I—oh!" The super's eyes bug at the word.

"I don't want to turn the power off." Gun swings his gaze back to the door. "I just need the information."

"Oh, well, probably not. That thing would be like the devil to break into. If the lights go out, it's probably just this old building with its—"

A shadow passes in front of the window, and quick, Gun says, "Button up!"

It goes quiet in the lobby.

The shadow slides across the glass and disappears behind the door.

One the Gun has one hand gripped around the pistol in his pocket and one hand back behind him, palm out at the super.

The shadow slips across the window on the other side of the door and is gone.

"Hang on a minute," Gun murmurs. Waits.

Nothing but the sharp stink of booze in the alcove.

It was probably someone passing by on the sidewalk.

Gun stays frozen, hand out behind him. Another moment. Another.

When he turns back, the super is asleep on the wooden chest, head lolled back against the wall, mouth wide open. The near-empty booze bottle sits between his legs.

Later, when the power goes out, the super doesn't stir. One the Gun gets the flashlight ready. He moves out from under the stairs to get closer to the door.

So the power going out has nothing to do with the main electrical panel. Nor the individual fuse boxes in the basement. At least as far as tampering with the lights on purpose is concerned. That means unless the killer climbed up some pole outside and cut some wire, which would be stupid and dangerous and something the layman wouldn't know how to do, the power going out was not on purpose.

Moonlight sits in the two windows flanking the door, making the windows float before his eyes.

Gun waits.

Gun waits.

No one comes.

DAY EIGHT. MIDAFTERNOON. ONE THE Gun sits across from the waitress in her booth at the café, lawbooks stacked around them on the table. He thinks these might be different books.

She's not drinking a milkshake today. She's got a grilled cheese sandwich and a piece of chocolate layer cake.

"You can eat anything you want!" she's saying. "Who cares about the calories or the sugar. You won't have eaten it tomorrow."

One the Gun is hunched over in his seat, arms crossed on the table, and staring down. "I don't understand what went wrong. I waited till nearly midnight."

"Your stakeout to try to catch the killer in the act?" the waitress says.

"I was right there at the front door where the killer had to come in. He never showed."

"He or she," she corrects.

"Or she."

"Gun, you're too obsessed," she says. "It's busting your judgment. Stop and think about it for a minute. You didn't set the bait. I was here at one o'clock yesterday when the doorman came in for your interview. You stood him up. I was at the Dive last night. I didn't see you there."

"I'm sick of that place."

"Gun, the guy's not going to try to kill you if he doesn't have reason to," she says. "Where's your brain these days?"

"Give me a break." He slips his hat off and runs his hand across the top of his head. "I haven't slept in over a week."

"Neither have I. What were you doing all day?"

Hanging around the office, regaling Miss Blue with his theories, trying unsuccessfully to sell her on dinner.

"Listen, Gun." The waitress points her cake fork at him. "I don't know what's going on with you, but if your goal is to discover who killed you, you've got to focus. You've got to set the bait. I think basically you have to go through the entire day as it was on that very first day. You have no idea what in that first day made the killer want to kill you, so if you want to catch him or her in the act, you have to do the whole day straight through."

"Don't you get how dangerous that is?" he asks. "Listen, whenever I stay on script and let time carry me along, I get sort of stuck in it. And the longer I let myself be stuck in it, the harder it is to pull away. That first night, well, the second night that was just like the first night, I couldn't get my feet to stop walking toward the basement. If I stay on script the whole day, I'm just"—he almost says the word *afraid*—"I might not be able to keep from really getting killed."

But what if Gun kills the preacher?

A zip of energy flashes up the back of his head.

What if he plays the day out exactly like it was except that, in the end, he kills his main suspect, then goes down into the basement, stands by the fuse boxes, and waits bravely for whatever comes?

If he's right about the preacher, nothing will happen. And he'll know for sure who the villain is.

If he's wrong about the preacher, of course . . .

But he's pretty sure he's right about the preacher.

This plan feels like something out of a radio show: gutsy. First-rate.

"What?" the waitress asks, watching him.

Could he do that? Could he just kill him?

If he's right about the preacher, it's justice.

If he's wrong about the preacher, he'll just put that day in a bubble and send it away, and then the next day the preacher will be good as new again. And it won't matter, that murder, will it?

SEVEN

THE BELLS ARE CHIMING AS he opens his eyes.

It's bright as day in the room. He's in his office.

Day nine.

He does what he always does, force of habit, force of time: Closes his eyes, listens to another strike of the bell, opens his eyes, waits for the room to stop spinning.

Two the True Blue is there in front of him. So is the bubble he always sees when one day drifts away from another.

Is he really going to do this? Run the day through on script and then kill the preacher?

"You looked so odd just now," Two the True Blue is saying. "Are you alright?"

"If you were given the chance to relive one day over and over," he says, "what would you do?"

The concerned tweak of her eyebrows softens. A small smile starts at the corners of her mouth, and her eyes blink off across the room. Then back to him. "Any day?"

Her enthusiasm at the question, her pretty innocence, pushes away his stress for a moment. He sits down on the couch. "No, today."

"I don't know," she says. "What if today turns out to be a horrible day?"

"But then you could start over and change it," he says. "Do anything you wanted inside it, good or bad. But only for that day. Then it would start over again."

"For everyone," she asks, "or just for me?"

"Well..." How to explain it? "Kind of for everyone, because they're there, too, doing what they do, but for them it's always day one, and for you it's always a new day."

Two the True Blue loves games and hypotheticals. The smile that runs its sun across her eyes is the same one that must have worked its shine on her big blues during her playground days. She drops her notepad on the desk and takes the chair opposite him, folds her fingers together over her knees, and leans in. "I'd eat at fancy restaurants! I'd eat cheese soufflés." She sits back, takes time to think again. "I'd order champagne. I'd order a bottle of the most expensive champagne, and I'd do it every day because I'd still have the same money in the morning. I'd take the day off whenever I wanted and just read books. Wait, would I remember what I read the next day, or could I only get so far and then—"

"No, the day would start over," One the Gun says, "but you'd remember."

She almost claps at this. "I'd read so many books!"

Look at that face. Faces are just stacks of features piled up against someone's head, and yes, smiles always take those features, even the homeliest of them, and turn them into something pretty. But when it happens with the eyes, the nose, the cheeks, the mouth of Two the True Blue, boy, you've got a smile that melts you like honey on a hot biscuit.

"And since it's Friday, I'd get to listen to my favorite radio show," she says. "But, oh. It would be the same one every day. Oh, that makes me so sad."

"There are some downsides."

She makes a cheering-herself-up face. "Well, I'd take a ride on a boat. And ride a horse. No, I don't think I'd like to ride a horse. But I'd do something different every day. Oh, I'd take all my money and buy all the jewels I could afford and just wear them around. I'd—but what would you do?"

"No, I want to hear yours," he says. "You weren't finished."

He wants to ask her, If you knew you could get away with it, would you do something bad?

"Well," her eyes arc across the room like she can see all the possibilities in the world. "I'd buy my mom a spaghetti dinner. And I'd rent my beau a fancy car he could ride around in. He loves fancy cars but can't afford one."

Of course she has to go and bring up that guy.

She leans forward to grin at him, her forearms folded across her knees. "I'd buy you a bottle of the best Scotch and tell you, 'Take the day off!'"

He laughs at that, and her eyes laugh back, pretty crescents. At this angle he can see a little down the front of her white blouse with the tiny eyelet flowers. He wants to take the day off, take the whole case off, try the kiss again, and more.

She sits back. "I guess none of that would mean anything, though. I'd want to do something good, something to change things for the better. Like I could take a whole day and pick up all the trash in the neglected part of town, or—but it would all be back the next day, wouldn't it?"

Her eyes blink up at Gun.

"Gosh, it's a dilemma, isn't it?" she says. "Because you couldn't really do anything meaningful, could you?"

One the Gun wants to beg to differ.

"Sure," she says, "you could buy someone a spaghetti dinner, but you couldn't do anything to make change in the world or in anyone's life. Nothing you did could ever change anything." She thinks a moment. "I guess the only thing you could change is yourself."

Gun's thinking this isn't true—but Two the True Blue doesn't know the whole of the situation. She doesn't know that if Gun solves this case and doesn't get killed, and the day turns over to tomorrow, maybe he can change her too. Make her fall for him because he will have changed into a first-rate gumshoe. When he first found himself here, in this strange situation, all he wanted was to solve his murder and save himself, but now he knows he doesn't want to get out without making his old life better.

So he gets the hell on script. Walks to the café and meets with the moose. Asks all the same questions, listens to all the same answers. Even here on day nine all he has to do is let time carry him along, and he remembers everything, can say everything exactly as he did on the very first day. In the beginning this felt fine, like he could relax in it, but now it feels creepy. Like he's not in control.

He heads from the café down along the square toward Our Lady of Immaculate Numbers to meet with the preacher. In his pocket is one of his little envelopes for collecting clues, but this one is filled with a scoop from the sample box of rat poison that's been sitting at the edge of his desk since day one. Murder weapon ready made. He could try to slip it to the preacher now in his chambers, of course, but no drinks are ever offered in this first interview. More importantly, if the preacher dies now and is absent from the Dive tonight, it changes the trajectory of the day. It would ruin the experiment. Anyway, Gun's been through this night enough times that he thinks he knows just the moment he can slip the poison into the preacher's drink with no one the wiser. Murders are far easier to commit when you know where everyone's attention is going to be focused.

He catches his image in a storefront window and stops a moment, looking at himself. Square jaw and small-brim fedora, brown suit. What will it feel like to kill the preacher? Will he feel guilt? Power? Will he feel like a man? Will he like it?

Stepping along the sidewalk just down from the funeral chapel, he can already see through the windows Six the Kicks standing in the center of the room, looking down on the casket of Five the No Longer Alive. Her simple black dress, her strong square shoulders. Red lipstick and black gloves.

But the preacher. He's already in the room. Standing long and tall in his holy vestments, hands folded, by one of the pillars holding up a marble urn. For cat's sake! When Gun arrived in the funeral chapel on that seminal day, the preacher hadn't been there yet.

Gun is late.

How late? Did he take too long at the café paying the bill? Stopping quick by the waitress's booth on his way out to brag that he's playing the day through on script—except that saying he's playing the day through on script is him jumping off script, and now he's late, and maybe he's already ruined this whole thing.

Through the windows of the funeral parlor, the preacher looks down at his watch.

Gun needs to get in there and have the conversation he had with the widow on that seminal day, introduce himself to the preacher, go with the preacher to—

Six the Kicks steps away from the casket and, with one small nod toward the preacher, crosses the room to the exit, steps out, and heads down the walkway. Straight for the sidewalk, straight for One the Gun.

Her eyes look past Gun, her face blank. Should he say something, try to recapture some of the exchange they were supposed to have already had?

Six the Kicks steps past him. Her perfume wraps around him like the gloss on a licorice whip. She turns and heads away along the sidewalk.

When Gun swings his gaze back to the funeral chapel, the preacher is standing at the open doorway on the back wall, leaning out like maybe he's talking to someone beyond. Now he comes back in, followed by a nun. They're chatting as they move across the room. And then she's the one standing by the marble pillar, and the preacher is leaving through the back doorway, heading off into the church.

One the Gun double-times it to the front door of the place and goes inside. He doesn't know what his plan is now, to try going forward with this experiment or not. Does he kill the preacher today, does he kill the preacher tomorrow? The nun smiles and crosses the room to him as he's crossing to her.

"Welcome," she says. She looks to be in her seventies with thin, colorless lips and a nose like a seashell stuck to her face. "Are you the man who has a two-thirty appointment with Father Heaven?"

"Uh, yes. Yes, I am."

"He told me to send you his way when you arrived," she says. "He's actually just gone through there. I'm sure you can catch him."

She stretches her black-draped nun arm toward the door on the back wall.

"Thank you," he says. "I will."

One the Gun steps out into the corridor. The preacher is already far down the hallway, stepping through a door at the other end.

Gun picks up the pace. Down the hall past framed paintings of shepherds and sheep and fishers of men. Then out into the wide, empty sanctuary with its rows of pews, shafts of amber and magenta light angling down through pictures of stained glass. The preacher is stepping up the center aisle, heading toward the front, probably to his chambers. It's fine, it's not all lost. Gun will just get back on script, run the day through. The only interaction he lost was the one with the widow. He'll interview her same as always at the Dive, then kill the preacher, and—

Wait. How the hell can he kill the preacher at the Dive without all the rest of the suspects knowing? They may not know Gun did it, but they'll see the man collapse—the entire night will be changed. The cops will be called and everyone detained for questioning. What has Gun been thinking?

He stops, standing at the back of the house. Okay, get a hold of yourself. No, the day isn't lost. Gun starts formulating a new plan. He can kill the preacher tomorrow. Maybe there's a longer-acting, less violent poison. Something that will send an under-the-weather preacher out of the Dive before he takes his dive. Gun will call Miss Blue and have her get him some data on the subject.

Only if he kills the preacher right can he prove that the preacher is the killer.

Meantime, let's throw a tail on the suspect, see what he does all day. Gun skirts the back of the house and starts up the center aisle. At the sound of Gun's shoes on the stone floor the preacher's head turns. He starts back down the aisle toward Gun. "Hello, my son. I'm Father Heaven. Are you the man here for my two-thirty appointment?"

"Oh, no." Gun points at the pew to his right. "I'm just here to pray."

"Ah. Well, by all means."

"Thank you."

Gun goes to the pew and sits down. The preacher continues up the aisle to his pulpit, steps behind it, bends down, and he must be opening that drawer in the back because now he brings out the notepad and sets it on the podium, paging through it.

Gun sits back and settles in. A church is not a bad spot for a stakeout. It's wide open, and anyone can be in here anytime they want, praying, reading the scriptures, consorting with the Lord.

There's a hymn book in the wooden rack fastened along the back side of the pew in front of Gun. He pulls it out and flips through it.

The preacher is making notes in the notepad, probably working on some sermon while he waits for his appointment. Couldn't he do something more interesting? Like go to the confession booth and let slip his sins to God for Gun to overhear?

Sins. Earlier Two the True Blue was talking about changing yourself. If Gun kills the preacher, even if only for one day, will that change him from hero to villain? Like how someone can be charged with attempted murder: They're still guilty even if they try and fail. Isn't the intent bad enough?

But if the preacher is Gun's killer, isn't it self-defense?

See, that's it. It's self-defense.

One the Gun has never killed anyone. In radio shows they make like detectives kill bad guys all the time, but Gun has spent most of his all-the-time working on very ordinary and unradiolike cases like *is my wife cheating on me?*, or *is my clerk siphoning twenty bucks a week from the company till?*

Hell, if the preacher doesn't stay dead, Gun's committing no sin. Sure, he's going to hurt the preacher, it can't be pleasant to die, but it's only temporary.

Gun flips a page in the hymnal. Has living in this one day over and over already changed him? Moved him down a peg from third-rate gumshoe to fourth-rate villain? It stands to reason that if you could do anything you wanted with no consequences, you might learn to be someone you didn't used to think you could be.

Nah! One the Gun wants to beg to differ. He bets he could kill the preacher, enjoy it even, enjoy being the bad guy, and then he could start the day over, and he'd still be the good guy he is now.

He's been reliving one day over and over for over a week. He figures it hasn't changed him yet.

WHEN THE PREACHER FINALLY GIVES up on waiting for his appointment and heads off, Gun gets up quietly from his pew stakeout and starts the tail job.

The preacher crosses to a door off the side of the back of the church and goes through. It's a wooden door with a plain round knob. No words or numbers painted on it. No window in or beside it to see what's on the other side.

Gun eases it open. The door leads outside to some sort of little courtyard bordered all around with stone walls and stained-glass windows. A patch of grass with small wrought-iron benches and here and there sprays of rosebushes making like holy-holy in the bright sunlight. Along his side of the courtyard runs a paved walkway. He lets the door close quietly behind him, and now he's following the preacher right out here in front of God and everybody, except that luckily it's just God and the preacher, or maybe just the preacher. And the preacher is already at the far side of the courtyard and opening another door and stepping through.

One the Gun hurries down the walkway. The sun flashes red, green, and gold along the facets of glass-cut apostles hoofing it across the arched windows. At the far side he tries looking through another stained-glass window into the place the preacher went, but he can only see the opposite wall. He waits a moment, then turns the knob and pushes. It opens silently, thanks be to God. He sneaks a look in.

His vision is pulled to the right and down a long corridor with low ceilings and white walls lined with framed portraits of nuns in their scapulars and cowls. Gun stays at the doorway, watching. Seven the Heaven strides down the hall, the long hem of his holy vestments swaying with his steps. There's another door at the end of the corridor, and this is where the preacher seems to be headed. Gun waits at his sliver of doorway.

The only sound is the rhythm of the preacher's shoes on the hardwood floor: *tack, tack, tack.*

Now the tiniest pause, more a hesitation than a stop, and just before the preacher goes out through the far door, his hand dips into his pocket, comes out with what looks like an envelope, and he slips that into one of a handful of what appear to be mailboxes lined up along the wall.

Gun waits. The preacher exits.

One the Gun enters and highballs down the hall past doorways and framed portraits. At the end, there to the left, are four small wooden mailboxes. One is blank but three have names:

Twenty-One the Nun
Thirty-Three the Chastity
Nine the Divine

Does One the Gun break into a nun's mailbox?

Does he pull out his key ring, select one at random, and

go to work on the little latch and jimmy it up and dent it in the process?

Does he steal a nun's mail?

Are you kidding?

Two the True Blue is on the phone at the desk when he gets to the office. He's had her working to try to track down any out-of-state Nines. She has a piece of paper with a few names on it.

"Thank you so much," she says into the phone with a hello glance up at him. "Goodbye." She hangs up. Then to Gun directly she says, "I haven't found much so far. You'd think I'd find more. Lots of things rhyme with Nine."

"Well, look no further." He makes a come-over-here gesture. "I found her."

"Great job, sir." Two the True Blue stands up from the desk they share and goes to the couch, sits down pretty.

One the Gun takes the chair across from her. Then, no. He gets up and sits next to her on the couch. At this move that Gun has never made before, Two the True Blue pulls the corners of her mouth back in a smile but shifts in her seat, settling a little farther away from him.

Gun reaches into his jacket pocket and brings out the single article of mail he stole from the nun's mailbox. Flashes it at Two the True Blue like it's a trio of aces, and she's the dame at the game table who's going to go home with the card sharp who's won it all.

"You remember how curious it was that we couldn't find her in the phone book?" he says.

No, Two the True Blue does not remember. In this today she knows nothing about Nine except that One the Gun asked her to try and track her down out of town.

"She's a nun!" he announces, a job-well-done grin on his face. He works his thumb through the flap of the envelope. "My theory? He's blackmailing her too. She may know all about the murder, and if so, she's going to be a very important witness."

As he reaches in, Gun shifts closer to Miss Blue. He can smell her jasmine perfume. He tips his head forward in a little nod and then pulls the letter out.

But the paper and handwriting are too familiar.

This letter is just like all the others.

Nine mine,

Forgive me; I had to send you one last note.

I understand why you have to go. I wish you well in your new, and secular, life. I think your new name suits you, but you'll always be divine to me. And don't worry, I mean that in the most unsecular of ways.

I want you to understand that you did nothing wrong. Yes, you took a vow. Yes, I took a vow. But what this affair has taught me is that God cannot deem any love a sin, not if it's pure.

"But the end of all things is at hand: be ye therefore of sound mind, and be sober unto prayer: above all things being fervent in your love among yourselves." 1 Peter 4:7–8

Again, I'm not saying it's wrong for you to go. I respect your choice to move on. It's best for both of us. But I hope you'll keep the memory of our love fondly and not bitterly. That's what I plan to do.

Maybe strangely, all of this has brought me closer to my calling. I've been feeling very low, yes, but I woke up this morning energized in my service to the Lord. I have asked His forgiveness, and I believe He will give it to me, and I will rededicate myself to His work.

Of course, one irony in all this is that, as I write to you, the man who first encouraged our love and gave us a place to express it lies in the funeral chapel. I'll go to the Dive tonight, take some flowers. Maybe play a few hands if they open the back room. I'll always want to go there because it's the place where our story, yours and mine, took place. As I move on, I'll always want to hold on to the things that remind me of what we had.

Like the letters. I wrote them to you; now you entrust them to me. I made a hiding place for them. I know that if they were to be found, it would mean the end of my time in the church, but I can't let them go. Because, forbidden or not, they tell our love story, and that's something I want to keep.

Maybe when you're out there in the world, you'll think to send a letter or two. I hope you do. You know where to reach me.

Go with God.

Your Ven.

V<small>EN</small>.

Short for *Seven*, maybe. Or for *Heaven*. Whatever it is, it's obviously what she called him. A nickname. A pet name. And so *V* was *V* after all, and not a Roman numeral, not *five*. Not Five.

"He didn't do it," Gun says.

He's in the café, sitting across from the waitress in what he's come to think of as her booth, hunched forward, elbows on the menu lying on the table. She's dressed in green today, another sweater set, a green so bright a bullfrog would probably mistake it for yellow.

"The preacher didn't kill Five?" she asks.

"Didn't kill Five, didn't kill me, didn't do any of it."

She's got a grilled cheese and a milkshake and a big plate of asparagus on toast and a dish of chocolate ice cream with hot fudge, and she looks to be working her way through all of them at the same time. More stacks of lawbooks are crammed in around the food.

"Don't uncount your chickens before they hatch, Gun," she says. "Just because it wasn't blackmail doesn't necessarily—"

"I thought you didn't believe the preacher did it."

"Well, true." She points her ice cream spoon at him. "But I'm saying you're way too impulsive in all this. You decide things too quick. Like some theory comes to you, so you think it must be true, you think you must be right. And you ignore all the rest. That doesn't seem like the most efficient modus operandi for a detective."

"I said I was a detective," he says. "I didn't say I was a good detective."

She's shoving her cheeks full of ice cream and talking at him through it, something Two the True Blue would never do. "At this point the way I see it"—spoon pointing at him again—"the killer could have been anyone."

Gun slumps back against the seat. He sighs. "All I know is I thought I knew who did it, and now I don't."

"Aren't you going to order something?" she asks.

He picks up the menu but doesn't look at it, just bends and unbends it between his hands. "How much time have I wasted on this preacher? What the hell is wrong with me?"

"You have all the time in the world" is her quip between bites.

He starts making little parallel rips along the edge of the menu.

"Listen, Gun," she says, "snap out of it. I thought you were going to run the day through on script. So you obviously didn't do that today. Do it tomorrow."

He's not going to tell her the reason he was going to run the day through was because he planned on killing the preacher. She tends to be judgy. She'd judge him for that. "I don't know."

"Well then, what's your next move? What's the plan?"

"How about to go get tight?"

She huffs at him. "Stop being a cliché. Whenever things don't go your way, you're out after the booze. It's getting annoying. Pick yourself up, dust yourself off, and get to it. Time's wasting."

"I thought you just said I have all the time in the world."

"Don't you want to catch the killer?" she asks. "Don't you want to have your trial?"

A heat runs up the back of his neck. "Like you can give me a trial. You're a waitress, alright? What is this insane obsession of yours about giving me some trial?"

Her mouth opens, closes. She's quiet for a second. Then her spoon fist hits the table between her stacks of books. She says, "Goddamn it, I die too."

The murmur of conversation in the café dims. But she continues nearly as loud.

"Did you ever stop to wonder why I'm here like you?" She waits to see if he's got a response to this, and when he just stares alarmed little pig eyes at her, she says it again, slower. "I die too. And it's not some murder. It's nothing I can solve or sidestep or change. There's nothing I can do about it."

"I, I," One the Gun stammers. "I mean, I didn't know that—"

She whaps herself on the chest with the ice cream spoon. It leaves a wet spot. "I want something out of my life, alright? I am not going to tell you stories of me as a little girl dreaming of being a judge and pounding the gavel and making the bad guys go to jail, and I'm not going to tell you how long I somehow thought I could save up my waitressing salary to go to law school." There seems to be something shiny in her eyes. "You got to be what you wanted to be in life, I didn't."

He's uncomfortable with how personal this all got and doesn't like how mad she seems, like it's all his fault. "Hey, I'm sorry you feel—"

"I don't care how silly it sounds," she says. "I know it's ridiculous, but it's something I need. Let me be your lawyer and argue your case. Let me have this."

Her mouth is closed now, so he can't see her big teeth. All he sees are her eyes, big and angry and hoping.

He snaps a nod. He says, "Alright."

EIGHT

THE BELLS ARE CHIMING AS she opens her eyes.

It's bright as day in the room. She's in her apartment.

Day ten.

The waitress with the doe eyes and the big teeth does what she always does, force of habit, force of time: Closes her eyes, listens to another strike of the bell, opens her eyes, waits for the room to stop spinning.

Yesterday's bubble bobs before her for a moment and then floats off and away.

Now she bends over the kitchen table and picks up the empty plate from the lunch she didn't get to eat, at least not in this today. She leaves it in the sink. On the first couple days of this she used to wash the dish, but now she figures, Why bother?

Living one day over and over is a little like living in a mansion with servants. You never have to wash the dishes, do the laundry, take out the trash. You can change your dress, drop the discard on the floor, and never bother to hang it up.

Pulling a glass down from the cabinet, she runs water into it, drinks, then leaves the glass on the counter for the time servants to take.

Such a mansion. Three small rooms and the tiniest bathroom this side of some river she'll never reach because you can't even drive there in a day.

Not that she has a car.

She picks up her pocketbook from the counter and crosses into the bedroom. A stuffed bear sits between the pillows on the bed she made on the last morning she had a morning. The bear is made of purple corduroy and has flowers embroidered on its belly. She picks it up and turns it over, pulls on a zipper, and reaches inside, bringing out a huge stack of bills. Sometimes she thinks of this as her mad money, sometimes as her savings. Right now she thinks, Isn't every mansion stuffed full of money? She hefts it in her hand. There's something exquisite about pulling out all the money she has in the world and holding it, knowing she can use it for anything she wants. She does what she does every new day, shoves the lot of it in her pocketbook.

She'll change clothes in a bit. First she has something to take care of. She goes out of her place and down the stairs to the lobby where she can get on the phone. The lobby is in need of a paint job. The floor is black and white hexagonal tiles, some broken. Embedded in the low ceiling is a wide, flat light set into a fixture shaped like a flower with a border of plaster petals all around. When she first moved in she thought that thing was so fancy.

She steps past the big front windows, where the noon light is making a pass at acting grand and new in a day full of yesterdays. One wall of the lobby is lined with wooden mailboxes and the other has a broom closet and a telephone in a little built-in booth where you can go and stand and close the door for privacy.

She calls her friend, the waitress with the mile-high hair. Lately she does this first thing in the new day so she can catch her friend in time to arrange to switch shifts at the café.

"Hello?"

"Hey, girl, it's me."

The waitress with the doe eyes and the big teeth has a name, of course. It's Ten. Ten the When, because for years she wondered when—ever since the first of the doctors told her she had a bad heart, told her she probably wouldn't live long, told her it could be any day.

What kind of a jerk doctor tells that to a little girl?

Yes, that first time with that first doctor was years ago, when she was, in fact, ten. When she used to have spells and her heart would race. When she'd get sent home from school and would have to spend the rest of the day, as the doctor called it, "being quiet."

She spent too much of her childhood being quiet and wondering when.

That was also when Ten the When started seriously dreaming about becoming a lawyer. Like Granddad, who used to tell her stories of grilling witnesses on the stand and wearing them down, catching the inconsistencies in their well-rehearsed testimonies, tossing their lies back at them so they had to admit their guilt.

"Doe," he'd say, "I took that fella's statement and turned it around so fast he confessed on the spot."

Doe was what Granddad sometimes called her. Because he said she had doe eyes, like the beautiful big brown eyes of a deer. Sometimes, when he was really talking to her man-to-man, not like granddad to granddaughter, he'd shorten it to *D*.

"D," he'd say, "here's the most important thing to know if you want to be a lawyer. Any person can be redeemed if they can look at their own guilt and really, truly want to change."

That was the reason she wanted to grow up and go into law. Not just to be like Granddad but because justice meant more than pronouncing sentence and turning crime into punishment.

She figured if you were as good a lawyer as Granddad, and you could make a guilty man see his guilt and want to change, you could change the world.

Granted Granddad got to be an old man, and she was probably going to die, and she didn't know when.

"When," he'd say when he wanted to use her formal name, when he wanted to make the really, really important pronouncements. "Let's you and I go to the soda fountain."

Yes, sometimes he'd call her *When*, and sometimes *D*, and one time *Wendy*, which was weird. What the heck kind of name is Wendy?

A tinny voice buzzes through the phone pressed to her ear. "Hey, When, what's up?" It's the waitress with the mile-high hair. Five and a Half the Always Good for a Laugh.

"Hey, you." When runs her hand along the phone cord. "I know this is absolutely last minute, but do you have plans for the rest of the day?"

She knows the answer because she's asked this question four times before.

"Oh, big plans. Starting at the laundromat and ending with a hot date."

"Ooh, a hot date?"

"Dinner with Forty the Tall, Dark, and Snorty."

Her bulldog.

"Why?" says Five and a Half. "You got something going on?"

When leans back against the corner of the little booth. "Well, I have a huge test tomorrow for my law class, and I haven't studied one whit."

She knows what her friend is going to say. She's going to say, "What, you're taking a class?" She's going to say, "Well, of course I can cover your shift." She's going to say, "Oh, come on, you don't have to take two of my shifts next week, I'm just happy to help."

And she does. And she does. And she does.

"Oh, you are a lifesaver! No, I swear I will take a double shift for you anytime you need it. Alright, I'd better go. Hey, and you may see me in the café studying. The guy upstairs is playing his saxophone nonstop, and I can't concentrate at all."

"Saxophone?" her friend says. "You do lead a glamorous life. Hope to see you there! Goodbye, When."

The phone clicks and leaves her in silence. Alright, that formality is taken care of. Now she has to pop back upstairs, figure out what to wear, cast off this yesterday dress, leave it for the time servants to take care of, and get on with the day.

It's a short walk down the square to the library where When has to go every morning to check out her books. It's a small branch but ornate compared to her usual digs—with a staircase and dark wood balustrades and high, high ceilings and endless walls of books—that do you know what she'd do one of these days? She'd break in after hours, drink herself glamorously silly on champagne, and fall asleep in the stacks. Yes, she'd do that if only she didn't know that to sleep would mean she'd die and never wake up.

What a bore.

She goes to the section with the lawbooks. She pulls each out from memory, almost without even having to look at the titles on the spines. Some she leaves behind. She doesn't need them anymore. She's a fast reader and a quick study.

She hefts the pile to the desk where the librarian with the pea-green eyes and the freckles says what she always says: "Wow, doing a little studying, are we?"

Sunlight sits in the window, a block of gold. It suddenly occurs to her, and she doesn't know why it never occurred to her before, that she'll never see rain again.

A knob of sadness presses the back of her throat.

Cheerily, she says to the librarian, "Sure am!"

OUTSIDE SHE WRAPS HER ARMS around her books and hauls them down the square, pocketbook hanging from one arm and thumping her elbow as she goes. She'd love to do her studying in the library, but she never knows when Gun is going to show at the café, and she wants to be there when he does to get the latest update.

She stops at the corner, waits for traffic to pass, crosses the street, and continues down the square. Snow too. She'll never see snow. These early autumn days: How very, very far away is winter.

As she walks she looks for the cat with the black coat and the one white ear. She doesn't see it. Unlike with all the other beings who move about this square (except for herself and One the Gun, of course) on their same trajectories every new old day, sometimes she sees the cat and sometimes she doesn't.

She's well aware of what this means.

She can't help but wonder: What happens to a creature with nine lives when it lives one day for eternity?

At the curb is a tree with long green leaves scattered with funny little cupped magenta flowers, each with a blue-colored berry inside. She passes the tree every day, but today she puts her stack of books down on the pavement and reaches out to touch a leaf. It's covered with a down of very fine fuzz.

Granddad taught her about this tree way back when, before she was When, back when she was Then. He said, "Rub the leaf between your fingers, Doe. Now smell."

She rubs the leaf between her fingers, brings her fingertips to her nose. Peanut butter.

If she can't see rain or snow ever again, if Halloween is never going to come around, nor Christmas, nor New Year's, she has to remember to stop and touch the peanut butter tree sometimes. Or touch that tree over there, the one with the pointy leaves. Or smell those flowers growing in the pot beside the café. She has to remember to take in the richness of the world she has left to her.

FIFTEEN MINUTES INTO HER STUDIES, Gun shows up at the café. Most of the day yesterday she didn't see him. She started to think she scared him off with her announcement of her impending death. Gun doesn't seem to be one for taking personal stuff very . . . personally. Today he looks like he always looks. The brown small-brimmed fedora and that little bit of beard shadow like he can't be bothered to shave all the way. But unlike how moody he appeared the last time she saw him, at least he looks focused again.

They're at a table instead of a booth. She thought she'd change things up a bit. Live a little. He's not eating. She's working through a plate of french fries, and she keeps offering him some, and he keeps shrugging her off.

"Seriously," she says, "what happened yesterday? You never came back with a progress report."

"I took the rest of the day off." He glances at her books. "You should, too, sometime."

"Took the day off where?" She thinks for a moment. "Oh. The Dive."

He's doing that thing where he makes little rips along the edge of the menu. "You could have joined me if you wanted."

"I was studying."

Truth is, admitting what she had to him had rattled her. Shoving those words out of her mouth had made them feel more real. She'd spent the rest of the day trying to stuff words about jurisprudence and due process and adjudication into her brain to push out the hurt.

She holds out a french fry again, but he doesn't take it. She shrugs. "Alright. So what's the plan?"

"The police said the type of poison that killed Five was found in the storeroom of the Dive, but it's common enough it also could have been brought in from outside. I'm wondering which of the suspects might have it in their homes."

She points the french fry at him. "You're going to do some more breaking and entering!"

"With two murder weapons, I have twice the chance of finding evidence, right? The way I look at it, the murder of Five was planned out, sneaky. But when the killer decided they had to eliminate me, it was rash. That makes me think they had a gun, probably for protection. It's probably at their home right now."

Ten the When sits up straight. "Well, great! Hop to it! The sooner you get the information, the sooner you can solve the case, and then you can finish this day safe and move on to tomorrow."

Tomorrow. If only she could follow him there.

"So get breaking and entering!" she says. "But you'd better stop in once in a while and give me a progress report."

He kicks another nod at her. He drops the tattered menu on the table and slides out of his chair. "Sure," he says. And as he goes to leave: "Don't study too hard."

"Oh, I will," she calls after him. "You know me."

But he doesn't, does he? If he did, he wouldn't crack some knock-off comment like that. He knows she has to study hard if she wants to know everything lawyers know.

One the Gun crosses the café through the sounds of silverware clinking on china and steps out through the open doorway without looking back.

***

SHE STUDIES FOR A BIT, but her heart isn't in it. She gathers up her books and lugs them back behind the counter, where she leaves them in stacks with the menus. She tells Five and a Half the Always Good for a Laugh that she's got to go out but will be back later.

She doesn't know where to go. She looks for the cat with the black coat and the one white ear and doesn't see it.

Dead center in the window of the dress shop is a mannequin wearing a cocktail dress, red satin with a peplum of black lace. A scalloped neckline. Off the shoulder. Very pretty, but When is tired of seeing it. Seeing the same thing every day on this square, knowing she'll see it every day forever and ever if she's lucky.

A little bell makes a *ting* as she opens the door. The shop is small with light blue painted walls covered with mirrors. On the racks are mostly simple dresses, cotton and rayon. The red job in the window looks to be the big guns.

A shop girl with cat-eye glasses grins at her from behind the counter. "Well, hello, welcome. Can I help you find anything?"

"Actually, I'd like to see the dress in the window," When says. "The red one."

"Oh?" The shop girl comes out from behind the counter. "Big date?"

When doesn't want to say no, so: "Yes!"

"Well, great!" The shop girl takes a pencil out from behind her ear and puts the end in her mouth, thinking. "Now I've got one more of those in stock, but I'm afraid it would be too small."

"That's fine. I'd like that one. The one in the window."

"It might need some adjustments," the shop girl says, "but sure. Why don't you come with me into the fitting room. This way."

***

THE BELL MAKES A TING as she goes back out into the day.

She's wearing the red dress. The blue skirt and top she had on before are folded up neatly in the fitting room. When she went to pay for the dress and wear it out the door without any alterations, with her altogether unmatching shoes and bag, the shop girl with the cat-eye glasses looked at her like she'd insisted on leaving the shop in her underwear. But When said she was late for her big date and wanted to look beautiful.

Just outside now, she stops to admire the shop window. The shop girl with the cat-eye glasses is climbing up to remove the naked mannequin. A new dress will go up, and at least for the next several hours something will look different on the square.

There's a chill on the air. The sunlight is deceiving this time of year. The red dress slips softly against her calves as When strides down the sidewalk. She thinks about the shop girl with the cat-eye glasses. She thinks what she thinks every time someone is nice to her: Maybe they could be friends. But the thing is, they can't. Not really. Because you can't build anything enduring when there's no tomorrow.

Even people she already knows. Say, Five and a Half the Always Good for a Laugh.

And she is. But these days it's always the same laugh. And what good's a conversation if one of you isn't going to remember it tomorrow? What good's a relationship if it can't progress beyond today?

The only one she has is One the Gun.

Even though he's kind of a jerk. Thinks he's always right, hardly sees beyond his own obsessions. At least what they have together is something that lasts.

What's going to happen after One the Gun finds out who his killer is, goes on to the end of the day, and passes through to the other side, leaving her here? She knows what will happen.

When she sees him in her day after day, he will just be the him he was on that very first day, that seminal day, coming in and sitting down with the doorman for their interview, only asking her for a hamburger.

How long can you stand to live if you can't experience enduring relationships?

Maybe when One the Gun is lost to the forward flow of time, she'll go out in search of someone new. How many people die in the city in one day? How many possibilities might there be to find someone who, like her, can't escape?

Maybe she can at least make friends with the cat.

WHEN SHE STEPS BACK INTO the café, Five and a Half the Always Good for a Laugh, head pointed down into the cash register, puts one eyebrow up at her. Ten the When goes behind the counter and grabs up her books, goes to an empty booth, her usual booth, and arranges them on the table.

Five and a Half comes over to her booth without a menu. "Girl, you are a nut. You're going to study in that?"

Off the top of her head, she says, "I'm studying trade dress law."

"Well, it's absolutely gorge! You want another plate of french fries? I had to clear the other away."

"No, thanks," she says. "I'll order something later."

She always sits on this side of the booth so she can watch the door for him. She's itching for an update to his snooping. She works through an hour. He doesn't arrive.

AT FOUR SHE RISKS MISSING him in order to take another stroll around the square. It's even chillier. She walks with her arms tucked in, hugging herself. She thinks about stopping up to her apartment to grab a wrap, but what's the point of popping down a wad of cash for something fancy if you're going to hide it under some mismatched sweater?

She passes shops, touches trees, turns at corners. A bearded man in a blue tailored coat, passing her coming the other way, gives her the eye. What she really wants to do, of course, is go by the dress shop with its new dress in the window. Take a gander at the tiny change she made on this square. What's life worth if you can't make change? Maybe tomorrow she can sneak into the display window of the refrigerator store and shut the doors of all the refrigerators. That would switch things up a bit.

But when she comes to the dress shop she stops cold.

They've put up the one remaining red dress.

SHE'S WORKING HER WAY THROUGH the three basic categories of tort law and a fresh plate of french fries when One the Gun finally shows at the café with an update. His suit is even more rumpled, and his hair is mussed under his hat with strands hanging across his forehead.

"What's that on your sleeve?" she says. "Grease?"

"I've been climbing in and out of windows, alright?"

The look on his face is somewhere between too focused and not focused enough. He tucks into the booth opposite her but doesn't slide all the way in, like he's not going to stick around long.

"So I started with the widow," he says. "I knew she'd be at the church at that time. I'd already done a thorough search of her wardrobe and jewelry and things, so I left that off. I checked under the sink in the kitchen, the hall closet, all the places where you might keep your rat poison. Is this a different dress than you were wearing before?"

"I don't think so," she says.

"I gave that place a wall-to-wall going over. Desks, cabinets, anything you might hide something inside. No poison, no gun."

"Say, don't you want something to eat?" She lifts the edge of the plate. "The french fries are really good here."

"Then I looked up Four the Door. I knew the place would be empty because he's at the Dive by three. He's got a room on the square. What a fleabag. That place is about the size of a business card. One room and a closet. Sink and a hot plate. Bathroom down the hall. Sure his boss is the best boss in the world. Must be paying him peanuts."

"Oh," she says, "how sad."

"There was hardly anything in the place. No pictures on the walls, no books. There were a few weights."

"No poison?"

"No poison, no gun," he says.

He looks around like he might be wanting to get his hands on a menu to tear up.

"I already went fishing in the preacher's chambers and came up zeroes," he says, "but I went back over to the church and poked around. I thought about the little kitchen room where they make coffee and put out doughnuts after services."

"Refectory?"

"Where there's food, there's rats," he says. "If the preacher poisoned Five, he could have gotten it from there. I looked under the sink, in the storeroom, everywhere. Checked the kitchen in the nuns' wing."

"Convent?"

Gun wheels his hand. "Whatever, some sort of building in the complex just dedicated to nuns. Anyway, no poison."

"No guns?" she asks, hoping he'll crack a smile.

"Okay, but then!" he says. "It hit me, if the preacher's chambers is where he lives, where's his bathroom? Where does the guy take a shower? Turns out that's not where he lives at all. You know that little building at the end of the church complex?"

"Clergy house?" she tosses out. "Rectory? Parsonage?"

He puts an eyebrow up at her like *are you finished?*

"Vicarage?"

"The guy's actual quarters aren't much different from the other place," he says. "Pretty tiny. Same cot, same blank walls with a cross here and there. He's got a closet for his priest duds. No poison, no guns."

He stands out of his seat. Looks down at her plate and finally picks up a french fry.

"Where to now?" she asks.

"Eight the First Mate. At least I can find out whether his place is decorated with all that nautical hoo-ha." Gun studies the french fry for a moment, then sets it back down on the edge of the plate. "I'll catch you later at the Dive."

AFTER SHE FINISHES HER FRENCH fries Ten the When goes to the phone booth just inside the drugstore and slides the door shut. Tosses some silver in the slot, asks the operator for long distance.

The phone rings. Picks up. The voice says, "Hello?"

"Hello, Granddad."

"When!" His voice is thin and crackly like two autumn leaves rubbed together. "Well, what a nice surprise!"

"I've been thinking of you and thought I'd give a call," she says.

"Well, how nice, how nice. It's been a little while, hasn't it?"

She called him yesterday and the day before and the day before, but of course how is he going to know that?

"What did you do today, Granddad?"

Some life comes into his voice. "Oh, well I had a nice walk in the garden. I saw a cedar waxwing! Pretty thing."

"That's lovely."

"Oh, it was, it was. Haven't seen one for years. Saw plenty of chickadees, too, but they're not much to write home about."

"I like chickadees," she says.

"So do I, Doe," he says. "They sound like tiny little trolls."

She laughs.

"And let's see," he says, "we had baked fish and spinach for lunch. And in a little bit is dominoes in the common room."

"That sounds like a nice full day," she says.

"It is, it is! And how about you, When?"

"Well, I've been studying law," she says.

Now his voice sounds almost as robust as it did twenty years ago: "What, When! You want to be a lawyer?"

"Just like you, Granddad."

"Well, how do you like that?" he says. A little pause, and then, "It's difficult, Doe. I'll have to say that. It's a lot to learn."

"Do you think I can do it?"

What a silly question. She knows what he's going to say, but she asks every time and waits with a weird dry lump in her throat for his answer.

"Oh, do you even have to ask? Of course you can do it. Of course you can. I have complete faith in you. Now here's what I want you to remember. It's the most important thing. Any person can be redeemed if they can look at their own guilt and really, truly want to change."

She doesn't tell him that for her becoming a lawyer is just learning about becoming a lawyer, that there'll be no passing of the bar, no office with her name stenciled on the glass. She's well aware that the whole thing is ridiculous. She's a smart woman. Smart enough to become a lawyer, smart enough to know that becoming a lawyer is impossible. But whenever the truth gets too close, she shoves another book in front of her face.

"I think I can do it, Granddad. I'm studying really hard."

"Of course you are," he says. "I have complete faith in you. Say, do you know what I did today?"

"What?"

"I had a nice walk in the garden," he says. "I saw a cedar waxwing! Pretty thing."

There's a tiny sting behind her eyes. She says, "Oh, you did? A cedar waxwing? That's lovely."

"Oh, it was, it was," he says. "Haven't seen one for years. Saw plenty of chickadees, too, but they're not much to write home about."

"Do you know what I did today, Granddad?" she says. "I smelled a peanut butter tree. Do you remember those? Do you remember how you taught me?"

There's a pause on the line. Then, "Oh, yes, oh, yes. And you smelled one today?"

"I sure did."

"Well, how do you like that?" he says. "And I suppose it smelled good."

"It sure did."

"Well, that's just fine," he says. There's another pause. And then, "Who is this again?"

She closes her eyes a moment. The booth feels tight and oppressive. She makes her voice bright. "It's me, Granddad. It's When."

"When! Well, what a nice surprise!"

"I was thinking about you," she says, "and I thought, heck, I'm just going to give him a call!"

"Well, how nice, how nice. It's been a little while, hasn't it?"

She called him yesterday and the day before and the day before, but of course how is he going to know that?

"I miss you," she says.

"I miss you, too, When. Will you come for a visit?"

Her throat twists. She tries to swallow. Through the glass of the phone booth, and out through the glass of the drugstore's big front window, a breeze shivers the sidewalk trees. "Yes, Granddad."

"When?"

"Yes, Granddad?"

"When will you come for a visit?"

"Very soon," she says. "In fact, I called the airline."

And she did. It was on a different today, but she called. There's a flight from here to there. She's taken it many times before. It's four hours with a one-hour layover. It would get her there at eight in the evening, which wouldn't give them many hours before the day circled back again.

That's fine, she told the man from the airline. *I'd like to reserve a one-way ticket. Do you have seats open today?*

Well, not today, he said, voice jolly, *but we can get you on tomorrow.*

"How about I come visit you for Thanksgiving, Granddad?" she says. "Would you like that?"

"Well, hot diggity," he says. "Hot diggity, indeed!"

"I'll take you out for a big turkey dinner, and we can talk about your old cases and walk in the garden together and look for birds."

"I had a nice walk in the garden today," he says. "I saw a cedar waxwing! Pretty thing."

She lets her head rest on the wall of the phone booth. "Oh, you did? A cedar waxwing? How wonderful."

"Oh, it was, it was," he says. "Haven't seen one for years. Saw plenty of chickadees, too, but they're not much to write home about."

"I think they are," she says. "I'd like to hear all about them."

"Well, you know, I have to admit, I do like chickadees. They sound like . . . oh, hold on a moment." A murmur of sound on the line. A pause. Then he's back. "I have to go now. That nurse is here. She says it's time to go down for dominoes."

"I understand," she says. "I love you, Granddad. I'll call you tomorrow."

NINE

THE BELLS ARE CHIMING AS he opens his eyes.

It's bright as day in the room. He's in his office.

Day eleven.

One the Gun does what he always does, force of habit, force of time: Closes his eyes, listens to another strike of the bell, opens his eyes, waits for the room to stop spinning.

Another day down, and what did it get him? No poison, no guns anywhere. At least he got to do some breaking and entering. Twelve days ago that would have made him feel sleazy. Now he has to admit that the kick of unlawful entry, the sense of power that comes from going through someone else's space uninvited, the little violation in it—he doesn't know if this new skill moves him up a notch to second-rate gumshoe or takes him down to fourth, but he knows he enjoys it.

So there was that, at least.

But then at the end of the night, it had taken him two tries to jump out of time. Weird.

***

THE BELLS ARE CHIMING AS she opens her eyes.

It's bright as day in the room. She's in her apartment.

Ten the When does what she always does, force of habit, force of time: Closes her eyes, listens to another strike of the bell, opens her eyes, waits for the room to stop spinning.

Another day down and another day up. Yes, why not think about a day being up? Why not try to be more up, herself? After all, the death she was supposed to have at the end of this day never comes. Isn't that the best gift someone could be given? Who needs Halloween and Christmas and New Year's Eve when you have today and today and today?

As she heads down to the lobby to get her shift covered at work, When remembers it took her two tries to jump out of time last night. Weird.

THIS TIME WHEN ONE THE Gun visits the police department it's a little later in the day, so he finds Detective Cinco the Toss 'Em in the Clinko in the lobby of the building, talking with the receptionist with the strawberry lips and the figure-eight curves.

"Gun!" the cop says. "You here to talk about the Five case? Come with me! Come to my office! This way!"

"I wanted to ask about something that wasn't on the police report," Gun says, walking. "I'm curious if Five himself had a record."

It's kind of an odd direction to take, but after yesterday's bust, grasping at straws seems a good plan.

"Are you kidding?" the cop says. "Guy was a cheap hood, a lowlife, a no-good! If you ask me, he deserves what he got! In here!" The cop opens the door and ushers Gun into his dingy little office with the scarred wooden desk and the two metal chairs. "Be right back!"

When Detective Clinko returns with Five's file, he opens the manila folder on the scatters of paperwork on his desk, and the two men stand over it, looking down.

The cop narrates One the Gun's read through. "Yeah, he was making book in that back room of his, and from what I gather, raking it in! He was run down two years ago on a fraud charge for supposedly rooking the clientele, but it didn't stick. Also he was buying cheap booze and decanting it into more expensive bottles."

"Seems like plenty of dope in here to make a wife cool it on her husband," Gun says.

"I'm ahead of you on that angle, Gun." The cop sits on the corner of the desk and crosses his arms. "She definitely could have wanted the mug out of the way because of this stuff. Or, for that matter, the bartender could have. Think about how it must feel to put your hopes and dreams into a business, only to have it corrupted by your less-than-upstanding so-called angel!"

One the Gun nods out of politeness, but really, it isn't anything he hasn't considered before.

"And!" The cop thrusts a finger at the ceiling. "Speaking of the devil!" He jumps to his feet. "This is hot off the press!" The cop moves the papers around on his desk and uncovers another manila folder, sets it on top. "I've been doing some research on these folks, and I just found out that, what do you know, Eight the First Mate has a record!"

This is interesting. "Oh?"

"Reason we didn't find it before is that, at the time, our friend the bartender had a different name! Eight the Not So Narrow, Not So Straight!"

"Oh?" More of a punch to the word this time.

The cop opens the file and leans in, angling his face down at the report but glancing up to give Gun the double-Os from under his eyebrows. "Seems our friend the whiskey slinger was accused of assaulting a man in a brawl, a man who later died."

"Wow!" One the Gun says.

"He was cleared of the charges for lack of sufficient evidence," the cop says, "but next thing we know, he skips town! I call that very suspicious!"

Gun points a finger at him. "I think you're right."

"And!" the cop says. "Then he drops out of sight for the next seven years. Not one trace of an Eight in either name. Who was he for those seven years? Where did he go? What is he hiding?"

A buzz of possibility hums in Gun's stomach. He says, "I'm going to find out."

ONE THE GUN GOES TO the phone booth just inside the drugstore and slides the door shut. Tosses some silver in the slot, calls his office. Two the True Blue picks up and says hello in her clear, bell-like voice.

"Checking in," he says. "And listen. I've got something for you. Apparently the bartender wasn't always called Eight the First Mate."

He tells her what he's learned. He doesn't know how all this new information fits together, but it's going to help him solve this case. He can feel it.

"Manslaughter!" she says. "Wow. Amazing. How did you track this down?"

"Oh, I've been interviewing folks, scouring the newspaper morgue, piecing things together."

"Impressive!" she says.

"Now I'm hot on the trail, so I'd like you to do a little research for me," he says. "See if you can track down anything about Eight during those seven mystery years. Any trace you might find will likely be out of town and under a different name. I know this is a tall order, but if anyone can find a needle in a haystack, I mean, you're the most capable person I know."

"Well, thank you, sir!" Obviously flattered.

"Alright, I'm off to beat the bushes for leads," Gun declares. "I'll see what I can smoke out on my end, you see what you can find on yours, and we'll solve this case together!"

TEN THE WHEN IS TRYING on dresses at the dress shop.

Each time she tries on a new one, she comes out from behind the white curtain of the changing room, stands in front of the full-length mirror, looks at herself, then takes a twirl.

She's tried on the yellow one with the long skirt, the blue one with the short skirt, the blue one with the long skirt, many-colored dresses with every manner of skirt—A-lines, straight skirts, circle skirts, pleated skirts; scoop necks, square necks, high necks, boat necks; mousseline, velveteen, zibeline, crepe de chine—and with each dress she tries on, with each twirl she takes, she's surprised by an emptiness in her gut. As if she expected one of these dresses to make her feel different, devil-may-care, which she doesn't, so she doesn't know why she should be surprised.

She leaves on the green one with the twirliest organdy skirt and the sequined bodice because you only live once, or so they say. She scoops up six or eight of the others, the ones that look expensive, and hauls them to the register.

The shop girl with the cat-eye glasses gives her the up and down with one raised eyebrow. "Um, all set? Do you want to change back into your clothes?"

"Thank you, no," Ten the When says, "and I'd like these. And that red one in the window."

The shop girl with the cat-eye glasses watches When dump the load of multicolored fabrics on the counter. A big, slightly perplexed smile starts spreading on her face.

When puts up a finger. "But on one condition. When you take that red dress out, you don't put another red dress in the window."

The shop girl looks at her blankly for a second. Then the eyes in those cat-eye glasses go from When to the window and back to the pile of dresses waiting to be rung up. Then she ticks her shoulders up by an inch and says, "You've got it."

IT MAY HAVE BEEN A fib before when One the Gun told Miss Blue he'd been to the newspaper office for research, but it's not a fib now as he steps through the door and checks in at the front desk. He's here at the same time he usually comes. Even his body knows it. His feet walking along the concrete floor of the back hallway toward the morgue room feel familiar, like he's slipped right into the same footsteps he made on that seminal day. This time his aim is to scour their records for any shred he can find of Eight the Not So Narrow, Not So Straight.

But then he glances through the small glass pane in a nondescript wooden door as he passes, lets his eyes fall on something inside, and—what?

Gun stops in his tracks as the realization hits him, and he turns back. He's walked this corridor how many times and never noticed until now?

He pushes the door open and the man inside looks up, a crate of mail in one hand and an envelope in the other, stopped in the act of slipping that envelope into one of the slots lined up along the wall of the newspaper office mail room.

Three the Goatee.

Oho.

Gun lets the door close behind him, takes another step in, and turns his head at the man, giving him a pointed sideways look. "Now wait a minute."

Three the Goatee is frozen in place, eyes bulging above his carefully coiffed whiskers. "Mr., uh," he says, "Gun."

"Now I thought you were a professor at the college," One the Gun says.

The so-called professor looks different than usual: regular work pants rather than his pressed slacks, no jacket, his shirt-sleeves rolled, and his tie loose. Gun makes a show of looking around. The room is long and thin, almost oppressive. Cracked paint on the walls and no windows. In the center are two long tables pushed together, covered with stacks of papers and envelopes. At one end of the table closest to Gun, shoved up against a crate full of more envelopes, is a pompous little tea setup: pot and matching cup in white and gold porcelain, a tiny silver spoon, and a slice of lemon.

Miss Blue has said the so-called professor drinks tea all day long. Fancy tea. Supposedly gets it imported. But this stuff is strictly grocery goods. You can tell; the box sitting there says *Econo-Royale*.

"You work in a mail room." One the Gun enjoys stating the obvious.

Three the Goatee is still standing there with the crate of mail. He's got it hugged to his chest now, like its bulk can protect him from anything Gun might say. "Uh, no, I—"

"Looks like you do," Gun says.

"The mail room is on the other side of the wall," Three the Goatee says. "This is the sorting room."

"Okay..."

Goatee's eyes are bouncing around in his head like he

doesn't know what to say but can't stop talking. "See, mail goes into these slots and then people go into the mail room on the other side to pick—"

"Does Two the True Blue know this?" Gun lifts the little ornate teapot, pretending to examine it.

"You put that down."

"Because I don't think she'd appreciate being lied to."

Goatee shoves the box of mail to the floor and skirts the table to Gun. "Listen, Gun, please. Don't tell her. I just—"

"Yeah, I guess you did."

"It wasn't a lie outright, not at first. She just thought, from my clothes and the way I know things—"

"Seems kind of insulting, professor." Gun sets the pot down. "Thinking Miss Blue wouldn't want to be your girl if you weren't some high-and-mighty professional egghead." (Gun's attempts to convince her he's a first-rate gumshoe notwithstanding.)

Three the Goatee's looking up at him with pleading eyes like a basset hound. "Please, Gun. Let it go, please. You don't know what it means to me. I never thought I'd rate a woman as smart and classy as her. I just—don't tell her, alright?"

Gun rocks back on his heels, crosses his arms, smiles amiably. He doesn't want the guy running off to Miss Blue with ready-made excuses. "Alright."

TEN THE WHEN HAS BEEN handing out dresses in the café. What an exchange it's been as ladies go in and out of the restroom trying things on. She gave the yellow one with the long skirt to the schoolteacher at the counter reading movie magazines over a plate of franks and beans. She gave the pink one with all the lace to the bookshop girl who always orders a lettuce and tomato sandwich and takes a beefsteak home for her Chihuahua. When she gave the blue one with the feathers to her friend Five and a Half the Always Good for a Laugh, she told her, "Promise me that as soon as you get off work, you'll change into it and go see your beau."

"I'll be seeing him tomorrow. You've got me working tonight, remember?"

"Please, tonight, if only for a little while!" When said. "Promise me! I want you to enjoy it tonight."

"Alright, you nut. I promise."

A good deed is worth it, isn't it, even if it's soon to be unremembered? Like when Ten the When calls Granddad. That schoolteacher with the fancy yellow dress headed off to prepare an extravagant surprise dinner for her husband for the anniversary of their first meeting. Maybe all sorts of lovely moments will be had today in fancy dresses. Moments that will be gone tomorrow but filled with joy in their present. And that's all we have, isn't it? The present?

In the present Ten the When is back in her booth with her books. The skirt of her green dress is so full she can hardly keep it squashed under the table. And sometimes, in this bright café light, when she shifts a certain way while looking down at her book, a beam banks off one of the big sequins on her bodice and hits her in the eye.

Now she glances out through the big café windows and spots One the Gun coming down the sidewalk. He's going at a brisk clip, looking determined. Standing in her seat, she waves big across the restaurant to catch his eye. His figure slows, his head swivels her way. She gives him a come-here wave.

He turns and heads into the café, making for her booth. She sits back down into the *shish* of her organdy skirt. "Wait till I tell you what I've been doing," she says. "I've been having such fun."

Gun shoves in opposite her. "I've just got a moment." His eyes blink down to her sequins. "Playing dress-up again? I hope you're not doing that on my account."

Ten the When feels her eyes trying to roll. Why do men always think if a woman dresses up, it's for them? "No, Gun. It's not for you."

"Because I've got a girl," he says.

"Did you pass it when you came here?" she asks. "The dress shop?"

"What? I guess."

"What color dress was in the window?"

He's lifting the skirt edge of one of the few remaining frocks draped over the back of his seat by the wall. "I don't know."

What Ten the When says pulls a grin up out of her. "It's orange! Do you know why? I bribed the shop girl to change it."

Gun's just looking at her blankly.

"It was red yesterday," she says, "and red the day before, and red the day before. I got her to put in the orange one."

"Why?"

When doesn't know why she needs to explain this. "To make change! I just . . . need to make change! Don't you want to make change?"

"Orange isn't that different from red," he says.

She drops it. She sits back in her seat. "So you've got a girl?"

One of the folks When gave a dress to, a man, comes over to their booth with his café receipt in one hand and the dress, peach crepe, in the other. "Heya, lady, thanks again." He bends into them, the grin on his face flashing both rows of teeth. "My sister Sixteen will love this. She's never had nothing so spiffy as this!"

Ten the When lobs his grin back at him. "I hope she likes it!" And as he starts to leave, she calls after, "Remember, make sure she wears it today!" Then back to Gun. "So what updates on the case?"

"She's the prime article," Gun is saying. "She'd wear the hell out of one of those dresses."

Gun seems odd these days. Different. She can't put her finger on it. It's like there's something different behind his eyes. He's never been one to be completely locked onto you when he's talking to you, but lately he seems even more remote. Inside his head.

She says, "Who? Your girl?"

"Well." He flips his hand. "It's moving in that direction."

"Ah, so it's a budding romance?" She could remind him that any progress he makes moving in that direction today will reverse itself tomorrow, but her cynicism wouldn't do him any good.

His eyes go merry. "I think so."

"Well"—she smiles but gives him an exaggerated waggle of the finger—"don't let it get in the way of solving your case."

Gun folds his hands on the tabletop, his thumbs side by side, and taps them together. "Why can't I have two goals? Wanting to get the girl is just making me more motivated. Solve the case and you get the girl. You're the hero."

"Oh, you want to be a hero."

"You know what I mean. Get the job done, and it greases the wheels."

Ten the When sits back and crosses her arms over her spangled chest. "Well, mister hero," she says. "Just be sure to keep your priorities straight."

WHEN GUN STEPS INTO HIS office, he has his coat draped over his arm. Hiding underneath it is the dress he got off of the waitress with the doe eyes and the big teeth. Two the True Blue is at the desk, on the phone, her eyes up at the ceiling, listening. As he closes the door behind him her eyes flick in his direction, and she gives him a quick hello bob of the head before turning her attention back to the call. "Correct. He went missing for seven years."

Gun drapes the coat and hidden dress across the back of the client couch and then stands there, waiting.

"Yes," Miss Blue is saying, "that would be very helpful. You have this number. And a good day to you too. Goodbye." She hangs up, makes a note on a pad on the desk. "Alright, not a whole lot yet, but I've made some calls to a few places. I heard from a police department north of here that there was a troublemaker by the name of Eight the Ingrate, but the timing doesn't quite add up, and it sounds like that man is quite a bit older."

"Come over here," Gun says. "See what I have."

Miss Blue slants her head a moment but rises and steps out from behind the desk, crossing to him. She has a polite smile on her face.

Gun reaches under the coat and pulls the dress out with a flourish. It's rose colored and slinky, almost like a slip but longer, with a sweetheart bodice. So sexy none of the customers in the café had felt comfortable choosing it, Gun figures. He loops a strap over each of his index fingers and holds the dress out so she can really see it.

"It's for you," he says.

Two the True Blue looks at the dress, then at him, her eyebrows pressed together.

"I was walking by the dress shop," he says, "and saw it in the window, and I thought, That would look perfect on Miss Blue."

He reaches for her hand. It's soft. He lays the dress over her palm, holds her hand a second longer before letting go.

Miss Blue stares down at the drape of rose. "Sir, I appreciate it, but—"

"Oh, think nothing of it. Just a little something to say thank you for all the hard work you do."

"Well, I..."

"Sure, now, you enjoy it." He sits on the back of the couch like casual. "Oh, I saw your boyfriend today."

"Oh?" She's looking down at the dress hanging over her hand.

"You know, I thought he was a professor at the college."

Miss Blue looks up. "He is."

"I saw him in the newspaper mail room, sorting mail," Gun says.

Miss Blue is just looking at him, a confused tweak between her pretty brows.

"He told me not to tell you because he knew you wouldn't appreciate that he lied to you, but I don't think it's right for you to be deceived like that. Here." Gun stands. He goes the few steps to her and lifts the dress from her hand. He holds it up to her, draping it across her chest like he's looking at the fit. "I think this will look nice."

Miss Blue takes a step back, flashes him a smile that looks uneasy.

"Seriously, Miss Blue." Gun folds the slink of dress over his hand and passes it back to her. "I'd think carefully about whether you want to be going out with someone who pretends to be something he's not. I was pretty shocked when I saw him there. I don't mean to be a stoolie. I just want what's best for you."

She looks far away and then back at him. A sort of blank look on her face. "Well... I'm sure he has his reasons."

Gun blinks. He says, "What?"

She smiles and drapes the dress over the arm of the couch. "If he felt like he had to pretend to be something he's not, I'm sure he had a good reason. He grew up poor and felt ashamed of it. He had to work two jobs while he was putting himself through school, you know."

Two the True Blue goes and sits down on the chair across from the couch. Gun turns to reorient himself toward her but can't think of what to do but stand there stupidly.

"We met on campus, actually," she says. "I was attending a public lecture on philosophy and bumped into him in the hall afterward. He had the cutest little briefcase." She slants her head. "Gosh, I must have given him the impression I thought he taught there and he just . . . oh, I feel sorry to think he felt like he had to keep up this charade." Her eyes look faraway again. Then she taps one hand on the armrest of the chair. "You know what? I'll go see him tonight and let him know it's all okay."

"You'll—"

She pops up from the seat. "He must have been feeling so ashamed. Well, if we clear the air, I'm sure our relationship will be better than ever. Thank you for telling me, sir. I appreciate it."

AT THE DIVE TEN THE When is on the dance floor, dancing. She feels like she should be studying—she still has so much to learn—but giving out dresses today, sending folks off to plan dates and dinners, made her happy at first and then lonely.

When she got here One the Gun was sitting at the bar nursing a Scotch. She started over there to join him, but something in his body language said he wanted to be left alone. The way he hunched over the drink, some tension along the curve of his back. She's come to know him well enough in these handful of days to know that that hunch means Gun is in a mood.

Ten the When has danced with this man before. She doesn't know him. She saw him on the first night she started looping back in time and impulsively asked him to dance and he politely agreed. But tonight, with When in this outlandish green dress, he was downright eager when she went up to his table and said, "Care to take a twirl on the dance floor, sailor?"

And here she is, twirling round and round to the repeating music in the *shish* of organdy. Below her feet is the elaborate, foot-worn nautical compass painted on the dance floor, but even if she looks down, she can't see anything but the green pouf of her skirt. Her partner is a short man, very light on his feet, elegant. He has thick, straight eyebrows like black caterpillars over his eyes. He wears a purple bow tie and smiles over her left ear as he turns her.

And as he turns her the suspects in the case revolve around her. Four the Door at the entrance chatting up some customers, Six the Kicks in her glittery mourning blacks at one end of the bar, Seven the Heaven at the other, and off across the room, bending over a table with a tray of drinks, is Eight the First Mate.

As light as her partner is on his feet, he doesn't move her across the dance floor. He just keeps the room turning around her. Four, Six, Seven, Eight; Four, Six, Seven, Eight.

This case isn't hers at all, but still she's obsessed with it. Wanting to find out who the villain is, wanting Gun to solve it and become the hero he wants to be. Wanting Gun to become a little more like the hero that, if radio has taught her anything, he should be.

Ten the When's feet on the dance floor feel weird, disconnected. It's the pull of time. It wants her body to be doing different things, doing the things it was doing on the night before she started looping back in time. She notices this pull during the day, a faint otherworldly quality about her movements, but she really feels it the later each day gets. The closer, maybe, that she gets to the death hour. Time wants to claim her.

Four, Six, Seven, Eight, twirling, twirling.

Lately she's been wondering if she's been feeling this pull even more.

ONE THE GUN TIPS HIS head back and drains his glass, setting it on the counter. Here at the bar the widow is far down the left of him and the preacher down right, in their usual spots, but Gun's got his sights set on the bartender. He's in the mood for a grilling. That little scene back at the office still has his hackles up. He's been biding his time—or at least biding his drink—while the bartender's been flitting around doing bartender things, but now Eight the First Mate steps up opposite the counter from him and nods at his empty. "Like another?"

"Eight the First Mate," Gun says. "That your real name?"

The bartender swivels to the far counter and grabs a bottle of Scotch. Now he turns back, smiling, amiable, like he didn't hear what Gun just said. "You're that detective, aren't you? Someone from your office called me and said you'd be in to talk to me about what happened on Wednesday."

The bartender clinks some fresh ice into Gun's glass and pours. He reaches out to push the freshened drink in Gun's direction.

"I found out a very interesting thing about you today," Gun says. "The police say you have a record."

The bartender's hand hovers above Gun's glass for a moment, and then he pulls it away. "Must be someone else," he says.

"A certain fight in a bar a number of years ago?"

The bartender's eyes twitch like a kitchen mouse caught in a flashlight beam. "I was never convicted on that. I never did that."

"Want to tell me about the incident?" Gun says.

"Hey, what is this? I don't see what it has to do with—"

"This is a murder investigation," Gun says. "I need you to cooperate."

The bartender turns away again. He catches the eye of a customer now standing halfway down the bar. He lifts his voice: "Red tonight?" Then ticks a nod at her. Bringing up a wineglass from below the counter, he reaches for a bottle, giving Gun a shrug with one shoulder, casual. "I happened to be in a tavern and there was a fight. I was taken in for questioning."

"Sounds like it was more than that," Gun says. "For instance, the victim died."

The bartender is pouring. Looking at the wine as it slips into the glass and not at Gun. "They told me that, yes."

Gun makes a little flip of the hand, impatient. "Come on, rewind this reel, give it to me slow."

The bartender heaves out a sigh that makes the curls of his moustache wobble, and he sets the glass down. "Okay, I was in a little tavern down by the docks. Having a drink at the bar, minding my own business. Two guys next to me started beefing, and pretty soon they were going at it. One got the other pinned down on the floor and he was lousing him up, and me and another guy pulled him off, and that was it. They both got up and the barkeep threw them both out."

He takes the glass of wine a few paces down along the bar, hands it to the woman standing there. Then keeps going, farther, to the cash register. Takes his time ringing her up.

Gun sits and drinks and waits. When the woman steps off, Eight the First Mate stands there a moment like he's hoping for more customers to serve. Gun raises his voice just enough to reach him. "And?"

A moment longer to scan the club, and the bartender comes shuffling back. "Well, that was it. I never knew the guy died until I was called in for questioning."

"Sounds like there were witnesses."

"The place was dark. The fight happened fast."

"So the man you said helped you pull the guy off . . ."

"Okay, yeah, he fingered me to the cops." Eight the First Mate flaps his hand like *who cares, it was nothing*. "But he must have gotten his signals crossed with the chaos. Anyway, he said he wasn't sure. Said it *could have been* me, not that it *was* me."

"This story isn't making me too certain you're innocent," Gun says.

The bartender's words start to come out fast, a little desperate. "It was stacked against me. They did this lineup. He picked me out, yes, but it was the moustache. I was the only one in the lineup with a moustache. If your suspect has a moustache, why would you get up a lineup with only one moustache?"

"Are you saying the police don't know how to do their jobs?"

"I didn't kill that guy in that fight, and I didn't kill my boss." The bartender sweeps his hand around the place. "He saved this business. He did me a huge favor."

"That's an interesting name, First Mate," Gun says. "Were you really the first mate on a ship?"

"No."

"Second mate? Third mate?"

"I like boats. Why does it matter?"

"Eight the Not So Narrow, Not So Straight," Gun says this one slowly. "That's an interesting name too."

The bartender's body doesn't move. "So names are interesting."

"If you were such an innocent guy, always minding your own business, not getting in bar fights, what were you doing with a name like that?"

"It's getting kind of busy," the bartender says. "Maybe we should find a time—"

"I don't know." Gun makes a show at scanning the room. "I don't see anyone signaling you for a drink. In fact, here." He finishes his. "I could use another."

He puts a bill down on the counter. The bartender looks at it, then takes the drained glass and puts more ice in it.

"So your former name," Gun reminds him. "Eight the Not So Narrow, Not So Straight."

"So I wasn't so narrow," the bartender says. "I was more portly in those days. I don't see why—"

"Well, okay." Gun waves this off. "Even if that is true, what about the rest?"

"I don't have to talk about this."

"I think you do," Gun says. "I mean, it looks pretty suspicious. What else could *not so straight* possibly imply than—"

The bartender's eyes are little black pellets in the middle of big white orbs. He turns away again. Steps down to the cash register, where he takes his time ringing Gun up, then crosses back, setting down change, and goes to the very opposite end of the bar, pulling a bottle from where it's displayed on the back wall. He looks at it like he needs to study its ingredients.

When he comes back, slowly twisting off the stopper, he's making a wistful face and listening to the piano lady go at it. "This was Five's favorite song."

He's trying to change the subject. Gun's not ready to let anything go. "Where were you after you dropped out of sight after that bar brawl?"

Eight the First Mate pulls over Gun's glass, looking down into the crush of ice. "Around."

"What was your name then?"

"I don't think I have to answer any more questions." He pours his drink.

Gun picks a coin off the counter and studies it a moment. "There are plenty of possibilities." He watches the bartender's eyes to see if anything sparks recognition. "Eight the Bait? You say you like boats so much. Eight the Freight? Maybe you were bumming around trains."

"I'm becoming Eight the Irate."

"Eight the Out of State? Eight the Bad Date?"

"It was Great, okay?" The bartender shoves the drink in Gun's direction. "I don't get how all this matters. I was called Eight the Great."

One the Gun turns the coin in his hand. Eight the Great. He can't make heads or tails of it.

The bartender says, "I was a magician."

Gun's eyes bounce up from the coin, then back down. Then they blink across to Six the Kicks sitting solo at her end of the bar.

"Yeah, she was my assistant," the bartender says. There's a pause. "Okay, fine, here's the short version, and then I'd like you to leave me the hell alone, alright?" He takes a breath into his thick chest and lets it out again. "It was just after . . . the bad time. I had to get away. I couldn't stand everyone's stares. They either pitied me or still thought I was some kind of tough. So I changed my name, hired Six, learned some tricks, and we got the hell out of town."

"Hold up," Gun says. "How does someone who's never done magic learn how to cut people in half and things?"

"I knew some guys. Those taverns down by the docks, they have loads of entertainers. They hooked me up with some training and props. Tricks of the trade. And costumes. Glitzy stuff—rhinestones and feathers. Before I knew it Six and I were on the road."

Tricks of the trade. One the Gun has been thinking that the bartender could easily have dumped some premixed poisoned whiskey into Five's glass and tossed the evidence, but now he finds out that the guy can do magic tricks too. Sleight of hand. Two possible ways to poison the boss with no one the wiser.

"Eight the Great." Gun turns the coin again. "I don't see why you were being so cagey about that name. Unless it contains a secret you don't want me to know."

The bartender starts wiping down the counter with a bar rag, face pointed down. "It just . . ." He lowers his voice. "I wasn't that great."

Gun sits back on his stool and sips his Scotch. He doesn't know whether to want the bartender as his main suspect or not at this point. There's something charming about Eight the First Mate, something that seems innocent, that makes you want to believe him—but no good detective assumes innocence based on appearances.

Eight the First Mate spreads the bar rag out on the counter, looks down at it. "It was nice while it lasted, though." A frown on his face. "But Six got tired of the one-night stand gigs. And I wanted to settle down, too, get a respectable job. We used to play plenty of dives. A little restaurant that serves fish and chips with a nautical theme, that was my dream."

"And Six met Five through you?"

Eight the First Mate starts folding the bar rag in long, thin increments from the bottom up. "No, he met her through Four the Door," he says. It seems like the little trip down memory lane has taken the edge off his indignation. "Or through Four's sister, actually. Before the Dive was the Dive. I'd just bought this place, was starting to fix it up. Five was running a jazz joint down by the docks, and Four the Door was his doorman there. Anyway, Four was in the hospital for his appendix. Both Five and Four's sister happened to visit at the same time. Five thought she was pretty and started flirting her up. She told him, 'Hold down, tiger. If you're looking for romance, you should meet my friend Six.' I guess that tells you something about Five—flirting up nuns in hospital rooms. But she introduced Six to Five, and the rest, I guess, is history."

Most of this speech has been sounding to Gun like nothing really but a pile of numbers, but now a realization spikes through. "Wait," he cuts in. "Four the Door's sister is a nun?"

"Was one," Eight the First Mate says. "Four tells me she's decided to leave the church."

Gun pulls on his ear. Did he never think to ask the bartender if he knew someone named Nine? He knows he asked the moose. He can't remember what the moose said now. He must have evaded the question. What did Six say? Did he ever even ask Six?

The bartender unrolls the bar rag, gathers it in a crumple, and tosses it in a bin on the far counter. "She used to come around here a lot, actually. Funny, a nun in a bar, but I guess she came to see her brother. Granted, we've got Father Heaven in here all the time, so."

Gun says, "Was she here on Wednesday night?"

"No, she hadn't been coming around as much." The bartender brings his voice down again. "There was word she was having a fling with someone she would meet here, but I never saw her talking to too many people except Four and maybe Father Heaven. Anyway, when she stopped showing up these last couple weeks, I figured she decided maybe her conduct wasn't too becoming for a nun, and she gave it up. Of course, then she gave up being a nun, too, so."

"Did Four the Door know about this fling?" Gun asks.

"Oh, I'm not saying I believe the gossip. Although Four did say he saw her slip into the boss's office one time, and that's weird. But if she was having a fling, it couldn't have been with

Five. She was much too pious to get hooked up with a ... well, Five wasn't exactly a saintly character." The bartender gives a shrug as if to excuse all the unsaintly stuff his boss ever did. "Four believed it, though. The gossip. Got pretty heated about it. He asked if it was me." Eight the First Mate rolls his eyes. "Like I'd go after a nun."

Eight the First Mate catches the eye of a cocktail waitress a few paces down along the bar, flicks an excuse-me look at Gun, and goes off to take care of an order. Gun sips his Scotch. Maybe tomorrow Gun can try a one-two punch on Miss Blue: Redrop the bomb about her so-called professor boyfriend, plus present his latest findings in the case at the same time. How much will it take to really impress her? He runs through the suspects in his head. Up until now he's had a widow with a wandering eye and designs on her husband's business, a doorman with an explosive temper, and a priest with an illicit love affair and a penchant for cheating at cards. Now add to that a bartender with not one but two ways to have easily dropped the poison in the glass in front of witnesses, a bartender who very well may have once killed another man. And suddenly Nine might be part of the equation again. Because if the moose thought Five was the one disrespecting not only the widow but also his own sister, that could be plenty motivation for murder.

"I THINK YOU'RE RIGHT," TEN the When tells him.

They're sitting at a two top together at the edge of the Dive dance floor. Whenever she looks down, she can see the pouf of her skirt erupting out from under the table on both sides. Gun's got a mostly drained drink that he keeps rolling between his fingertips. He's got that weird mix of too much and too little focus on his face, like he's half inside his head, turning things over in his mind, and only half sitting here with her.

"Four the Door seems too naïve to be a killer," she says, "but that very well may be a ruse. Did you hear the episode of *Who Is the Villain?* where the villain turns out to be the washed-up boxer with the poodle dog? That character was a dead ringer for Four the Door."

"Thing is," Gun says, "I have all these leads but no clear direction. All it seems to say is that any one of them might have done it."

"Alright, so onward and upward," When says. "What's the plan?"

He's going to say, How about to get tight?

He says, "How about to get tight?"

"Gun, drinking yourself stupid isn't going to get this case solved and get you out of this day alive," she says.

"Trying to get rid of me?" he says, more to his glass than her.

When puts her elbow on the table and her chin in her hand and leans into him. "Would it be strange if I said I kind of want to help save you?"

He raises an eyebrow.

"That probably sounds stupid, and I'm sure you're well able to save yourself, but think about it this way," she says. "I'll be here for the rest of my life, and sure, I can kind of do what I want, I can go out and buy some extravagant dress or eat myself silly, but nothing I ever do will amount to anything. Because nothing I ever do will change anything."

One the Gun stares at her a moment, then looks down into his glass as he rolls it.

"I want to help you save yourself and get out of here because it's the right thing to do," she says. "But for me it's my one chance to do something that means something. When you go I want the fact that you met me to have made a difference."

She sits back, looks down at her hands in her lap. She's

embarrassed at getting all personal, but she kind of hopes what she's said has moved him in some way.

He says, "My assistant Miss Blue said that same thing the other day."

"Which?"

"That thing about there being no way you can change anything in here."

"You told your assistant?" she asks.

"No." He bounces his shoulders. "I just asked, 'If you were given the chance to relive one day over and over, what would you do?' She was all focused on eating just like you. But then she said the problem is you couldn't make any change in the world."

Hearing this truth spoken back to her presses a lump of pain into that place behind her eyes. She says, "It's sort of killing me, the fact that I've basically lost all purpose in my existence." She kicks her gaze to him again, leans her face in closer. "But you haven't. Because you can escape."

The word itself seems to escape her lips. To not want to have been spoken.

They're both quiet. The piano player is pounding the keys like a flyweight in the fourth round.

One the Gun says, "She also said that the only thing you could change is yourself."

"Who?"

"Miss Blue. She's a very brainy type of person, always thinks all the angles."

When shifts in her seat and her skirt rustles like dry paper. "Part of me feels like, why change yourself if you can't use that to do good in the world? Why change in a vacuum?"

She tips her head back. Old pipes snake along the ceiling.

"But again, Gun, you." She turns back to him. "You can

change and then take that change with you. Be better in the world that's beyond."

"I just want to catch the killer."

"But you could do more. You could take more out of here. What are you guilty of?"

He blinks and cranks his head back on his neck. "Me?"

"My Granddad says," she says, "everyone's guilty. He was a lawyer too. He says everyone's guilty of something, but any person can be redeemed if they can look at their own guilt and really, truly want to change."

"Mmm." Gun tosses back a slug of Scotch.

"I mean, sure," she says. "You can be a hero like some radio detective, but the real heroism is reaching down into yourself, into the places you don't like to touch, the guilty places, and being willing to examine and change them. That's the real hero stuff, Gun."

His eyes go off hers for a moment and stare into the middle distance. Nothing in particular on his face. It's hard to know if she's reaching him. She waits to see if he has something to say.

Gun raises his drink again, clinks the ice at the bottom, and sets it down. "I'm all out," he says. "Want a drink? I'll buy us a round."

He's already standing out of his chair.

"Gin fizz," she says as he moves off.

And that's the thing. Not the gin fizz. But the other reason When keeps hanging around this man who can't seem to see past the brim of his hat. And the reason she keeps finding herself nagging him about things like those half-assed apologies he likes to make.

It's about purpose. Her purpose. If she lets herself admit it, she's spent far too much time on her obsession with acting the lawyer. What if the one thing she's able to do in here is change this man for the better, and then let him take that change out into the world?

L ATE. S HE'S DANCING AGAIN WITH the man with the purple bow tie. Gun's already headed out for the night. He wasn't much interested in talking further about her theories of right and wrong, but she'll get through to him. She'll be patient and persistent. She's got time.

The pull of time makes her feet feel dopey on the dance floor. Heavy and slow. Her feet don't want to be dancing. They want to be doing what they were doing at this same time on that seminal night. Lying tucked in her bed where, an hour from now, at just about midnight, her heart is scheduled to seize and lurch and die.

An hour from now? Less than an hour? She's honestly not sure. Last time she looked at the little clock on the wall hidden by that post halfway to the bar it was ten thirty, but the difference between ten thirty and eleven is huge when you only have until twelve. Ten the When is usually very conscientious about what time it is at night, but those gin fizzes have made her irresponsible. She should hurry up and jump out of this day before it gets away from her.

The dancer with the purple bow tie smiles over her left ear as he turns her.

Just jump out now. In the middle of the dance. Wouldn't that give her partner a surprise. Or, when the day circles back on itself, do the people in this day, too, just vanish?

It bothers her that she'll never know the answer to this question. But there are lots of mysteries of life that you never learn the answer to. She just knows she needs to get on with it before she finds that it's suddenly midnight and too late.

She closes her eyes and reaches down into herself to rip herself away from the forward flow of time.

Go.

Go.

Go.

But she's still spinning. Her feet on the dance floor. The strange, dopey, heavy feel of them. She opens her eyes.

The dancer with the purple bow tie is looking at her with his caterpillar eyebrows pressed together in the center. She should probably say something, like she's having such a good time dancing with him that she closed her eyes out of sheer pleasure, but right now she doesn't care. Why isn't this working?

It took two tries last night. She told herself she was just distracted, but what if that's not it?

She closes her eyes again, tries again.

But time keeps moving forward.

This time when she opens her eyes the dancer is looking more concerned than confused. Criminy! She cranes her neck and scans for the clock on the wall, but all she sees is the post studded with papier-mâché sea stars.

She's suddenly sure it's rounding on midnight. The death hour. She can almost feel the stirrings of pain in her chest, or is that simple mortal terror?

She can't concentrate. She's got to get the hell out. She jerks back from the man. His eyes go wide. She doesn't take the time to apologize, just turns and rushes across the dance floor to the entrance where Four the Door tries to say, "And a grand good night to—" as she blows past.

Outside the air is cool. How late is it? A heap of moonlight throws long shadows through the sidewalk trees to the pavement at her feet. Her feet don't stop even though she wants to now that she's free of the noise of the club. Just stop and make the jump, but they won't stop. Her feet are obeying the pull of time. Her feet are walking her home. Taking her to the place where she's supposed to be when her heart is scheduled to seize and lurch and die.

    Oh god. Get out now. She's afraid to trip and fall, but still walking, she squeezes her eyes shut. Reaches down into herself to rip herself away from the forward flow of time, doing her damnedest to ignore the fear that maybe she just can't do it anymore, that maybe this is it.

TEN

DAY TWELVE.

"It's getting harder, isn't it?"

The waitress with the doe eyes and the big teeth sounds oddly monotone, not the bold, animated voice Gun is used to. They're in her booth at the café, but she doesn't have all those books piled around like always. She's got one of those milkshakes she seems to love so much. She looks tired, a little washed of color, although it might be because she's wearing that faded lemonade dress again.

"It took three tries for me last night," One the Gun says.

"I can feel the pull of time all day now," she says. "I mean more than before. I mean a lot. It's probably been gradual, and I haven't noticed."

"I keep thinking maybe it's because I haven't slept in . . . how many days is it? Eleven?"

"Time is healing itself," the waitress says. She sucks milkshake through the straw in some sort of extra hungry way, like she's trying to drink the whole thing in one go. "Knitting itself back together. Like blood cells in a wound. Making things sluggish. Soon the hole will heal and time will move forward. And take you with it."

One the Gun doesn't like talking about this. He makes a little flip of the hand. "It'll take you too."

She studies the straw as she bobs it up and down through her milkshake. "I die, remember? You can save yourself. I can't."

"You don't know for sure. We both might just wake up in tomorrow."

The straw goes up and down.

One the Gun sweeps his hand over the empty table. "Where are all the books?"

"Life's too short!" She's grinning cheerily, showing him her big teeth, but her eyes are shiny. "Don't you think I should live a little?"

"I don't even have a game plan for today," Gun says. "I feel like I've scooped up everything there is to know, and I still don't have a clue. Or I have all the clues but still no idea."

The waitress mimics the radio announcer's voice: "Who! Is! The Villain!" She takes another long pull on the milkshake, then slides out of her side of the booth and stands. "Gun. Take a walk with me."

His eyes up at her are confused. She's leaving half that milkshake.

"I'm tired of this place," she says. "Let's walk around."

He slides out beside her. Follows her across the café, weaving through tables, to the door.

Outside the sun is doing what the sun has been doing at this time of day for twelve days straight, putting in only a cursory effort against the early-autumn chill, sending short shadows to pool under the trees that grow at the edge of the street, and running a shine along the planes of the bronze statue of the man on the leaping horse that stands at the very center of the square.

They walk side by side, the waitress on the right, Gun on the left by the street. He's worried she's right, that time is healing itself, that time is running short. He wants to talk through how to get a move on with this case, but now she's being chatty.

"Is it true, what you told me once, that when you were young your name was Fun?"

"Everyone's more fun when they're young," Gun says.

"It's got to be strange to have a name like Gun," she says. "Like there's something dark inside you."

"No one's going to hire a detective named One the Fun," he says.

"You know, we all have dark things inside us," she says. "We wouldn't be human if we didn't."

Oh, great. She's starting in on the lecture series again. The pull of time is a weight on each of Gun's footsteps. Time wants him to be somewhere else. Time wants him to be where he was in this moment on that seminal day. "Do you feel it now?" he asks. "The sluggishness?"

She stops and turns, and her eyes on his are too wide. "Listen, if today's all there is, and then time takes you out of this place and the hole closes up—"

"You keep acting like you know you're not getting out," he says. Starts walking again and she follows. "You don't know for sure you die. I mean, we both came awfully close, but we didn't actually get to the moment where—"

"Can you just promise me you'll use this experience to make yourself better?"

They pass the Dive; its heavy wooden door is shut. A sign hanging from it says *The Gangplank Is Up*. Then *Please Come Again*. Then, smaller, *Hours: Three to Late*. The ship-hull neon sign is dead in the early-afternoon sun.

"Think about all the maybe motives of your maybe killers,"

the waitress says. "Avarice, lust, rage. Think about what it is in these people that makes you believe each of them could possibly be a villain. And then look inside yourself to find the kernels of those things in you. My granddad says, 'Watch a trial sometime, but take what you learn about the accused and turn it back on yourself. Use it to make yourself better.'"

"Having lust doesn't make you a killer," Gun says.

"I'm not saying learn to stop being a killer," she says. "I'm saying we all have the potential for bad stuff hidden inside, and most of us aren't willing to look at it. We can get worse and we can get better. If you're a hero, you get better."

Gun doesn't see how any of this applies to him. They turn at the corner and continue down the square. Past the building where Six the Kicks has her apartment. Where Two the True Blue has her apartment.

"Just," the waitress says, "if you get out and I don't, take my granddad's advice with you, alright?"

He makes a short shrug. "Alright."

"Promise?"

His shrug turns into a desperate toss of the hands. "Alright, but I don't know who the killer is! I need more time."

Urgency is a fist pressing up against his ribcage.

"Time," the waitress says, like the word is funny, like the word is sad.

One the Gun realizes what he has to do. He doesn't want to, but he can think of nothing else to try to bring the killer to light.

He says it as if it wasn't something she herself suggested on some other today. "I need to play the entire day through like on that first day and find the clue I'm missing. Find whatever it was I said to the killer or the killer let loose to me that made him or her decide I needed to be eliminated."

The nod the waitress gives him says she knows this is what he needs to do even though doing this will be dangerous.

Because whenever he goes on script and lets time carry him along, time grabs hold. With time healing itself, with the hole closing up, they both know that time's hold on them is ever stronger. Will he be able to find the clue without time locking on and hauling him down to the basement?

Now something softens in her face. "Don't worry," she says. "The clue is there. The killer killed you for a reason and that reason happened somewhere in that day. You will find it. All you need to do is clear your mind and pay attention."

One the Gun wishes he were better at paying attention these days.

"And then," she says, "you don't make the time jump and start the day over. You go through to the other side. You get out of here. Whether the hole closes up completely or not, you get out of here. You save yourself."

Strange, to think about getting out of here. Does he remember how to live in a world where time does nothing but move forward?

She turns back to her walking but shoots one word at him. "Tomorrow?"

He doesn't feel ready, but he has to be ready, so: "Tomorrow."

They step past the church. The cat with the black coat and the one white ear is sitting on a paver before the door to the funeral chapel, watching them go.

"And I need you to do me a favor," he says. "I need you to play the day through too. Be the waitress at my table when I interview the moose and then later when I have dinner. Come to the Dive like you did on that first night. If your path isn't exactly the same, I'm worried my path won't be either."

That has to hurt if she believes, like she seems to, that time will be over for her very soon. But she snaps another nod at him, pushes a smile onto her face, and they walk on.

***

A SHORT TIME LATER GUN is sitting on a wrought-iron bench just down from the door to the funeral chapel, hunched over, elbows on his knees, hands clasped. He's alone. The waitress with the doe eyes and the big teeth has gone off to make a day of it. A last hurrah, she said, before she's got to throw the apron back on. The cat with the black coat and the one white ear is sitting on the paver like before, in a content little curl, tail making a leisurely thumping against the stone.

Gun closes his eyes, squeezes the bridge of his nose between his thumb and forefinger. The waitress is so sure all he has to do is pay attention and the clue will fall in his lap.

No, he's got to try and hunt down that clue today. He'll think through every detail he can remember from that seminal day. Not at the office; Miss Blue would be too distracting. Maybe he'll go to the café. He'll get a pad of paper and a pen. Write it all out. Study it.

His body feels strange in space. Some heaviness pressing on him. Like time is a ghost at his back with creeping tendrils reaching around, grabbing hold.

Who knows if he can even jump out of time tonight.

What if today is all there is?

What if, alright, today is not all there is, but then tomorrow he runs the day through and time drags him to his death?

Because see, there are other things he wants as much as solving this murder case.

One the Gun stands. He points himself in the direction of his office.

"WHAT IF YOU WERE GIVEN the chance to relive one day over and over?" One the Gun says. "What would you do?"

He's sitting on the client couch in his office. Two the True

Blue is sitting opposite in the chair, legs crossed prettily under her pale peach cotton skirt. At this question she starts to smile at the corners of her mouth, and her eyes blink off and away for a moment. Then back to him. "Any day?"

"No, today."

"I don't know. What if today turns out to be a horrible day?"

"But it won't," he says. "And anyway, then the day would start over, and you could do anything you wanted inside it, change the day completely. But only for that day. Then it would start over again."

"For everyone," she asks, "or just for me?"

"Kind of for everyone, because they're having a day, too, doing whatever they do, but for them it's always day one, and for you it's always a new day."

Two the True Blue grins full-out at this lovely game. "Well, let's see!" She folds her fingers together over her knees and leans in. "I'd eat at fancy restaurants! I'd eat cheese soufflés." She takes time to think again, but he knows what she's going to say. People are such creatures of habit, he's found, with their brains working like their brains tend to work. "I'd order champagne. I'd order a bottle of the most expensive champagne, and I'd do it every day because I'd still have the same money in the morning. I'd take the day off whenever I wanted and just read books. Wait, would I remember what I read the next day or could I only get so far and then—"

"No, the day would start over," One the Gun says, "but you'd remember."

She almost claps at this. "I'd read so many books! Oh, and since it's Friday, I'd get to listen to my favorite radio show. But wait. It would be the same one every day, wouldn't it? Oh, that makes me so sad." She frowns for two full beats. Then she makes a cheering-herself-up face. "Well, I'd take a ride on a boat."

"And a ride on a horse?" he asks, remembering. She's going to say no, she doesn't think she'd like to ride a horse.

"Maybe," she says. "Well, no, I don't think I'd like to ride a horse. Let's see. Oh, I'd take all my money and buy all the jewels I could afford and just wear them around."

"What jewels would you buy?" This is not a question he thought to ask before.

"Different ones every day."

"What would your favorites be, though?"

"Sapphires," she says. She sinks her head a little into her shoulders like she doesn't think she rates sapphires. "I've never had jewels like that. But what would you do?"

"No, I want to hear yours," he says. "You weren't finished."

"Well," her eyes arc across the room like she can see all the possibilities in the world. "I'd—"

"Buy your mom a spaghetti dinner," he cuts in.

Her eyes blink back to his and stay there.

"Sorry," he says. "Go on."

Two the True Blue tips her head slanty for a second. "But I would. Spaghetti's her favorite. Have I told you that?"

"No," he says.

"Well, I would. Just the two of us. And I'd rent—"

"You'd rent your beau a fancy car he could drive around in because he loves them but can't afford one."

A smile starts to pull at the edges of her mouth, and her eyebrows press in together. "That is exactly what I was going to say!"

"And then what?"

He folds his hands and lays his forearms across his knees, leans into her. He wants to give her time for the thought to form before he springs it.

"Well, I'd—"

"Buy me a bottle of good Scotch and tell me to take the day off."

The smile drops from her face, and she sits back. She's turning her head like she's trying to look at him out of her ear. "What are you—"

"I know what you're going to say because we've had this conversation before," he says. "We had it today, only it was also three days ago."

A surge of pride wells up inside Gun's chest like he's not a guy caught in a dangerous anomaly of time but a magic man. Telling her this feels like power.

The smile on her pretty heart-shaped face says she doesn't believe him, says she thinks he's off his trolley and doesn't want to say so but doesn't know what to say instead.

He plows ahead. "I've lived today eleven times already. One full day and then ten repeats and today will be twelve. I've been working on the case this whole time. For instance, I know the preacher has a hollowed-out Bible where he has this secret stash of letters he wrote to a nun he's in love with. I know the doorman is secretly in love with the widow and gets irate when anyone disrespects her. I know the victim is missing a bead off the front of the sailor uniform he's wearing in his casket right now—and another off the back, and believe me, I didn't pull him out of the casket to discover that one."

He can see Two the True Blue trying to make all of this make sense in her brain. "Hmm, I think there might have been something in the police report about them finding a bead—"

"You know that radio show that comes on every Saturday night called *The Rim of Beyond*?" Gun says. "You remember that story they did once about a man who wakes up in the same day every day, and he can't get out of the endless looping of time until he makes an important discovery?"

Two the True Blue stands, taking a couple steps away from him. "Sir, I think you're making fun of me or something, and I don't understand—"

"No, not at all." He jumps to his feet. He's screwing this up. "I would never make fun of you. You're the smartest, most capable person I know."

She likes that. It makes her sapphire-blue eyes just about twinkle. "Well, gosh, sir."

"Listen, I know this all sounds ridiculous," he says. How can he prove this? He kind of thought the mind-reading routine would be enough. He needs some time to think this through without her staring at him with those gorgeous big eyes. Not to mention he really needs time to think through the case. "Can I just ask that you keep an open mind, and we can talk about this later?" He grabs his hat from the floor at the foot of the chair and shoves it on his head. Picks up the pad of paper and pen sitting nearby. "But first do me a favor. Get on the phone and call the police station. Ask for the detective on this case."

"Cinco the—"

"Yeah, yeah, him. Ask him if he's found any new information about any of the suspects."

She's following him to the office door, still looking confused. "Alright, sir."

"I'll bet," he says, "he'll tell you he's discovered that the bartender, Eight the First Mate, has a record. That he was accused of beating up a man in a brawl, a man who later died. That he was acquitted of the charges but then dropped out of sight."

He opens the office door but pauses before heading out.

"Do it now before there's any chance I could get over there or call that cop myself. And feel free to ask him if he's told me any of this," he says. "I'll bet he'll say he hasn't."

***

AND THE DAY MOVES AS days tend to move: forward.

Ten the When gets together with a friend at the teahouse, the two women chatting over elegant cups and saucers.

One the Gun sits at the café with a pen and paper, making a list of every clue he can think of in the case.

Ten the When bribes the owner of the tea shop to move all the tea cans around in her display window, bribes the shop girl with the cat-eye glasses to take down the red dress again, bribes the man from the refrigerator shop to close the doors of all his display refrigerators.

One the Gun goes to the phone booth just inside the drugstore and slides the door shut, calls his office to get Miss Blue's reaction to the phone call he asked her to make.

"It's all true, sir! The bartender was tried for manslaughter, but he got off, and then he dropped out of sight. Before that, though, I also learned he had a different name."

"Eight the Not So Narrow, Not So Straight," Gun says.

"Yes! Such an interesting development. From his name alone he seems like a prime suspect."

"Did you ask Detective Clinko if he'd told me any of this?" Gun asks.

"Oh, yes," she says. "He said he hasn't told you."

"So then . . . ?"

"Sir, with all due respect—"

"Oh, come on," Gun says, "if Clinko didn't tell me, and I'm *not* looping back in time, then how do I know?"

"I don't know," she says. "Maybe from your interview with the doorman."

"Okay, but he didn't."

"Oh, sir." The lilt in Two the True Blue's voice is like she knows they're both in on the fact that this is all an amusing bit of drollery. "Alright, you're a time traveler. I think it's time for you to travel to your next interview and see what else you can find out."

Ten the When goes to the roof of the highest building on the square, the bank building, and has a look at the view.

One the Gun goes back to the café and makes more notes on the case. Then he makes a list of Two the True Blue's answers to his what-would-you-do game. He asks the waitress with the mile-high hair if they have expensive champagne, if they can make a cheese soufflé, but no dice.

Ten the When buys a bag of peanuts from a vendor and sits under the statue of the man on the leaping horse in the center of the square, eating her peanuts and feeding the pigeons. Loving the peace of it all and wondering if she might just take a little time for herself tomorrow when she knows Gun won't be around. What harm could it do?

One the Gun goes to the phone booth just inside the drugstore and slides the door shut, calls his office again.

"Alright, Miss Blue, listen to what I know. Eight the First Mate used to be a magician. Six the Kicks was his assistant. Six the Kicks and Eight the First Mate currently have joint ownership in the Dive. Before it was the Dive it was a fish and chips restaurant and it belonged to the bartender."

Gun goes down his list, reading off everything he's learned in the case. All the possible motives of the suspects. Their exact whereabouts on the night in question.

"The thing I told you about, where the preacher's in love with that nun? The nun is Four the Door's sister. Five the No Longer Alive has a police record. Seven the Heaven has a twin brother, fraternal. Eleven the Leaven. A baker. I mean, how could I learn all of this in less than a day if I'm not looping back in time?"

She says, "To me it sounds like you're having some really amazing interviews."

When One the Gun hangs up, he changes tack and calls the police station.

"Say, Detective Clinko, I'd like you to check on someone for me, find out if he has a record. Name's Three the Goatee."

"Oh yeah? Why?"

Gun makes it up as he goes along. "It's for the Five case. It may be nothing, but this guy was seen coming out of the alley beside the Dive not long before the body was found."

"Bing bang bull's-eye! Alright, hang on!"

There's a buzz in Gun's gut. Why didn't he think of this before? The guy lying about his job is one thing, but if he has any blots on his record . . .

Gun waits. Through the drugstore's big front window comes the muffled *clop-clop-clop* of horse hooves and a jingling of bells. It's the man with the novelty carriage ride who works his way around the city. He hasn't come through the square in any of these repeating days, which means today he's gotten a fare he never got before. The horse is white with black trappings trimmed with jingle bells. The buggy is white, too, open in the back so you can see the red-velvet upholstery, and so you can see, too, a certain waitress laughing with her head thrown back.

Now the cop is back on the line. "No record."

Nuts.

One the Gun goes to the bank and fills his pockets with change, then goes back to the phone booth. With the patient help of the operator, he calls everyone he can think of to try to drag up some dirt on Three the Goatee. He calls One-Third the Jailbird. He calls Twenty-Eight the Reprobate. He calls every available woman he knows, from Thirty the Little Bit Flirty all the way to Googolplex the Sell You Some Sex, but every call is a dead end.

One the Gun spends far too long on this pointless departure, but then something occurs to him. It's a bolt from the blue—the true blue, as it were. And suddenly he knows exactly how he can get her.

Outside the drugstore, the sun already getting low in the sky, One the Gun and Ten the When, by chance, come together on the sidewalk. She's carrying a paper bag with a loaf of bread peeking out from the top.

"Gun! Anything new on the case?"

"Nothing new," he says.

"Oh well, don't worry," she says. "It'll all come out tomorrow. Say, I'm glad I came across you. I'm throwing a party! I'm going to call all my friends to bring hors d'oeuvres and booze. I'm making canapés! Come by anytime after seven. Or before, if you want to help me blow up balloons."

She tells him her address. It's a short walk down the square.

"Well, I have some plans this evening," he says, "but I'll try to make it."

"Please try. I'd like to touch base before tomorrow. Alright, off with you. I've got a party to prepare, and you've got a case to crack!"

Ten the When goes off to start making canapés.

One the Gun goes to the barber for a haircut and a decent shave, gets rid of that bit of scruff he always carries around.

One the Gun goes to the men's shop for a new suit.

One the Gun goes to the pawnshop and smiles down at the gray guy behind the counter. "Hello. You got anything with sapphires?"

WHEN TWO THE TRUE BLUE opens her apartment door that evening to find One the Gun standing there, the eyebrows tick up on her face. "Oh! Well . . . hello." Music is playing softly somewhere behind her.

One the Gun has his hands up, palms out, *wait till you hear this*. He gives them a shake for emphasis. "Okay! I've figured out how I can prove this to you."

She slants her head at him. A bit of smile starts at one corner of her mouth. "Sir, did you eat Welsh rarebit before you went to bed last night?"

"All I ask," he says, "is that you keep an open mind. The openest mind you've ever had."

"Okay?"

"It is now"—he looks at his watch for dramatic effect—"ten minutes to seven. Ten minutes to our favorite radio show."

"Really?" She seems genuinely pleased at this. "It's your favorite too?"

"I like it so much I could listen to it over and over," he says. "In fact, I *have* listened to it over and over. The episode that's about to come on? I've heard that thing so many times I'll bet I could recite it word for word."

She's got that head-slanted half smile on her face again. Skeptical but willing to humor him, maybe. Skeptical but willing to politely enjoy watching him make a fool of himself, maybe. She steps back to invite him inside and closes the door behind him. As she leads him into the living room she's grinning and shaking her head. "I'll say, that was pretty amazing earlier at the office. It was like you were reading my mind."

She puts her hand out at the couch and he takes a seat. She takes the matching chair kitty-corner to him.

"I must have told you those things before," she says. "About my mom's favorite food being spaghetti and all."

Gun takes off his hat and leaves it on the arm of the couch. "Don't you believe there's a possibility of the world being different than the way we perceive it? That there might possibly be ghosts out there, or psychics, or science we don't understand?"

"My mom went to a séance once."

"Wait till the show starts," Gun says. "You'll see."

He tries to sit back, casual, but his body wants to pace laps in the room. The little box in his pants pocket—he's not sure, anymore, about that part of the plan. It might seem too premeditated, make this all seem like a setup. She hasn't said a word about his suit or his haircut. Time wants him to get the hell out of this place, to be at the café alone. He can feel it in his hands, how they want to reach up to an invisible coffee cup on an invisible table.

"You'll really be able to recite the show word for word?" Two the True Blue asks.

"Well, maybe not word for word, but I remember a lot of it. For example, the opener is something like . . . the night was darker than a bootblack's bag, and every once in a while the clouds let the light through . . . let's see . . . something about how it was just enough light to close the door on the day that came before."

As he says this there suddenly comes an unspooling of organ music into the room, and his heart kicks him in the chest. It's time. Now the voice of the announcer issues sharp through the speaker of the radio sitting on top of the cabinet on the far wall: "Handi-luxe brings you another transcribed tale of crime and justice as it asks the question: Who! Is! The Villain!"

Two the True Blue grins at him like *okay, let me have it*. The theme music is playing. One the Gun's leg starts a fidgety bounce. What if he chokes and can't remember anything?

The thrum of the organ keens to a high note and then stops abruptly.

And as he opens his mouth to recite the opening lines along with the show's narrator, Gun finds that time has taken a deeper hold on him than he thought. The spiel comes tumbling out of his mouth right along with the narrator, indeed word for word.

"The city was a heap of vacant windows piled up against a sky full of more black than a bootblack's knapsack. Here and there the clouds parted and let some light through—but only just enough to show the old day to the door."

His eyes on hers and her eyes on his, and she looks as shocked as he feels.

And it just keeps coming.

"I'd just returned to the office after a day snooping under old garbage can lids for some zero named Fourteen who'd been eighty-sixed by his wife, who now suddenly wanted him back. Who could say why? It was a worthless job for a worthless client, but it was better than shining up the vacancy sign in my wallet."

Just look at Two the True Blue's face. That wide-eyed wonder. She believes him.

More organ music. Footstep sound effects, *tack, tack, tack*. The opening of a door. One the Gun sits back against the couch and starts reciting again.

"He blustered into the office like a bad wind that took a wrong turn from the right side of town. He looked like an upstanding businessman, but he had larceny in his eyes."

One the Gun's voice trades dialogue between the radio detective and the businessman, pauses for each burst of music or sound effect, then jumps in again. Every line comes out of his mouth perfectly. Every syllable, every break, the timing so exact that he and the radio could be one and the same. For a bit Miss Blue just sits staring at him, her lips parted, eyes big. Then suddenly she stands and is walking across the room away from him. She goes to the radio and snaps it off.

Gun is still reciting, "The body pitched forward like a busted sugar sack in a—" but then his voice, too, cuts to silence.

Miss Blue turns and looks at him with a mix of confusion and amazement on her face. "I just don't . . . this is too, too weird! Golly, I can't even concentrate on what's happening in the show, I just. I mean how . . ."

"I told you how," he says.

"You must have memorized it somehow."

"How could I?" he says. "This is broadcasting now."

"But it's impossible. It's—"

She stops and then, quick, switches the radio on again. The broken bit of narration jumps from Gun's mouth just as it jumps from the radio speaker:

"—mitts like waffle irons. I stepped toward him, knowing I might need to use my fists before the night was out."

Now Miss Blue is outright gaping at him. Organ music rises with a dramatic tremolo. She looks at the radio like it might explain what's happening. One the Gun stands from the couch and crosses to her.

She snaps the radio off again. A pause. Silence. She puts her eyes to his. Snaps it back on.

"Light up, golden boy, I'm sick of being left in the dark. And don't reach for that gun or I'll tune your glockenspiel."

This makes Miss Blue laugh. Which makes Gun laugh. And he feels that thing he rarely feels. How he and she are here together, sharing a moment.

She's looking at him with wonder again. Wonder looks sexy on her face. She's so close. Her jasmine perfume. He wants her so bad.

Again she switches the radio off. "If it *is* real," she asks, "what does it feel like when the day starts over? Is it like waking up in the morning?"

"No," he says. "It's like . . . one second it's night and one second it's day. And I'm dizzy because the light's changed and everything around me's changed. I squeeze my eyes shut and then open them again, and you know what I see first?"

"Hmm?"

He steps closer. Close enough to kiss her. "You."

The wonder turns to something else on her face, and she slips away from him, taking a few steps across the room. "Because you're in the office?"

He follows. "Being stuck in this one repeating day has made me realize things I wish I'd done with my life." He reaches back to their what-would-you-do game to mine a little more of Miss Blue's answers, the ones he didn't already use up this afternoon. "I wish I'd done more good things, like take a day and pick up all the trash in the neglected part of town."

He tries to get close to her again. She keeps stepping away.

"And I wish I'd had a real relationship, not just silly flirtations all the time," he says. "I wish I'd meant something to someone. So I could do things for her and know her deeply." He reaches into his pants pocket, touches the small box.

"Shall we listen some more?" she says, eyes away from his. "I want to hear you do it again."

She starts back toward the radio. Worry is rising inside him. She seems disturbed. He feels like he's losing the headway he gained.

He blurts, "Miss Blue. There's something I haven't told you yet about my situation. I die at the end of the night."

She turns back, looks at him a moment. "I don't understand."

"That first night," he says, "just before the day looped back on itself, I was down in the basement of the office. It was about midnight. The power had gone off in the building, and I'd taken a flashlight down to fiddle with the fuse boxes. Five's killer was there and . . . shot me."

Two the True Blue is staring at him, blank faced. He has no idea what she's thinking.

"I was lying on the floor, dying," he says, "and then I was in the office again. The day had started over."

"I don't know, sir, that sounds very . . ."

"What I'm saying is, if you knew you were going to die, wouldn't you want to do the things you'd always wanted to do?"

It isn't working. She just seems disbelieving again.

He crosses to her.

She angles her body away from him. "Sir, I'm starting to feel uncomfortable with—"

He puts his hands on her shoulders. "Two, I can't keep making excuses. I need you to know how I feel."

She tries to step back, but he holds on.

She says, "I think you need to go."

"Don't you understand," he says, "I don't know how much time I've got. It could all end tonight with a bullet in my back."

She twists like she's politely trying to extract herself. "Please—"

He holds tighter. "Don't make me beg, Miss Blue."

"Sir!" She puts her hands flat on his chest and shoves. He stumbles a step back, and his hands come free of her. "You need to go," she says, louder than he expects. "Now."

Anger is a flash up the back of his neck.

He lunges forward, clamps his hands around her arms just below the shoulders.

He can do it. He can do anything he wants, make her kiss him, take her into the bedroom, rip open her blouse right here and let the buttons fly. Those buttons will be intact tomorrow.

Two the True Blue stares at him with her lips parted. Such a look on her face. Eyes the color and size of oceans.

One the Gun doesn't move, his hands still clamped on her.

What the hell is he doing?

Just over her shoulder, sitting next to the radio, is a small picture in a discreet wooden frame. Three the Goatee.

"Get out," Two the True Blue says, her voice froggy, "or you'll never see me again."

One the Gun lets go.

He steps back.

He moves quickly away, across the room, leaving his hat, and double-times it to the door without looking back.

WHEN THE DOORBELL RINGS, TEN the When weaves herself and the swishy skirt of her red cocktail dress through chatting friends to the door of her apartment and pulls it wide.

And surprise: It's Gun. She didn't really expect to see him. She wouldn't have been surprised if he forgot her party completely.

She grins. "You came! Come in, come in."

He's hatless and looks a little strange. His eyes are unfocused. Maybe he's been having a drink or two like she's been having a drink or two, maybe he's been making a day of it just like she has. Or maybe he's worried about tomorrow.

"Come meet my friends." She pulls him inside. Champagne has made her body loose—makes it a little easier to ignore the constantly increasing pull of time—and she does a half pirouette, closing the door. "I'm going to introduce you as One the Fun. How about that!"

She leads him into the noise of the party, the gabble of conversation and music, a hoot of laughter. A few folks look up from their threesomes and fivesomes. She sweeps her hand out like *behold*: White balloons on the furniture, on the bookcases, on the floor, white and silver streamers hang from the ceiling and curl on people's shoulders. A few of her guests wear shiny paper hats. "It's a New Year's Eve party! I figured, hell, if I'm never going to reach the holidays, I can bring the holidays to me! Although I told everyone we'll have to do the toast at eleven instead of twelve. I'll get you a drink. Have a canapé!"

She looks around for the tray. It's on the coffee table in front of the couch. It's nearly empty. "Oh, I have to get more. Gun, come help me."

Ten the When pulls Gun into the kitchen where the table and counter are full of glasses and bottles and mismatched trays of hors d'oeuvres. She grabs a glass and chunks some ice into it from the sink full of ice and bottles, then pours Scotch. She presses it into his hand. "Drink!"

He stares at the glass with a weird sort of nothing on his face.

When pulls an open bottle of champagne out of the sink, pours some in a water cup.

"I should have been drinking champagne all along." She makes her voice into a half whisper and pretends to shout: "Happy New Year!"

She lifts the cup in a toast and drinks. He toasts her back.

"I'm trying your trick about getting tight and then not having a hangover." She drinks again.

Gun puts his glass down and sticks his hands in his pockets. Something crosses his face. He seems to think for a moment, then, "Hey, I brought you something."

"For me?"

He pulls it out. It's a small box, unwrapped. He hands it to her. His shoulders make a little shrug. "From one friend to another."

The word puts a pang into that place just under her ribcage. Is it true? Is this man she didn't know two weeks ago her friend?

She opens the box. A flash of blue. A brooch. It looks like two flowers, one big, one small, linked together and made of real—she thinks they're real—sapphires set in gold. She pulls it out and gazes at it in her hand. Somehow it seems the most beautiful thing she's ever seen.

"Gun, that's lovely."

She pins it to her dress even though it doesn't go.

"I can't believe you thought to give me a gift," she stares down at her chest. "It's so thoughtful." Her eyes flick back up to his. "Gun, thank you. I wish I had something for you."

He waves this off. "Think nothing of it. Remember the whole unlimited-money thing."

"True, true." She drinks to that. "Oh, Gun, I had the most amazing day! I had tea with a girlfriend, and I took this carriage ride, and I ate peanuts on the lawn under the horseman statue and fed the pigeons. I went to the highest building on the square and looked at the view. I got my hair done." She turns her head this way and that. "I got a present from a friend."

She lobs him a big smile. She thinks maybe she's been judging him too harshly. Telling herself he's kind of a jerk. How can she presume to have any idea what's been going on inside his head? Here he is on the brink of a dangerous assignment, and he comes to her party, and he brings her a gift.

Ten the When smacks the counter. "And you know what? I've decided not to believe this will all be over. Maybe once the hole closes up, time will let me go, and I won't die, and you'll just be on one side and I'll be on the other."

She grins desperate joy at him.

"And you!" she says. "What did you do today?"

His eyes bounce around in his head like he's ashamed of something. "Nothing."

"Nothing? I'm sure you didn't do nothing. Every day is more precious than we know. Did you know that?" Something wells up inside her. She points her champagne cup at him. "Why don't we ever know that? So, so precious, Gun! Every little moment you had today was precious, Gun! Tell me about it."

"Oh," he says, "I've mostly been going over the clues so they're fresh in my mind for tomorrow."

Ten the When puts her cup on the counter. "Well, that does sound a little boring for your penultimate day." She lifts a domed lid off a tray of canapés. "Don't you like that word? Penultimate? Oh, but you're not going to die, I forgot."

She pulls a canapé from the tray and hands it to him.

"Here," she says, "ham and olive."

He puts it in his mouth.

"Oh," she says, "but I'm not going to die either. See, I forgot too. The hole will close up, and you'll be on one side, and I'll be on the other."

She turns quickly to the sink, hauls out the champagne, and tops off her cup.

"And you'll have gone back into time and will take Granddad's advice with you," she says. "And maybe you'll do all sorts of great things on the other side." She toasts to that. "Don't forget, Gun. Any person can be redeemed if they can look at their own guilt and really, truly want to change."

A gust of party laughter comes in from the next room.

When gestures toward the sound with her cup. "Everyone has stuff they're guilty of. My friend Twenty the Plenty? She shoplifts! Constantly! My neighbor Zero the Hero? He may be a hero when it comes to fixing your sink, but that guy's a zero in the family department, let me tell you. He and his son had some falling out, and Zero hasn't spoken to him in seven years. It plagues him." She points at Gun with her cup. "And no amount of fixing people's sinks can take that guilt away. But one call to his son, and he'd go from zero to hero again in no time."

She picks up a canapé, this one apple and cheddar, but doesn't put it in her mouth because it would get in the way of her words.

"My granddad's advice could save the world," she says. "And you're going to take it with you to the other side, aren't you? You really did mean it, right? Because when I said promise, you just said . . . I don't remember what you said, but I don't think you said promise." She points at him. "Hey, Gun! I want you to promise."

She leans forward to get her earnest face closer to his.

He looks down at the brooch and then back up to her. She can't tell what's on his face. His eyes look stony and his jaw is clenched.

"You really believe that?" he asks. "Anyone can be redeemed? You don't think some people are just bad?"

She thinks maybe he's thinking of that crack she made earlier, that there's something dark inside him. "Anyone. Even the murderer." She does believe this. "But they *have* to recognize their guilt and they *have* to want to change. To pay their debt. To become new. Think about it, Gun. Think about how much better the world would be if we didn't just kill and lock up our criminals. If we really, truly wanted to help them change. Help the world change. That's my granddad's advice on the grand scale, really. That's what you have to take out of here."

She doesn't understand why this speech doesn't seem to move him.

"I just," he says. "Anyway, what if I can't make it out?"

"Oh, that." She grabs her champagne cup and uses it to point emphasis at him. "The clue to the killer is there, waiting in tomorrow. You'll find it. I believe in you."

She has to believe in him. He's all she's got.

LATE. THE WAITRESS WITH THE doe eyes and the big teeth is gathering all her friends in the center of her apartment for the countdown. People shuffle around Gun, sidling in, shooting him grins and lifting drinks in his direction in silent Happy-

New-Year toasts. Neighbor Zero the Hero pats him on the back like they're old friends. Twenty the Plenty seems to be eyeing up the silver candlestick on the coffee table. Everyone thinks his name is One the Fun. And everyone seems totally game to count down to midnight and shout "Happy New Year!" at eleven o'clock in the middle of October.

Kooky broad with her canapés and her lawbooks and her grandfather's advice. All Gun cares about right now is Miss Blue. He keeps running that scene at her apartment over in his head. What he maybe almost did tonight. Could he really have been capable of that?

Nah. One the Gun wants to beg to differ. He just got a little excited. He wouldn't have actually done anything.

He throws back a slug of Scotch from the cup in his hand. He wants to feel relieved that nothing happened, but a low panic is rising in him. How the hell can he ever get her now? And not for some one-time fling, either, but for keeps?

He can't, can he? There's always something that gets in the way.

"Here, you need a hat." The waitress with the doe eyes and the big teeth sticks a little silver party hat on his head and pulls the string under his chin. He forces a smile, and then she's off to assault someone else with her cheer, a stack of pointed paper hats in her hand.

That damn Three the Goatee smirking his mealymouthed mug in that framed portrait on Miss Blue's cabinet. He's the real monkey wrench in the works. Gun can solve the case and become the big hero, but the so-called professor is always going to be standing in the way.

Unless.

A tingle runs up his neck and spreads across the back of his head.

What if Gun were to just . . . eliminate him?

"Alright, alright!" The waitress is flapping her hands in a come-here motion to get the gaggle of people standing around her to move in closer. "It's almost time." She stares down at the watch on her wrist. "Get ready to shout your hearts out! And don't worry about the neighbors. This won't have happened tomorrow."

Someone in the crowd says, "What?"

Could he just do that? Eliminate the competition? Get rid of the one thing that's been holding him back from getting what he wants most in the world?

"Okay, here we go!" And as she leads the group in the first number, she blinks her doe eyes through the crowd to One the Gun and shoots him a grin.

"Ten!"

The sound is louder than Gun expects, a crash in his ears.

Kooky broad with her starry-eyed morality lectures. *My Granddad says everyone's guilty.* Gun can't remember how the rest of it goes, but it's true, damn it. Gun isn't the only person who's ever had an improper thought. Everyone does bad things.

The numbers blasting by him just prove that it's true.

"Nine!"

See? Even that nun. Forsaking her vow of chastity and lying about it.

"Eight!"

Yes, the bartender. Beating people up in bars. Keeping secrets about his identity. Maybe murdering Five.

"Seven!"

Oh, the preacher for sure. Fleecing those poor saps down at the Dive just to add cabbage to his own personal collection plate. Not to mention the whole seducing-nuns thing. And again with the maybe murder.

"Six!"

The widow, always getting her kicks, probably fooling around on her old man the whole time. Possibly killing him.

"Five!"

Yeah, even him. Sure, he's the victim, but that guy was as corrupt as they come, making book in the back room of the Dive and rooking the clientele. Nothing but a cheap hood. Really, is the world worse off with Five not in it? That's what Gun wants to know.

What if he just did it? Killed Three the Goatee. Killed him tomorrow, solved the case, and then turned the day over to the next. Got out of this looping of time and moved on with his life without Three the Goatee dogging his heels. Because if he killed him tomorrow, the guy would be gone for good. Because tomorrow would become the yesterday for the new tomorrow after that. And then Gun would console the grieving Two the True Blue, become her counselor, her guardian angel. He'd be even more of the hero.

Out through the window the moon is doing what the moon has been doing at this time of night for twelve nights straight, shoveling heaps of silver moonlight down across the square to scare shadows out from under parked cars and sidewalk trees.

Down on that sidewalk a cat paints a long shadow across a brick wall: little points of ears, sleek curve of back, a swish of tail. And even on the street the sound of the countdown carries, the players in this strange mystery rolling in names across the night.

"Four!"

Is it a surprise, what Gun is contemplating? It certainly goes against what radio would have us believe about heroes. Consider the episode of Two the True Blue's Saturday-night radio show *The Rim of Beyond*, the one where the man wakes up in the same day every day. Consider how, over the course of the episode, that man becomes a better person. Radio likes to teach us that the hero of a dilemma like this is supposed to be improving himself.

But in truth, reality doesn't tend to work that way. The chance to relive the day over and over is a power.

And power doesn't tend to make people better.

"Three!"

"Two!"

"One!"

ELEVEN

THE BELLS ARE CHIMING AS he opens his eyes.

It's bright as day in the room. He's in his office.

Day thirteen.

He does what he always does, force of habit, force of time: Closes his eyes, listens to another strike of the bell, opens his eyes, waits for the room to stop spinning.

Even standing here at the very beginning of this day he can feel time's pull on him. And if he had any doubts before that the waitress's theory is true, those doubts are gone: He feels it deep in his elbows and knees now; the hole is closing up.

Two the True Blue is standing in front of him. Such a look on her face. Eyes the color and size of oceans.

Today's the day, Miss Blue. I'm going to make it happen. I'm going to get you once and for keeps.

That's what he thinks but not what he says. Instead he says what he always says as yesterday's bubble, floating above and between them, takes yesterday's dangers off and away and leaves today's dangers behind. "Miss Blue?"

"You looked so odd just now," she says. "Are you alright?"

He thinks he's alright. He has a plan. Last night after the countdown, he slipped out before the waitress could corner him, and he went and sat on a bench in the center of the square to work out exactly the best time and place to do the deed. To do it quick and easy so no one will see him, so he doesn't mess up the trajectory of the day, and so the body won't be discovered at least for a while. He thinks he has everything worked out perfectly—which is pretty great for the short time he had to think things through. He knows what happens in the day, after all. Time magic is quite convenient to have on your side if you want to commit a murder.

"I'm fine," he says. "Please do go on."

Two the True Blue smiles, and the day moves forward. Like it always does. She reads him her notes on the case and tells him about the poison. She mispronounces its name. She tells him the victim probably suffered a few shocking moments of agony followed by violent convulsions, followed by unconsciousness, and finally death. She details his appointments for the day, her finger with a clean, filed nail pointing at a notation on the calendar open on his desk. One o'clock time slot. *Meet with doorman at café.*

But when she reaches to the high shelf of his bookcase, standing on one foot, to work out the huge volume of *The Compleat Illustrated Pharmacopeia*, when she grabs hold and drops back on both feet, teetering, One the Gun takes a step back, keeps his tripping foot away from her heel, and lets her catch her balance on her own.

"Here we go," she says, and opens the book over the appointment calendar on the desk. "Let me find the page."

No, no tripping trick today, no matter how much his body aches to have hold of her. Instead he plays the gentleman, so that when the office door opens and Three the Goatee walks in, all annoyingly dashing with his gray tailored coat, homburg, and neatly trimmed whiskers, all looks completely innocent.

"Sweetie," Miss Blue raises her voice to Three the Goatee as he steps in from the door. "I'm almost ready. I was just giving my boss an overview of the case."

Gun tosses his hands up, cheery. "Oh, I'll read up on the poison. You kids go get some lunch. Professor, how are you today?"

A handshake and a hearty pat on the back. Three the Goatee's eyes positively shine at this friendly interaction. Then as Miss Blue goes to retrieve her light jacket and pocketbook from the hook on the wall by the door, Gun pretends a thought is occurring to him. "Say, professor, come over here." He takes Three the Goatee to the desk, to the corner where the sample box of rat poison sits. Points down at it. "That's the kind of poison that killed our victim. Now you work at the college. Is there anyone you can put me in touch with in the science lab who might get this under a microscope so we can look a little deeper into what makes it tick?"

At the mention of his sham job at the college Three the Goatee's eyes bug and give a blink.

"You do teach at the college, right?" Gun repeats.

"Uh, of course . . ."

Gun moves around behind him, leaving him standing next to the edge of the table and the poison. "You know what? Just think about it. I don't want you two to be late for lunch. I'll come down and find your office tomorrow, and we can chat."

"Oh, well, I, that is, I—"

"Oh, right," Gun says. "Tomorrow's Saturday. Do you even have classes on Saturday?" He tosses a casual glance across the room to make sure Miss Blue is paying attention.

As she catches his eye, Miss Blue smiles. "He's often in his office on Saturday preparing lecture notes."

"Saturday, Monday, we'll find a time. I'll give you a call. Be fun to see where you work. I know Miss Blue's awful proud of your accomplishments. Okay, you two have a good lunch." He pats the so-called professor on the back again and ushers him, still bug-eyed and blinking, to the door.

Once the two are out of the way One the Gun goes back to the desk. He closes the volume of *The Compleat Illustrated Pharmacopeia* and slides it back onto the high shelf. He opens the desk and pulls out a little clue envelope and a pair of evidence gloves, puts them on. Reaches for the box of poison.

His hands feel stiff, ungainly. Time doesn't want him doing this. Time wants him to be walking across the room to head out for his first interview. He quickly scoops a bit of poison into the envelope, tucks the lip of the envelope inside to seal it, and then slides that into his pocket. He takes off the gloves and puts them, too, in his pocket. Recloses the box, checks the desk for residue, straightens. Starts walking. The heaviness in his limbs relaxes as he finds his way back to where his footsteps should be, and then time carries him along into this final day.

"I APPRECIATE YOU MEETING ME like this," One the Gun is saying to the moose in their booth in the café.

"The pleasures are all on me," the moose says. "Gee, when your girl called me I never would have thought I'd get grub in the deal."

The waitress with the doe eyes and the big teeth steps up to their table, hands them each a menu. She deadpans a hello nod at Gun, but her eyes flash a tiny acknowledgment at him over the menu as if to say, *Here we go*.

His last chance. He has to focus and find the clue that's hidden in this day and solve the case. Only if he finds the killer will he become a gumshoe worthy of Miss Blue, only if he finds the killer will killing Three the Goatee be worth it.

He and the moose make small talk and order lunch, a burger and coffee for Gun, a plate of chicken and a glass of milk for Four the Door. On script like this, locked into the forward flow of time, One the Gun almost doesn't need to think in order to do and say things. Time carries him along. And he has to remind himself to pay attention. It's so easy to get lost in the slippery stream of it all.

"Sure, yeah," the moose is saying, "if some lout's got to start in on some beef and the boss gives me the eyes, I take care of it—I take care of it but good—but that's all part of being a doorman, get me?"

Gun's hands move freely—burger to napkin to coffee. It's only when he deviates from the script that he can feel the drag on his body, the hold time has on him. "And you were on duty the night your boss was killed?"

The moose talks about the last time he saw his boss alive, and One the Gun listens hard for anything that might be the clue.

"He tags by me at the door like always, says he's closing up. I ask who's still in. He says just his wife and the preacher. I don't get why that preacher's got to always be around so late. Don't he have to get up early and say his catechisms?"

"What was his mood when you saw him last?" Gun says.

"Like a pussycat in a parakeet cage," Four the Door says, matter of fact.

One the Gun still doesn't know if this means happy (lots of parakeets to eat) or sad (not a lot of space in a parakeet cage for a cat).

"Not like sick, if that's what you mean," Four the Door says. "Not like he was getting ready to pitch the big snooze. But anyway, then the boss goes off to his office to count the take like always. I stick and let out the last of them, then lock up, go to the bar, fix myself a short one. I'm sagged, I mean, my egg is fried. You try standing all night on these cat sticks."

One the Gun is way more used to the moose's slangy lingo now, but he stays on script and stares blankly at the moose like he doesn't understand.

Four the Door says, "You getting all this, shamus?"

"Well, it's just you're a little hard to—"

"Listen," the moose says, "if you just took the hedgehogs out of your head holes, you could quit tossing horseshoes with your dear old auntie's flapjacks."

One the Gun's thinking this is going to be a long day. "Um. So then what happened?"

"I wait for the boss. I always pitch him good night last of all. He doesn't come out. Finally I go to the office door, knock. Nothing. Open the door and there he is."

The moose's smile is gone. He looks down into his milk.

"Best boss I ever had."

INSIDE THE FUNERAL PARLOR OF Our Lady of Immaculate Numbers, standing a few paces back from the pedestal in the center of the room, One the Gun casts a slant down into the casket of Five the No Longer Alive like there might be some sort of clue to be found in there. But he's still just a stiff in a stupid costume.

Six the Kicks, standing at the edge of the casket in her morning mourning wear, the plain black dress and black gloves, no hat or veil, gives Gun the quick glance she gave him on that first day. Then the preacher comes in from the back doorway.

"May I help you?" The preacher's long-fingered handshake. "Seven the Heaven."

When One the Gun introduces himself, the woman's head snaps up. "Another cop?" she bleats. The look on her face jumps from hurt to offended, closing in on indignant. "Please tell me you're not here to question me in the presence of my dead husband."

One the Gun starts, "Well, ma'am, I—"

"You have no right to suspect me." Sticking her chin out at him.

"Why do you think I suspect you?" he asks. Other than, you know, it's my job.

"You don't fool me," she says. "You know he wasn't the only man in my life. You know I like to get my kicks. But kicks don't kill husbands."

They do if you kick hard enough, he says.

Not out loud.

ONE THE GUN AND SEVEN the Heaven take their long walk down the church corridor and out into the wide sanctuary. Rows of pews, shafts of amber and magenta light angling down through pictures of stained glass. Gun dips his hand into the raised dish with the holy water and walks on, letting the wetness sit there on his fingerprints.

In the preacher's chambers it's just like before, verbal sparring and Bible quotations.

"If you're a man of God, I'm a millionaire playboy with a yacht and a pony."

"'When I applied mine heart to know wisdom, and to see the business that is done upon the earth (for also there is that neither day nor night seeth sleep with his eyes).' Ecclesiastes 8:16."

That God lingo is about as easy to interpret as the moose's slang.

Gun is already tired of having to play this day straight through. What could this interview tell him about who killed him? He figures the real meat of things came later in the day, when they were all at the Dive. Why else would whoever killed him wait to kill him until the end of the night?

"And so that whole time on Wednesday night you were in the back room saving souls?" he's asking the preacher.

"I played a few rounds, yes."

"That how you come up with stuff like that green sparkler, there?" Nodding toward the ring on the preacher's pinky. "Playing a few rounds?"

"This ring? Not at all. It was a gift from a parishioner."

"Looks expensive."

The preacher puts his hands in his lap, out of Gun's sight line. "It's glass. A trinket. I wear it in her memory. She left it in the church donation box not long before her death. She said it was the only thing she had. Her graciousness warmed my heart."

One the Gun tries to think the case through in the back of his mind while performing the conversation with the front of his mind, but no, he has to pay attention. Maybe a pretend emerald ring can be important. Maybe having Bible verses shoved into his ears can be important.

The script continues to spool out of him. "Did you interact with the victim on the night of his death?"

"Yes, yes, I did. He was in and out of the back room where we were playing a few rounds. He was always a very gracious host."

"You talk to him directly?"

"Well, here and there. You know, to say thank you for being a gracious host."

For God's sake, God-man, give me a little help here. If you killed me, just give me the clue already. I'm tired of your smug face and your tired old verses. Can't you just toss me some little kernel of a clue so this insufferable interview can be worth it?

"'That which hath been is that which shall be,'" the preacher recites, "'and that which hath been done is that which shall be done: and there is no new thing under the sun.'"

After his interview with Seven the Heaven, One the Gun goes to the phone booth just inside the drugstore and slides the door shut. Tosses some silver in the slot, calls his office. Two the True Blue picks up and says hello in her clear, bell-like voice.

"Checking in," he says. "Got anything new for me?"

He knows what's she's going to say. She's going to tell him that the police have reported back that traces of the poison were indeed found on the glass that was discovered on the desk in the office following the victim's death, but that the glass contained no fingerprints, not even partials. She's going to tell him her beau was a little perturbed at catching them in what looked like a clinch—but wait. She's not going to say that because it didn't happen today. He changed the script. Is that going to be a problem? If their conversation is shorter, will it throw his timing off?

Okay, calm down, it can't be that big a deal. Just center yourself back into time, and time will take you where you're supposed to be.

"Thanks for this information," he hears himself say, just as on that seminal day. "I'm heading over to—"

But through the drugstore's big front window comes the muffled *clop-clop-clop* of horse hooves and a jingling of bells. It's that novelty carriage ride. And sitting in the open buggy, just like yesterday, is the waitress.

Son of a bitch!

She promised. And here she is out having fun. Off script. How can she be so selfish?

"Sir?" Two the True Blue says in his ear.

He rushes to complete the sentence he started. "Um, heading over to the newspaper office to have a look in their morgue. Will check in again later if I can."

Gun hangs up and hurries out of the booth, out of the drugstore. He's out of sync with time, he can feel it. Every move of his body is leaden. Labored. He speeds up along the pavement. In a moment his footsteps find their way back to where they should be, and as time carries him, his body relaxes again.

TIME CARRIES GUN TO THE newspaper office. He tries to ignore the simmer of anxiety in his stomach—focuses, instead, on the waitress taking that carriage ride. That muttonheaded dame. Selfish. Gun deviating from the script is different than the waitress deviating from the script. After all, he's the one who has to solve this case. All she has to do is come along for the ride. Gun is going to make this one last departure quickly and easily, and then he'll find his way back to his footsteps, and time won't be the wiser.

He lets time carry him through the door of the newspaper office, down the back hallway toward the morgue, but then, quick, with no one in the corridor in either direction, he stops at the door to the sorting room.

Feeling the pull of time in his hands again, he reaches into his pocket, brings out the gloves, and puts them on. Pushes the door open. Goes inside.

Three the Goatee looks up, a stack of mail in one hand and an envelope in the other, stopped in the act of slipping that envelope into one of the slots lined up along the wall.

"Well, hello, professor," Gun says, making like innocent. The words are gluey in his mouth as they work against time. "Fancy seeing you here. I was just heading to the morgue for a little research and happened to see you through the glass."

Three the Goatee is frozen, eyes bulging above his carefully coiffed whiskers. "Mr., uh," he says, "Gun."

One the Gun walks over to the two pressed-together tables that take up most of the center of the long, thin room. He positions himself at the table edge with the pompous little tea setup: pot and matching cup in white and gold porcelain, the tiny silver spoon, and the slice of lemon. It couldn't be more perfect. Not only a table but also piles of papers and a crate of mail between Gun and Three the Goatee, blocking the so-called professor's sight line from what's about to happen.

Three the Goatee is still frozen, envelope pointed toward the mail slot. "So . . ." His words come out slow, almost monotone at first, but pick up the pace as they go. "You know my . . . little secret now. Listen, you—you can't tell Two, okay?"

Gun makes a flip of his visible hand and reaches into his jacket pocket with the other, pulling the poison packet out, keeping it below the lip of the mail crate. He wants to glance down at what he's doing, but the so-called professor's eyes are locked on his. "Oh, hey, I understand," Gun says, nonchalant. "Women. Always wanting us to be more than we are. Don't worry about it, I can keep a secret. Go ahead, you keep working. Just thought I'd say hello."

Three the Goatee's whole body relaxes, and his limbs start to work again. He shoves the envelope in the slot. "Really? Wow. Thank you so much."

Gun fumbles with the flap that's tucked into the poison packet to seal it. His hands feel heavy, stiff. He can't make them work right.

Three the Goatee lowers his stack of mail to the floor. "You don't know what a relief this is. Really. Today when you said you were coming to my office, well, I didn't know what I was going to do."

Suddenly the guy is starting across the room to Gun. Gun blinks, and his stiff fingers grope at the poison packet hidden behind the mail crate. Those gloves he put on to hide his fingerprints aren't helping either.

"I never wanted to deceive her," Three the Goatee is saying. "It just happened, and then I didn't know how to tell her the truth."

He's skirting the table, heading right for Gun with his hand out to shake.

Gun's hand jerks, hitting the corner of the crate.

The packet falls from his fingers. Lands with a little *thwap* on the floor.

"Really, I can't thank you enough." Three the Goatee is almost to him. "She means the world to me. You probably have a girl. You probably understand."

His hand is grabbing Gun's hand, pumping up and down. Gun's trying to glance down to see if the packet busted open on impact, if there's poison spread across the floor.

"Say," Three the Goatee says, "care to sit a bit, have some tea?" He looks down. "Drop something?" Stooping to reach for it.

A buzz jumps through Gun's body. "Uh, yeah, that's evidence." He lunges for it. "I'd better take that." He snatches it up. It's all intact. It's not all lost.

"Evidence," Goatee muses. "You sure have a neat job."

His smile at Gun is pleasant. He does seem, when no one's trying to steal his girl, like a pretty nice guy.

"I must have another cup around here." Three the Goatee turns away.

Opportunity is a prickle across Gun's forehead. His fingers scrabble at the packet again.

"This is sort of my office." Three the Goatee is opening up a cabinet, his back mostly turned to Gun, but Gun can still see one of his eyes. "It's only me in here, so I sort of took it over. Hmm, I thought I had a mug somewhere."

The flap on the packet comes open. Quickly Gun pours the contents in the teacup. The stuff is going to fall to the bottom, so even quicker, he takes the silver spoon and gives a stir, careful to keep it away from the edges.

The poison powder turns into a little cloud in the caramel-colored liquid.

He sets the spoon on the saucer as quiet as possible, tiny *tink*. Did Goatee hear? Gun straightens, tries to let his breath out silently. It comes out in a labored shiver.

Goatee is turning back to him. "Here." Looking at a coffee cup with a chip in the rim. He gestures toward the teacup. "You take that one. I just poured it, it's fresh. I'll drink from this."

Gun blinks down at the just-so-slightly cloudy caramel-colored liquid.

"Oh, I . . ." He throws a pointed look at his watch. "I should probably . . ."

Three the Goatee, smiling, raises the poisoned tea toward Gun.

"How about," Gun says, "tomorrow when you come to pick up Miss Blue for lunch, the three of us can have some together. How does that sound?"

He doesn't wait. He high-tails it to the door. It's good, it's fine, the plan is in place: The poison is in the tea, and if the cops come to question Gun, he'll tell them he showed the poison to the victim earlier in the day. Gun will tell them he told the victim he would come by his office at the college to discuss it. What a surprise that the victim didn't work at the college after all, that he was just a lowly clerk at the newspaper office, lying to his girlfriend for years. That must have been the reason for his suicide.

Hidden in this remote little room where no one else routinely goes, the body won't be found until late tonight or tomorrow. The cops won't be out questioning folks until at least tomorrow, and by then Gun will have found his own killer and turned the day over, escaped this place, and he'll be able to speak freely without feeling the pull of time on his words: *Oh, officers, this is all my fault. I said I was coming to his office. He knew his lies would be exposed. I feel terrible.* And Miss Blue will corroborate the whole thing.

"Lunch tomorrow sounds great, Gun," Goatee is saying behind him. "Thank you. And you won't forget? You promise to keep my little secret?"

Gun opens the door. "Of course. You can trust me."

Ten the When is delivering a ham and swiss on rye to a table, just like on that seminal day, when Gun comes through the door of the café at dinnertime.

She grabs a menu and steps up to his table. "Here you go, sir."

He shoots her a glare. "I saw you."

When opens her mouth, closes it, opens it again. Her off-script words feel thick and awkward. "Saw me what?"

He reels it out fast, and she can hear the pull of time in his speech. "You said you'd play today exactly as before."

"I have been, within the bounds of—"

"I saw you in that carriage, and it threw me off," he says. "Any departure could ruin everything, did you think of that?"

She hisses, "Did you think of the fact that I probably die tonight?"

"Alright, fine, but just stick to the script, okay?" he says. "I'll have a hamburger with grilled onions. Coffee."

Slightly bent into him, When jerks up straight. She kicks her chin up. "Right away."

As she turns away the heaviness of her limbs, the stiffness of her movements, relaxes, and she finds her way back to where her footsteps should be. Time carries her along again. But her stomach feels like that time a peach pit fell into the kitchen drainpipe and nothing would go down. She trudges across the café to the back counter, open to the kitchen, and tells the cook, "Hamburger, grilled onions."

What difference could it make that she took a little time for herself today? Gun has to understand how things work by now, how easy it is to step back into the forward flow of time. Once he's locked in it carries him along, and who cares what she does with her own time? Alright, so he saw her in the buggy, and maybe it threw him off, but then he locked back in and here he is. Exactly where and when he's supposed to be.

It's unfortunate that the carriage driver took her through the square. She told him not to. Could she be wrong? If Gun stews on this thing, could it really throw the whole thing off? It wasn't even as fun a ride as before. With time pulling on her as much as it's been today, she didn't have that same lovely free feeling. It was like she was hugging a bowling ball to her lap as the horse dragged her along. Still. She's glad she convinced her friend to take a partial shift so she could do the off-script things she did midday, and now she's back on duty just as she said she'd be.

Ten the When pulls a coffee cup up from under the counter, then a saucer, clink of china on china. She feels like slipping a little ipecac into his brew. See what that does to his pretty little investigation.

But she needs to protect her investment.

That sounds crass, but really, that's what it is: an investment in humanity. Okay, now it sounds melodramatic. But if she sends him out of here different than he came in, she will have done something good for the world.

Even with all his moodiness, she has to believe her efforts have been teaching him something.

She pours coffee. Over the buzz and clatter of table noise in the restaurant comes an unspooling of organ music. Then the voice of the announcer issuing sharp through the speaker of the radio on the shelf above the cash register: "Handi-luxe brings you another transcribed tale of crime and justice as it asks the question: Who! Is! The Villain!"

AT THE DIVE, STANDING INSIDE the entryway in all his gold-button ritzy-like finery, Four the Door snaps a salute and says what he always says: "Welcome aboard!"

One the Gun steps off to the side. "Business good tonight?"

"Sure, sure," Four the Door says, "folks been coming by to make with the respects. Look at all them flowers there in the corner."

"Very nice," One the Gun says.

They make the same small talk they made on that seminal night, and then Gun asks the moose for more details on the night of the murder. He asks whether the victim could have poured his own drink even though he knows the answer.

"Yeah, yeah, no, I told you, the bartender. Every night he pours the boss a whiskey, puts it neat on one of them little napkins, leaves it on the bar."

"And then goes home," One the Gun says.

"Yeah, it's an agreement they have. When he spills his last slug, he's done. Every night. He pours the boss a short one, then he heaves ho. That's how he always puts it, 'heaves ho.' He's the one with the boat fix."

"The bartender?"

"Yeah, yeah, he talks kind of funny. He's back at the bar if you want to have a, you know, a palaver."

Moving off into the club, Gun tunes his eyes through the half-full scatter of tables straight to the spot where Three the Goatee should be sitting and drinking his martini, pinky all a-perch, if he's still alive.

It's empty.

Gun pulls in a deep glug of air and lets it out slowly.

He weaves through tables, through the cannonade of piano chords, heading for the bar.

It's true, right? If Goatee's not here, it means it must have worked, right? Now all Gun needs to do is solve the case, right?

At the leftmost edge of the bar, nursing her glass of something red, is the widow. Six the Kicks dressed to some sort of nines, still in mourning black, but this particular black, with its slink and sparkle, is doing a better job on her curves than her daywear.

And all the way to the right side of the bar is the preacher in his holy blacks, making slow communion with his whiskey. Bless us, O Lord, for these thy gifts. Gun wants to say a prayer of his own, that somewhere in this slog he'll come across the clue he needs. He's hauled his sorry carcass through most of this day already for nothing.

He bellies up to the counter and orders a Scotch on the rocks.

The widow is behind him right on cue. Her perfume wraps round him like the pink on an ice pop. "Put it on my tab."

They exchange their reintroductions, and she takes both their drinks, one in each hand, her tiny black beaded handbag dangling from her wrist, and he follows her across the room to the booth that's too damn close to the woman taking a meat pulverizer to the piano. They slide in, and she pushes his drink across the table. "I want to do all I can to help find the person who did this to my husband."

"I appreciate that." The Scotch is just as he likes it—fresh and medicinal, like the scent of the swab before the needle. "So, if I may, I'd like to start with the moment just before your husband went into the office at the end of the night."

And actually, he absolutely would not like to start with the moment just before her husband went into the office at the end of the night—a dead horse he's dragged out over and over, over the course of these too-many days.

"Well, it was just like always," she says. "He went to the front, told Four the Door he was closing up, then came back to the bar. I remember he said, 'What a Wednesday, my friends! What a Wednesday!'"

"What did he mean by that?"

"Oh, I don't know," she says, "I guess business was pretty good."

Is there a clue in that statement? What a Wednesday? Something to be gleaned from his good mood?

"And then?"

"He took the cash drawer from the register and went off to the office," she says. "I was at the bar chatting with Father Heaven. First Mate finished cleaning up and poured my husband his drink. Three fingers of the good stuff and a squirt of soda. Set it on the bar to mellow. My husband likes . . . liked . . . to let it mellow."

Is there a clue in the fact that he liked to let it mellow?

Is there a clue in the fact that the widow slipped up at first and used the present tense to talk about her husband?

No, Gun, they didn't fake his death to collect the insurance. This isn't a radio show.

Six the Kicks leans over the tabletop toward One the Gun, ticking her chin in the direction of Eight the First Mate across the room behind the bar. "He's always been jealous."

"The bartender?"

"Let me give you a little information," she says. "This whole place? Used to belong to the bartender."

"Oh?"

"Couldn't make a go of it," she says. "He was running it into the ground. No planning. All he did was think up ways to play ship captain. Pretend he was on a boat. Throw fishing nets all over the place. But he couldn't keep it afloat."

Her eyebrows bounce like she notices the pun.

"Anyway, my husband came along and bankrolled the club," she says. "Saved this place from ruin. And what thanks does he get? I think you know."

Gun needs to remember to focus on more than just looking for clues he may have missed. He needs to be looking for places where a clue that gets dropped is recognized by the one who dropped it. He needs to focus on the faces to find the moment when the realization happened: When the killer knew they would have to eliminate Gun too.

"First Mate thinks my husband turned his sweet little restaurant into a dive," she says. "He always resented it. And he wanted it back. And he knew if my husband was out of the way, it would come right back to him."

Across the club Eight the First Mate is mixing a drink in one of those silver shakers. What happened between Six and Eight to give her such a belly full of venom for the guy after their early connection with the magic act?

Does she resent the fact that he was always the star and she the assistant? Did he grow to resent the help she gave him by talking Five into buying the Dive, and did their relationship hit the rocks because of it? Or is she just a coldhearted crow who hopes a murder charge for the bartender means complete control of the Dive for her?

Or does she know something about Eight the First Mate she hasn't yet told Gun?

He finds his mouth opening to question this and quickly shuts it.

Focus, Gun, focus. Stay on script, listen for the things she doesn't mean to say, listen for contradictions, watch her face.

"And"—Six the Kicks sits back in her seat—"the cop told me he was poisoned."

"True," Gun says, "whether willfully or by accident."

Is it weird that she never presses the possibility that he could have been poisoned by accident?

"He said it probably came from the storeroom," Six the Kicks says. "The poison used to kill rats. Who do you think uses poison in this place to kill rats? The bartender. And who better to know all about poisons than someone who mixes drinks for a living?"

She's pushing it—and she's pushing his buttons. He's kind of pleased that he gets to move on to the part of the conversation where he gives her the business. "You said you saw the bartender pour the drink. You didn't mention seeing him put anything in it. And if you did see that but didn't question it, you may be complicit."

Okay, watch her face, Gun. Look for inklings of guilt.

"Well, no," she says, "but he could have. I wasn't watching him with an eagle eye."

"You said, 'Three fingers of the good stuff and a squirt of soda,'" Gun says. "That's pretty specific."

Her face doesn't change. "That's my husband's drink. And anything could have happened to it between the bar and the office."

One the Gun thinks either what she's saying is true, or she has as good a poker face as the preacher.

But here's another possibility to bring into the mix. If the suspect spills something they shouldn't, they may not notice when it happens. It could be later tonight that they realize and come up with the plan to make with the trigger.

And what of the trigger? This gun that wasn't found in Six's apartment, Four's apartment, Eight's apartment, Seven's quarters. What of this seemingly nonexistent murder weapon? Of course, the suspect could have had it on their person when Gun was conducting his searches. Of course, the suspect could have it on their person now.

The widow's black beaded handbag is sitting on the table. No way she could fit a gun in that dinky thing. Do beaded gowns have pockets? Probably not gowns that hug like hers.

Gun keeps going with the script. "Doesn't the bartender generally pour the drink and then take off? Doesn't someone else, maybe even you, generally take that drink to the office?"

Six the Kicks gets a suspicious squint in her eyes. "Generally. Doesn't mean he didn't take it on Wednesday."

"You saw this?"

She blinks and her eyes shift to the side. "Well, no. Doesn't mean he didn't."

Of course, it would be weird for the killer to have the gun on their person now, because why take it to the Dive in the first place? It's not like they knew, when they were getting ready to go out, that they would be wanting to kill a detective at the end of the night. Unless they planned it earlier in the day, but the only one who knew Gun was coming to the Dive tonight was the bartender.

The pawnshop's just around the corner. Could any of these four, upon realizing they need to eliminate a certain detective, slip out and come back with the gun? One the Gun scans the club like looking might give him the answer. Time does not want him to turn his head. Time pushes back. But he pushes harder. And look.

At the front door of the place.

The doorman is gone.

The surprise sends a little shock up inside him. That shock seems to temporarily loosen time's grip. He swings his head. The moose is not at the bar. The moose is not by the piano.

Is he standing outside like he likes to do at the end of the night? Is he in the restroom?

Time takes Gun's head and swings it back to Six the Kicks. He pushes ahead with the script. "I thought you were right there at the bar. You didn't see who took it?"

"After he poured it I went to the ladies' room to powder my nose."

"And you didn't take it yourself?"

Her eyes narrow. "I went to the ladies' room to powder my nose."

The piano is louder, clanking in his ears. The player hits a particularly brisk series of chords that makes the widow wince.

"The preacher—" he says.

"Preacher?"

"Well, priest. You said he was sitting with you at the bar. So he'll corroborate your statement that you went to the ladies' room?"

"Sure, I'm sure he will, yes." Six the Kicks is up, grabbing her handbag. Leaving her wineglass. "I can't concentrate in here. I'll come to your office if you have any more questions."

Time takes his hand and pulls a card from his wallet, gives it to her. They exchange the final pleasantries, a handshake, and he's heading back, past the woman giving a shellacking to the piano, toward the bar.

At the door the moose is still missing in action.

Also, where is the waitress with the doe eyes and the big teeth? He can't remember what time she arrived on that first night. She'd better not cross him up. She'd better be here.

Ten the When leaves the café, pulling her apron off and folding it as she goes. On script, she hardly has to think to make her body move. Time and her feet are stepping her home to change out of this work dress and throw on the frock she's supposed to wear to the Dive. All she wants to do is anything else—squeeze out another drop of joy from this life that is waning. What didn't she do yesterday when she was making a day of it?

Eat a sundae, visit a museum, ride a bike, fly a kite, shoot a picture, play a piano, pet a puppy, write a poem, catch a butterfly, hike a trail, see a play, play a game, pound a drum, pick a flower, plant a tree, ruin a cream sauce, pitch a tent, build a birdhouse, bury a treasure, kick a football, sing a song, save a life, take a nap.

She passes the dress shop with the red dress in the window. She wants to march in there and buy that dress one last time, change the window one last time, but she hasn't the time. Time is carrying her toward home so she can change out of this dress and into another dress that is not the red dress, and it's fine, it's good, she's going to go to the Dive so she can keep her promise and keep Gun on the path toward solving this case, if he hasn't solved it already, so he can take Granddad's advice to the other side.

Granddad. That's what she'd like to do, phone Granddad.

She'll do that. There will be time after the Dive. There'll be a little time.

***

ONE THE GUN RESTS HIS wrists on the bar top with his glass between both hands. He's questioning the preacher again, although all he wants to do is turn around and take another scan of the house, look for Four the Door—look, if he lets himself admit it, for Three the Goatee, who he shouldn't have to look for. Who's dead for sure, but he wants to look anyway.

Just wait, Gun. You're scheduled to turn backward in, oh, two minutes.

And speaking of dead, Gun is launching again into that dead horse: Tell me about the last time you saw the deceased alive.

"Well, let's see," Seven the Heaven is saying, "it was just like always. He went to the front to tell the doorman he was going to be closing up, and then he came back to the bar. I remember he said, 'What a Wednesday, my friends!' Then he pulled out the money drawer from the cash register and headed to the office."

Gun doesn't think any of this is going to get him his clue. "And then?"

"Oh, the bartender poured him his usual drink. A whiskey and soda. Set it on the bar."

"And then?"

A little shoulder bounce from the preacher. "That's it. That's all I saw. I went to the back room. I'd left my Bible in there."

"You bring a Bible to card games?"

"It's my lucky Bible," the preacher says. "I went and got it and then headed out for the night."

Is Three the Goatee simply home in bed with a bad headache, having drunk only a sip or two of the poison?

He says, "Was the widow still at the bar when you left to go to the back room?"

"I believe so."

Is Three the Goatee here right now, having skipped the tea altogether?

He says, "She didn't go to the bathroom to powder her nose?"

"I don't know. I suppose she could have done that when I left." The preacher thinks a moment. "No, I can't say I recall her doing that. If you're wondering if she took the drink to the office, she may have. Or the bartender may have. It's possible the doorman did too. I didn't see if the drink was still there before I headed out for the night."

One the Gun turns away from the counter, leans back with his elbows on it, and finally he can comfortably scan the room. Three the Goatee is, of course, nowhere to be seen. Four the Door is back at his station. No way to know how long he was gone for. Or where he went.

He's bidding a snappy salute to the waitress with the doe eyes and the big teeth. Good.

Six the Kicks is over in the corner past the piano, alone, picking up bouquets of flowers and smelling them one at a time. Swaying to the piano music. Light glitters on her dress.

"You seem to know the deceased's widow," One the Gun says. "Does she always dress that way?"

"In black? She's in mourning."

"But all fancy in like a thousand beads?"

The preacher shifts on his feet, looks toward her. "That's Six, always. Beaded gowns, jewelry, gloves, the whole nine yards."

"But in a dive?"

"Oh, yes, always," the preacher says. "That, to Six, is class. She's the reason the Dive's sailor costumes are full of beads and sequins." His chin nods toward the moose at his station at the front of the house. The moose wearing that bulky sailor uniform. So easy to conceal a pistol in that thing. "She got the doorman to wear gloves, too, told him it would make him look ritzy—and believe me, he'd do anything to appear ritzy to her."

Gun still has gloves shoved in his own pocket. Gloves are evidence. He's going to have to get rid of them. God, and the little poison packet. For cat's sake. Is he as good a murderer as he is a gumshoe, meaning third-rate? He scours the crowd again for Three the Goatee. He's starting to worry that less than an hour might not be adequate time to plan out a good murder. "Oh? Are you saying he's sweet on her?"

The preacher raises his glass. "'There hath no temptation taken you but such as man can bear: but God is faithful, who will not suffer you to be tempted above that ye are able.' First Corinthians 10:13."

There are a few couples on the dance floor now. It's time for the preacher to catch the eye of the three shady-looking guys at the game table and shove off to join them. Gun turns back to his drink, but it's empty. Piano music is a rollicking roll in his ears: Up and down, up and down, and always that crash of notes at the end of the measure like waves against a bow. Gun needs to stop obsessing over Three the Goatee and knuckle down on his investigation. A low-grade panic is starting to churn inside him.

The bartender comes over. "Can I get you another?"

"Thanks. Scotch on the rocks."

"You're that detective, aren't you?" Eight the First Mate pulls a bottle from the back wall and works on the drink.

Gun strains his neck for another scan of the house, of the suspects, of the absence of Three the Goatee.

He says, "I believe my assistant contacted you about an interview."

The bartender slides the new Scotch to him. "We can talk here if you don't mind an occasional interruption."

"Thanks, yes."

"Looks like we've got time now. What do you want to know?"

Gun takes a seat on the barstool. "I'm told this used to be your place."

And it's all well and good as Eight the First Mate waxes nostalgic about his little original restaurant, fish and chips with a nautical theme, but it's not long before it's time again for that dead horse of all dead horses, the question Gun asks just like always, so he can listen to the suspect answer just like always.

"Well," the bartender says, "it was just like always. He'd gone to the front to tell Four the Door he was closing up, and then he came back here. All I remember him saying was, 'Ah, friends, what a Wednesday!' Seemed very chipper. He took the cash drawer and went off to the office to count it. I poured him his usual. Three fingers of rye and some soda. Left it on the bar."

One the Gun wants to care about this speech, but it's just like always, and he's starting to think this whole scheme of sticking close to the script was completely worthless and he's wasted what might be his last good day in here.

A cocktail waitress in a sailor dress hands the bartender a tray with three empty glasses on it. He takes the tray, discards the empties, and hands her the tray back without a word.

Gun pushes ahead with the script. "You didn't take the drink to the office?"

"No."

"Did you see who took it?"

"No."

"The deceased's widow and the priest were sitting at the bar at the time," One the Gun says. "She says after you poured the drink, she went to the ladies' room. He says he went to the back room. Can you confirm either of these things?"

"Well, I just grabbed my coat and headed off. I suppose they could have as I was leaving. Sorry, I guess I wasn't paying attention."

One the Gun is paying attention, has been paying attention all damn day, and what has it got him? Panic is creeping up the walls of his stomach. He's running out of time.

The dance floor is full of dancers now. As the song comes to a particularly raucous end the dancers cheer and the customers at tables raise their glasses.

"It was his favorite song," Eight the First Mate says. Eyes wistful over his curled moustache. He reaches below the counter. Raises the fifty-dollar bill. Across the bar the piano lady gives a nod and starts playing the song again.

And dear god, One the Gun does not want to hear the song again. A whole day wasted. He doesn't know what to do. Could the clue have been dropped and he didn't even notice? Is he just too stupid? Someone killed him for a reason. That reason happened today.

Why can't he find it?

He hears himself thank the bartender and order another drink. He scans the house again. It's becoming even harder to move against time. He gives the bartender his business card. Then time is leading him to the table of the cute little trick with the turned-up nose who he flirted with on that seminal night. He doesn't care about flirting with her, here, at the end of this last-chance day, but he doesn't know what else to do.

And the flirting feels interminable. It seemed so quick and frothy on that seminal night, but here, as time ticks his chances down, and he listens to the needless charming quips that come out of his mouth, all he wants to do is run. But he can't.

Her dark hair is piled up on her head like a load of chocolate-dipped cream puffs. She says, "I just love candlelit dinners in expensive restaurants, don't you? They're so romantic."

At the door the waitress with the doe eyes and the big teeth is chatting with Four the Door, looking like she's on her way out. Gun didn't even notice her much while she was here. He probably could have let her have the evening to herself.

He tries to catch her eye, but she leaves without looking back.

OUTSIDE THE DIVE THE STREETLAMPS are on all down the square, thumbing their noses at the deep purple of night. Ten the When pulls the fresh air into her lungs. Her duties are over. The rest of the short time she has left to her is free. She heads right for the phone booth just inside the drugstore. It's late but she knows the drugstore's still open. It's late for Granddad, too, but she's going to call anyway, wake him up if need be.

She steps toward the drugstore.

She steps past the drugstore.

She tries to grope with her hand toward the door, but her hand won't obey.

In the dark of the alley just beyond, the cat with the black coat and the one white ear watches her go. But the cat can't do anything about it either. Because Ten the When is locked into the forward flow of time. She hasn't strayed from it at all since One the Gun gave her the business at dinner. Whereas Gun has been straying a little here, a little there all night, swinging his head to watch his suspects, to search the crowd for Three the Goatee, Ten the When has stuck to the script loyally, completely—and now she can't get free.

All she can do is let time carry her along. Past the drugstore, past the dress shop, past Gun's office, turning at the corner, heading up to her apartment building. Her shoes are a rhythmic patter on the stone floor past the phone booth in the lobby and onward to her destiny.

***

ONE THE GUN WATCHES THE suspects around him. In his chair he's angled so that he can scan the room and catch all four of them in one sweep: The doorman standing at the front door, the bartender filling orders and wiping tables, the preacher playing endless card games with those shady guys, the widow back at the bar, alone, hunched over a bit, and nursing a glass of red.

Gun can only manage a quick scan before time pulls his gaze back to the cute little trick with the turned-up nose. He flirts with her and then scans again, straining his neck muscles against time. He makes like casual but looks hard. Four, Six, Seven, Eight. Gun knows the suspects will all still be here when he leaves—that's how it happened before. If one of them goes missing in action in the meantime, it might mean they've slipped out to procure the gun.

He flirts with the cute little trick with the turned-up nose. Scans the room. They're all still here. He flirts with the cute little trick with the turned-up nose. Scans the room. They're all still here.

The piano lady has moved on to the rest of her repertoire, but she's still working the instrument over like a mugger in a back alley. Gun tries to watch the eyes of the suspects to see if they're watching him. No one pays him any attention.

He flirts with the cute little trick with the turned-up nose. Scans the room. Maybe the gun belongs to the Dive. Protection for the business. Maybe it's kept in the office. Maybe it's kept in the storeroom.

The piano lady folds up and someone switches on the radio. No one's on the dance floor now. More tables are empty. The doorman stands alone at the door, gazing out. The preacher is bent over a handful of cards in his circle of gamblers. Not far away the bartender is clearing glasses from a vacated table.

The widow is still at the bar, staring at a half-full glass of wine. Maybe she doesn't want to go home alone. Maybe she's waiting to follow Gun to his death.

To hell with it. He's going to go up to the suspects one by one and search them. If one of them has a weapon, he's going to find it.

He tries to stand. Time has him magnetized to his seat. The closer he gets to the end of the night, the harder a hold time has on him. He grabs the end of the table, hefts himself up. Collapses back down. The cute little trick with the turned-up nose slants her head at him.

"Well, anyway," she says, "I just love moonlit walks on the beach, don't you? They're just so, I don't know, shiny."

He listens to himself talk about moonlit walks on the beach.

He listens to himself talk about boat rides on the river.

Someone at the game table must have hit something good because the men erupt in whoops and groans. Gun has finished another drink. Bits of ice melt in the bottom of the glass.

"Shall we have another round?" she asks. And he does what he did on that seminal night, politely begs off and pulls out one of his business cards, tells her to give him a call at the office sometime.

The doorman at the door, the bartender wiping down a table—say, wait a minute. Neither of them could have followed Gun to the office, could they, because both have to stick around to close up. For cat's sake, does that narrow the suspects to two? Because whoever killed Gun had to have followed him to the office at the end of the night, right? To know where he'd be in order to kill him there. Sure, Gun gave each of the suspects his card; sure, they all know where his office is—but why the hell would anyone expect him to go there tonight? It's way beyond working hours.

The cute little trick with the turned-up nose is pouting as she puts his card in her pocketbook. "Oh, why couldn't we have just one more little drink?"

"I'd love to," he hears himself say, "but I've got to get some work done at my office."

Oh, yeah, that.

And then just in case one of the suspects might not have heard, she raises her voice in a whine. "Your office? Who goes to their office in the middle of the night?"

One the Gun stands. Tells her he'll give her a call sometime. Time is leading him to the door, where Four the Door grins down and thanks him for coming by. Is there any hint of menace behind that big vacant grin? Gun is a chump to think the moose wouldn't leave his post to follow him to the office. If the moose is a desperate killer aiming to dish the detective the deed to a cemetery plot, the last thing he's going to worry his pretty little head about is the Dive. Plus, look: The place is clearing out early tonight. Maybe in deference to Wednesday's tragedy. Who's to say it won't shut down with plenty of time for the moose or the bartender to head to the office?

"Have a good evening," the moose says.

"I will," Gun says.

It's debatable.

OUTSIDE IT'S QUIET. HIS FEET turn in the direction of the office. The pavement is mottled shadow and dim streetlamp amber. Storefronts are dark all along the square.

He tries to will his body to stop. His fists clench, but his feet keep walking.

The suspects and clues are behind him now. He failed. All he can do now is somehow break this time spell and stay the hell away from the office. Ride the night out and go into tomorrow as the third-rate gumshoe he'll always be.

Unless.

What if all he has to do is go to the office and listen to himself reciting the details of the day into the dictation machine?

Everything he just experienced he will soon be reciting into the dictation machine. That's what happened on that seminal day.

And maybe while he's reciting the killer will be there, too, lurking outside his door. Listening. Trying to find out whether this detective knows anything, whether this detective is a threat. And maybe One the Gun blurts out the clue that could prove the killer is the killer, some clue that causes the killer to decide Gun must be eliminated.

Could this be the way it all went down? The way it will go down tonight?

Remember, Gun, you found out from that drunken superintendent that unless the killer were to hike himself up some electrical pole and cut some wire—something a layman wouldn't know how to do—the power outage was a coincidence. Which points away from the scenario of the killer cutting the power to lure you down into the basement. Which points, again, toward the scenario of the killer listening outside the door and following you in the dark.

The clue is there.

Now Gun hears what sounds like footsteps somewhere behind him.

Faint enough that he could be imagining it.

Just like on that seminal night, Gun turns back, peers down the block. Dark shapes and shadows. There are too many nooks and crevices along this street, recessed doorways, alleys to duck into.

In a flash under streetlamp gold, the cat with the black coat and the one white ear scurries out from an alley and across the sidewalk, a tiny figure bounding through the empty street and to the other side where it keeps going, off toward the monument of the man on the leaping horse that stands at the very center of the square.

Time carries One the Gun along. To his office building. To the elevator and up to the sixth floor. All down the hallway the office doors are closed, the glass dark.

Gun reaches his office, opens up, goes inside, and closes the door behind him. Time controls these movements, but all the while he's thinking: What does he have that he can use to defend himself? All he sees are papers and books. There's the pyramid-shaped paperweight over there on the bookshelf. Could he even heft and wield the thing in his state? He tries to listen for someone moving outside. Someone coming down the hall. Nothing. Time carries him across the room.

But wait. On his desk something is different. There's a box sitting on the open appointment calendar. On top is a note in Two the True Blue's small, precise hand:

A woman dropped this off for you. She said she thought you could use it. I think it was the waitress from the café. —2

A slug of energy zips up inside him. He doesn't know if it's this burst of adrenaline or the simple fact that he has encountered something different, something off script, but in this moment, time's grip loosens. His hands feel like they're dragging through sand, but he grabs the box. Snaps the tape, pulls open the lid.

It's a pistol.

Fingers that don't want to move grasp it, lift it out. The weight of it in his hand.

Lord. He gave her the business for being out and about, and here the waitress had been delivering him protection.

He tries to hold on to the thing, but it slips from his grip and clunks onto the desk.

He makes a reach for it again. His hand only moves a couple inches, and then time tows the hand over to the dictation machine. A finger presses a lever, starts it humming.

No, it's okay, he's okay. The gun is there, close enough to grab if he needs it.

One the Gun's hand feels more relaxed settling back into time, taking the horn and bringing it to his mouth. Time sits him down. He hears, and feels, himself recite: "Notes on day one of the Five the No Longer Alive matter. Interview number one. Met with Four the Door at the café."

Locked in this close, he hardly has to think about what to say. The words form in his brain and pop out of his mouth.

"For expense account: Lunch of one hamburger with grilled onions, one cup of coffee . . ."

The script unspools out of him. As he speaks he tries to reach for the pistol with his free hand—and it's so close, just a couple feet away—but his hand is anchored to the desk now and only twitches.

He's going to have to be able to grab that thing as soon as he finds the clue. How does he think he's going to be able to reach it, let alone aim it at a killer?

He needs something to keep himself not quite locked in.

Gun tries to tap his foot under the desk. At first it won't move. Then it does. A tiny, almost imperceptible tap, then another, slightly larger, then another, larger. Feels like there's an iron weight on top of it.

But when he's tapping that foot, does the rest of his body feel less encumbered too? He tests his free hand. Lifts it from the suck of the desk surface. It's still like fighting against some unseen force, but yes, keeping that foot tapping, keeping something moving, as hard as it is, keeps him less tethered to time.

"Four the Door has an unnatural aversion to being low-class," his mouth is saying. "He kept correcting me if I called it the Dive, and he kept talking about how he's an ambassador in a fancy uniform. He also seems to have a yen for Six the Kicks."

Tapping his foot. Listening across the room for sounds out in the hall. Listening hard to the words that come out of his mouth.

Time streams onward. Gun is feeling pretty good about himself right now. He's going to find the clue, set his tapping foot to walking, and get the hell out of here.

"Seven the Heaven is pure sleaze in my opinion. The doorman claimed he spends his nights duping the gamblers out of money in the back room of the Dive, and when I questioned him about it, he basically admitted it."

Gun recites and recites.

Tapping, tapping his foot.

Trying, trying not to notice how tight a hold time still has on him.

IN THE SHADOWS OF HER bedroom, in her bed, Ten the When lies looking at the ceiling.

She doesn't know how long she has. The world feels thin, like bread dough stretched to near transparency.

But look. She has her eyes open. She's awake. On that seminal night she had been sleeping, had been awakened by the crash in her chest. The pain had flung her eyes open, and she'd gasped for breath. Lurching up from her blankets. Watching the darkness of the room bleach out white before the day turned over on itself.

She doesn't understand why she's awake now. She couldn't stop herself from walking home from the Dive, couldn't get to the phone booth to call Granddad, yet here she is, finding traces of moonlight hugging the crags in her ceiling. When guesses she can be proud of that, at least. She has a will strong enough to keep herself awake.

She wants to be at peace. Doesn't everyone deserve to be at peace before they go? But she didn't get what she wanted. She's not a lawyer, and she's not a hero.

The quiet surprise of a laugh quacks up from her chest. She'd always smiled to herself about Gun's juvenile desire to be the big hero, and here she is wanting to be a kind of hero herself. Save the day. And for reasons probably just as egotistical as Gun's.

Hell, why did she ever think she could change him for the better? With a few silly lectures? She's pretty sure nothing she said took hold. Otherwise, why would he have been so unreasonable about the carriage ride? Like his was the only day that mattered.

But there was the gift he gave her last night. And how he called her *friend*.

Maybe she at least helped save him. God knows with the way time has hold, he's not making it out alive without that pistol she bought at the pawnshop before the offending carriage ride. Well, that's her being egotistical again. He doesn't necessarily need it. Maybe he can keep himself from being pulled down to the basement. Maybe he's even already solved his case and jumped out of time and—but no. She's not thinking straight. There are no more jumps out of time, she's sure of it.

It felt so weird buying that gun. Holding it in her hand. Cold and heavy and terrible. Like what she'd bought him wasn't a tool for protection but murder. Not that Gun's a murderer, she's not wishing to save a man who could be a murderer. She pictures it: There Gun would be, at the end of the night in the basement, standing with the pistol trained on the killer.

Don't move, he'd say, *I have you covered.*

Aha, he'd say, *you thought you'd have the drop on me. But I had help from a friend.*

A cold dread seeps into When's useless limbs. What has she been thinking? Has time, which has hold of her body, dulled her thoughts too? If Gun's even close to as bad off as she is, there's no way he's reaching that gun.

She's the one who originally suggested he play the day through. She's the one who doomed him. Going along with his stupid obsession to solve this case, the stupid hero obsession. Why couldn't he have just locked himself in a room somewhere and waited for the hole to close up and the day to turn over? Why did he have to solve the case at all? What the hell is wrong with people and their priorities?

It's her fault. She's sent him to his death.

She has to do something.

She tries to get up. It sends a ripple through her body but nothing more. She tries again. Nothing. She strains her muscles, pushing against time.

She doesn't know what she can do if she does manage to move. How could she get all the way to Gun's office?

She tries again. Time is a boulder pinning her to the mattress.

But it's my fault, it's my fault. She strains, and a low guttural moan comes out of her mouth.

The sound sends a shock through her limbs, and for a moment she swears time's grip loosens.

Her voice. It's the power she has left.

She tries to open her mouth. It's glued shut.

She starts to hum. Some song she doesn't quite remember. She heaves her voice out. It's like wrenching wet cement from her lungs. The sound is shaky and flat, but she's making it against the odds, against time's clawlike hold on her. She comes to the end of the ditty and starts over. Louder.

She doesn't know what the tune is, doesn't care. Outside a car shushes by on the street. If she can keep humming, keep her voice moving, yes, see? She feels a stirring in her arms. She can almost move them.

She hums louder.

Now she recognizes the tune, something Granddad sang to her when she was a child. Some lullaby.

Her arm lifts an inch from the bed, drops. It's futile. Ridiculous. All she can do is hum. Louder and louder like the sound could somehow lift her. It whangs back into her ears, less a humming, more a moaning, and it creaks her mouth open so that the sound is pouring into the room from the hollow of her head. Pouring out, more a calling than a moaning, but a calling that rises and falls with the notes of the tune. A ludicrous, keening sound. She presses with all that she has, her arms against the bed, and lifts her back from the mattress. A good six inches from the mattress. Collapses again. Her throat pushing the sound out feels raw. This is useless. What a way to spend your last hour of life, wailing like a peacock.

A sudden sound in the apartment—her front door flinging open—sends a shock through her, and time's grip loosens more. She finds herself upright, forearms braced against the bed, head up in the room. Footsteps pound the floor, and now a figure shoots into the bedroom. Her neighbor, Zero the Hero.

Thank the lord she never locks her front door.

Her hero is in striped pajamas and his hair is sticking up. His eyes are wide. "What's wrong? What's going on?"

Somehow she never thought of calling for help. But here it comes. Her neighbor who always fixes her sink and shouted the countdown the loudest at last night's party, which seems so far away.

Her mouth is clumsy around the words. "Please. Need help."

"Are you sick? Are you in pain?"

But Ten the When has suddenly thought of the one way she could maybe save the day. "Hero," she starts.

"Zero," he corrects. He always does this. He prefers to be called by his first name. But she doesn't really notice.

"Hero," she starts again.

If the sound of her own voice, if the shock of her neighbor's arrival, can break time's grip, maybe sound can save Gun.

"Do you need to go to the hospital?" her neighbor asks.

"Can you just get me," she says, "down to the telephone?"

A SHRED OF MOONLIGHT THROUGH the window blinds falls across the telephone on One the Gun's desk.

"In my opinion the widow could have killed him as much as any of these other characters. I mean, she is one tough tomato."

Gun is leaned back in his chair, his body a picture of casual relaxation, but all inside he's tight as a stoolie in front of a lineup. His foot is working hard under the desk, *tap, tap, tap.* Is the killer listening outside the door right now?

"Then she comes right out and accuses the bartender. Gives him a motive: Apparently he used to own the Dive, and she thinks he wants it back. It does make sense. She claims he must have killed Five because he's the one who uses that same poison to kill rats in the place, and because apparently bartenders should have PhDs in poisons."

He tests his free hand again. It wrenches loose from the desk. The hand, the wrist, the whole forearm lifts a good six inches before it's sucked down again. If he can get free, will he wait to solve the case or just bolt?

"After interviewing the widow I talked a little more with Seven the Heaven. I asked, 'Does she always dress like that?' Apparently she does. Beads, jewelry, gloves, the whole nine yards. He said the reason the doorman wears gloves, too, is that he wants to appear ritzy to her—which, again, points to him having a crush, but it also means both of them would easily be able to take the glass—"

Wait.

A whoosh goes up through Gun. Time wants him to keep talking, but he clamps his jaw shut. Thinks.

Four the Door, gloves. Six the Kicks, gloves. Seven the Heaven, no gloves. But here's the thing. Eight the First Mate, no gloves.

The bartender does not wear gloves.

So why was the glass spotless? Sure, no prints from Five as he was found still wearing the gloves he always wore to count money. But why no bartender prints, or even smudges from when he poured the drink?

Gun saw that glass at the police station. It was pristine.

It was wiped clean.

Which Four the Door would have no reason to do because he was wearing gloves. Which Six the Kicks would have no reason to do because she was wearing gloves. Which Eight the First Mate would have no reason to do because even though he wasn't wearing gloves, everyone would know he touched the glass in the first place.

The preacher. After all this time it's the preacher.

But why?

There's no sound in the office but the hum of the dictation machine. Through the slats of the window blinds, the moon sits in cut ribbons in the black sky.

Time hiccups Gun forward in his recitation and starts him talking again, but he's not listening now. He lets the script run out of his mouth as he works the details out underneath.

The preacher's corrupt, okay. Doesn't give him a reason to kill the Dive owner. The preacher's a card sharp, maybe a compulsive gambler. Certainly doesn't give him a reason to kill the Dive owner. He doesn't have any stake in the business, doesn't have any designs on the widow. Gun once thought the preacher was blackmailing the guy, but you generally don't kill someone you're blackmailing. You kill someone who's blackmailing you.

Wait.

The letters hidden in the Bible. What if it was the other way around? What if Five was using them to blackmail Seven?

Okay, think this through. Seven wrote those letters to the nun. Yet Seven had them in his possession, hidden in his Bible. What if Five was the one who got hold of the letters, and he had been holding them to blackmail Seven?

Try this scenario on for size: Seven the Heaven is sweet on the nun Nine the Divine. They meet sometimes at the Dive. Five gets wind and offers to let them use his office with the chaise longue. Seven the Heaven writes her love notes inviting her to meet him for their assignations, but she can't leave these letters in her church quarters. She probably bunks with other nuns and surely doesn't want to get caught with evidence of such an un-nunly sin as sex. So she takes the letters to the Dive. To dispose of safely, or maybe Five has offered to keep them for her. Either way, Five gets hold of them and discovers a way to make some easy sugar.

This is starting to sound very plausible. Five had the preacher hooked good. Yeah, Seven was probably crooking the gamblers in the back room just to give the money right back to Five. That's a nice little turnabout of unfair play. Silence on the installment plan. Until Seven decides to eliminate his blackmailer.

Now Seven didn't mention any of this in his last letter to Nine. But he didn't need to, did he? Either she knew all about it and the subject was unspoken, or she was innocent and he was keeping it from her. Gun's thinking it's the former. That she knew and the whole sordid affair—the blackmail/murder one, not the love one—is why she left. What was it Seven said in his last letter? That he had written the letters to her and she now entrusted them to him. He must have killed Five, retrieved the letters, and offered them to her. And she refused them. One the Gun wishes he had the letter now—any of the letters—to look for other places to read between the lines, passages that seemed to say one thing but really say another, but who cares? He knows the preacher did it, and he's pretty damn sure he knows why. He's going to try like hell to rip himself off script and get out of here right now. Get far away from this place, ride the rest of the night through, and let the day finally, finally turn over, because he got what he came for—

Wait.

No, it doesn't all check out, does it? Because if Seven killed Five to get the letters back, how did he get the letters back? The poison took at least twenty minutes, Miss Blue said. The guy wasn't dead before Seven left the office. Seven wouldn't have gone in there, demanded and received the letters, and then killed Five. He wouldn't have gone in there, handed Five the glass, waited for Five to drink, then said, *Yeah, I just poisoned you, how about you give me those letters.* Seven surely didn't even know where the letters were kept, in the office or somewhere else at the Dive or at Five's home or in some safety deposit box.

No, no, nuts! It doesn't check out.

It goddamn doesn't check out.

Unless Seven had help.

Okay, yeah, that could be a possibility. The preacher kills Five and then one of the others retrieves the letters for him. But again: Why?

Maybe Seven was coerced. Someone wanted Five dead, didn't want to be the one to do it, knew about the blackmail, and essentially, well, further blackmailed Seven into doing the deed in exchange for returning the letters. That would check out, wouldn't it?

If the letters were kept at Five's home, it sounds like the widow. If the letters were kept at the Dive, it sounds like the bartender or the moose. Don't forget the moose is the nun's brother. That might figure somehow. Then again, it might not.

So One the Gun is back to square one. Or at least square two. And he's coming to the end of the line.

Across the room the glass pane in the door is blank, showing nothing but the wall beyond. Gun listens to himself saying something about Eight the First Mate tipping the piano player to play that stupid song. He hasn't been listening to the script as it's been tumbling out of him. And god. He's forgotten to tap his foot.

When did he last tap his foot?

He tries to get it started again. It feels like it's glued to the floor.

Now the lights go out.

Alarm crashes in his chest. He drops the horn of the dictation machine. Gropes for the pistol. His hand reaching for it feels like a dead hand. It brushes the gun. The gun clatters to the floor somewhere in the black.

All wrong, this has all gone wrong.

As on that seminal night, he fumbles along the worn spines of books on the bookcase until he finds the flashlight. A beam of light cuts the dark.

He tries to angle it down to the floor, to the gun, but time won't let him. Time makes him walk across the room, following the bobbing white sphere, which zeroes in on the door, and then his hand is on the knob, turning, opening.

Stepping through, pulling the door shut, he tries to point the flashlight into the dark where the door was, where the killer might be, but time pushes him the other way down the hall. He can't stop. He's too caught up in it.

Down the dark corridor. His body is carrying him toward his death.

Somewhere behind him, muffled, is a sound like a telephone ringing in one of the offices. Too quiet to really catch his ear. His feet keep walking.

The telephone in When's hand rings and rings.

Here, half in and half out of the phone booth in her apartment lobby, in the arms of her sturdy neighbor, Ten the When feels the little bit of strength draining out of her.

Is she too late? Is Gun already in the basement? If he's still in the office, is the power still on? No, that wouldn't matter, the phones would still work. She can only hope that he's there and the sound of the telephone ringing in his ears has jarred him out of the grip of time.

He may pick up, he may not. He may simply run. Or he may lock his office door against himself and walk the floor to ride the time out.

She repeats her building's address into the receiver, hoping Zero the Hero can't hear the rhythmic buzz in the earpiece pressed against her ear. She doesn't want to hang up. The longer it's ringing on the other end, the better.

But she can't hold the phone any longer. Her hand trying to grasp the thing feels like a block of wood. She can't think of anything else to say. She says, "Thank you. I will," the words stiff in her mouth.

A weight pulls her arm down and drops the phone from her grip to clunk and dangle from its cord. She looks up at her neighbor, his gray beard shadow, his concerned brown eyes.

"Ambulance is on the way." She hopes her voice obscures any tiny buzzing he may hear emitting from the hanging phone.

"Here," Zero the Hero shifts her in his arms and makes a reach for the phone. No, please let it ring, she thinks, but before she can say anything, he grabs the receiver and, still speaking, hangs it up. "Let's get you to that bench over there. Relax. It'll be okay."

He's shepherding them out of the phone stall. Her arm dangles from her shoulder, useless now. It gets her goat a little, being made to feel like a damsel in distress. Carried by a man. A hero. She doesn't want to die a cliché.

He carries her to a wooden bench across the way and lifts her down. She's scared she'll slip over, but the cold wall at her back holds her up. He sits beside her.

Has she saved Gun? Or has she lost her last chance to do something good in the world?

It's too much effort to turn her head, so she says it to the wide, quiet stretch of the lobby, "Hero?"

"Zero," he corrects, force of habit.

"I have something important to tell you. Will you listen? Listen hard?"

Zero the Hero sounds confused. "Sure, When."

"My granddad used to say." Time doesn't want her speaking, but she forces the words out. "Any person can be redeemed. If they can look at their own guilt. And really, truly want to change."

"Okay."

Urgency is a balloon rising against her ribcage. "Hurry. What are you guilty of?"

"What?"

"Granddad says everyone's guilty of something. Any person can be redeemed. Look at their guilt. Really, truly want to change."

And of course she does know what her neighbor feels guilty of. If she's honest with herself, her lawyer brain—her wishful hero brain—has logged all sorts of feelings of guilt in her friends and loved ones that she wanted to fix, to eradicate, to make better in a Granddad sort of way. And she hopes she did, at least for some of them, while she had the chance.

"I don't know," her neighbor says.

"Your son," she says.

Her neighbor hasn't spoken to his son in seven years. She doesn't know what the rift was, just that he's said how bad he feels about it, yet he's been unwilling to break the silence.

"I," he says, "that's not—"

"Can you remember? What Granddad said?"

Quiet beside her. She starts to try to turn her head, but it takes too much effort.

"Can you recite for me? What Granddad said? So I know you remember?"

Another beat of quiet. "Well, uh. Everyone can be redeemed?"

"If?"

"If they know their sins and want to change?"

Close enough. "Hero," she says. "Promise me something. If I die—"

The bench creaks. He's starting to stand. When's body slumps sideways, and he sits again fast. Her shoulder into his. He twists, hands on her shoulders holding her up, his eyes wide.

She smiles. "My dying wish. So you have to do it. Promise."

"I . . . okay?"

"Call your son."

THE FLASHLIGHT BEAM RUNS SHADOWS along the dark corridor walls of Gun's office building. Time pulling him ever onward, Gun tries to listen for footfalls behind him. He steps by the dead elevator, and there at the end of the passage is the door to the stairwell that leads to the basement.

Who's waiting for him down there? Or who's following him right here, right now? The preacher or his accomplice? Four the Door, who may have slipped out to the pawnshop earlier in the evening to buy a gun? Eight the First Mate, who may have had a gun at the Dive under the counter or somewhere in the storeroom or—

The storeroom.

The flashlight beam banks off the pane of glass in the stairwell door that is suddenly right in front of him and blinks in his face like the idea that has just gone off in his head.

The poison.

He said it probably came from the storeroom. The poison used to kill rats. That's what the widow said the cop had told her. But that was a lie.

Why did you disclose to one of the suspects that the method of murder was poison? Gun asked Detective Clinko down at the station on an earlier today.

May have been poison. Four little words, that's all I said, Gun.

The cop told her nothing about rat poison specifically and nothing about the storeroom. She lied. And the only way she'd know it was the poison kept in the storeroom was if she was in on the whole thing.

The widow and the preacher, in it together.

He figured it out. One the Gun figured it out at last.

Standing here in front of the stairwell door, he wants to stop and take the time to rejoice in the first-rate gumshoe-ness of it all, the hero-ness of it all, but his free hand pulls the door open and he steps inside. Starts down.

The widow and the preacher, in it together. She probably worked both ends to the middle. She's that coldhearted, at least so it seems to Gun. The way it stacks up to him, she found the letters, found out about the blackmail, and both hated her husband for it and decided to get in on the action. She wanted her husband dead, probably for more reasons than that, but didn't want to do the deed. So she put the squeeze on Seven, told him, *You kill Five, and I'll get your letters back.* Figuring if either of them went up for the crime, it would be Seven. He was the trigger man, so to speak. Then she chose the rat poison from the storeroom, because if Seven didn't get pinched, it would be Eight, who she'd love to get out of the way.

The widow and the preacher—Gun has no idea which one of them, maybe both—might be gunning for him now.

Skip it, who cares? He has to untether himself from time. That's all he has to do. He can ride the night out and turn this day over to tomorrow, the real tomorrow, where glory and Miss Blue await him if he can just untether himself enough to get off script and get the hell away from here.

The sound of his shoes on concrete echo in the enclosed chamber: *tack, tack, tack.* A turn at a landing and down. He can't tap his foot while he's walking, of course. He struggles to pull the fingers of his hand from the railing. Starts to tap it with his hand.

Just a tiny movement at first, but as he goes it gets easier.

A turn at another landing and continuing down.

Tapping, tapping his hand.

He has to concentrate everything on that hand to keep it going.

The flashlight paints a ghostly glow of reflected light along the edges of walls, the ceiling, and stairs before him. The bobbing sphere of concentrated light in the center and farther down is like a target he's pointed at.

Is the killer below him or above? He doesn't remember

hearing the door close at the top of the stairwell. He tries to listen for someone following. Sound of his own footsteps: *tack, tack, tack.* Sound of his hand on the railing: *tink, tink, tink.*

But why would someone follow him all the way to the basement? They wouldn't, would they? They'd kill him in the stairwell. They'd kill him in the hallway outside his office. There'd be no reason to wait. Which means the killer's in the basement.

And now he's almost there.

Panic floods him. Should he try to jump out of time? Start this day over? Is that even possible now? And if he does, and the hole closes up, what then? He can't think. There's a door in front of his face with red stenciled letters reading *Basement*. He doesn't have any railing to tap anymore. The hand reaches out and grabs the doorknob, twists, pushes into the room.

Strong smell of must and dust. Something metallic. It's blacker in here. The space is so wide the flashlight beam disappears into the dark. He tries to scan with his periphery to catch a glimpse, a shadow of who might be waiting. Time sweeps the flashlight beam around casually, like this is just any normal night where the power has gone out in the building.

He fights to make a fist with his free hand. His fingers curl, the press of the muscles, then he lets go. Tries again. Gets further. Lets go.

He has to keep it moving.

As he steps farther in, flashlight scanning, the basement materializes around him in pieces. A post running ceiling to floor with a fire extinguisher mounted to it. A big industrial mop bucket on wheels. A cot with a bedroll over there at the end of the room where the fuse boxes are starting to appear in the faint light coming in from a ground-level window. The fuse boxes where he knows it happens.

Gun makes a fist, lets go. The presence of the killer, or killers, somewhere in this dark whispers along his skin.

He has to jump out. Start the day over. He fights to reach down into him to rip himself away from the forward flow of time.

Go.

Go.

Go.

But he's still walking.

His eyes are getting used to the dark. Shadows find shape. The dim edges of a cabinet on one wall, a box against the other below the window. He doesn't see the shape of the killer because the killer is somewhere behind him. He knows this because he knows he gets shot in the back. The killer is probably in place with the gun aimed and ready. Gun makes a fist with his free hand, lets go. Makes a fist, lets go. It's getting easier. He tries to listen for the sound of the killer and hears nothing.

If the killer got him to the basement, why do they wait for him to get all the way to the fuse boxes?

The closer he gets to this death, the less it makes sense.

He tries again to reach down into himself to rip himself away from the forward flow of time, but time is not something he can jump out of anymore. He makes a fist, lets go.

His flashlight is making him a great target. Drop the thing, just drop it, but his hand won't obey.

If he can just get out of the way. Hide in the dark. Soon it will be midnight and a new day, right? Time will let him go, right?

Gun tries to reach for the flashlight with his free hand. He can hardly get the arm to move.

There's a sound somewhere behind him, a rustling of paper.

He's here, right in front of the fuse boxes where he knows it's going to happen. The flashlight does what the flashlight did that seminal night, angles down to the empty cot just beside him. Lights up the blue-and-white checked bedroll, the hole in the corner where some dollar bills are peeking out.

His heart whams his chest. He remembers the shot happens just after the flashlight beams on the cot.

The moment elongates. The light sprays across the cot.

And by god, he feels it: A rush of lightness runs through him as time's grip begins to let go.

Today is shifting to tomorrow.

Fast as he can, he tries to hit the deck.

He doesn't make it.

Crack of the pistol.

This time it takes him two inches to the left of where it took him on that seminal night.

Blast of pain. The blow, less centered this time, spins Gun backward. And in the moment before his hand lets go of the flashlight, the beam lights up a figure half lying not far away in a pile of newspapers—looking just roused from sleeping off a bender, gray hair sticking up, stained work shirt, pistol in one hand still aimed at Gun, and eyes wide with fear and fury.

From outside comes the first gong of the midnight bell.

It's the building superintendent. The old guy who interrupted Gun's stakeout that one night. Drunk on money he'd obviously gotten sneaking in and out of offices.

This broken-down small-time thief, this is who killed One the Gun.

The flashlight drops from his hand.

He collapses onto the floor on top of more bills and some stray coins that have fallen from the secret stash in the super's bedroll.

Another chime of the tower bell.

What a goddamn stupid death.

Not about his beloved mystery at all.

One the Gun's breathing grows shallow.

And outside on the street, having had a grand day of slinking and skulking and mousing and napping, the cat with the black coat and the one white ear makes one last leap off the curb and into a rush of blinding white headlights.

And down the square in the lobby of Ten the When's apartment building, Zero the Hero sits on the bench with When's body cradled in his arms. He thinks he can feel her breathing, but he's not sure. His eyes blink toward the lobby doors, looking for the lights of the yet-to-arrive ambulance, then down to his wallet sitting on the bench beside her and open to the photo of his son she was admiring just before the pains shook her body.

And the tower bells go on chiming.

TWELVE

It's quiet as he opens his eyes.

Now he is standing.

He doesn't remember making a jump out of time, but here he is, not where he was before.

He does what he always does, force of habit: Closes his eyes, listens for another strike of the bell.

But he hears nothing.

He opens his eyes.

He expects the room to be spinning, but nothing is spinning. Nothing is nothing, it's all nothing. No walls, no ceiling, no room.

And Two the True Blue is not standing in front of him like usual. No one is.

One the Gun rolls his shoulder in its socket. No pain from a bullet wound. And time has indeed let go of him. He moves his hand in space, and it slips through freely.

Out of nowhere comes an unspooling of organ music.

Gun swings his head but can't figure out where the sound is coming from.

The announcer's voice calls, "Handi-luxe brings you another transcribed tale of crime and justice as it asks the question: Who! Is! The Villain!"

More organ music. First the drone of a single bass note that starts at Gun's feet and spreads out around him in all directions. A floor where there wasn't a floor before.

Then chords grow and start to form shape. Notes tumble upward to make a surface, then bank a half-octave turn to create an adjoining surface. More chords—a D-minor seventh, an F diminished—reverberating into outline and plane, sound rising. The architecture of a room rising around One the Gun.

Tables, a wide desk, rows of bench seating like the pews in a church.

No. A courtroom.

Sound effect: crowd noise.

Sound effect: shoes walking across a polished stone floor, clop, clop, clop.

The waitress with the doe eyes and the big teeth steps into view. She is wearing a business suit, including slacks and a tie, and looks very different than usual, with none of the animation he generally sees on her face. She looks like he feels: dazed by confusion. Her eyes meet his, then blink around her, then land on the briefcase she holds in her hand like she doesn't know how it got there.

"We're dead, aren't we?" she asks.

A little zip jitters in his chest at that question. One the Gun does not want to be dead. If he's dead, then dead at least isn't the nothingness he expected it to be, but what about all that he was working toward in his life? What about solving the case and getting the girl?

Now a realization dawns on the waitress. Her eyes come back up to his, and they get big and full of something he doesn't know. Like eagerness, maybe, or wonder. She's quick to cross the courtroom to one of the tables set up in front of the long bank of empty seating. A triangular folded card on the table reads *Prosecution*. She thumps the briefcase down and snaps it open. Pulls out a manila folder. Flips that open.

Gun can see her face in profile as she reads. He can't tell what's on her face. It's mostly blank now. She turns pages.

He steps closer. Not close enough to read what she's reading. He's not sure he's ready to read what she's reading. He waits.

He starts to get impatient. "Well?" he asks.

She glances up. A beat. She looks back down. "It's what I said. We're dead."

Restless feet take Gun away from that statement to the far end of the other table, where he runs his hand along the edge, almost expecting not to be able to feel this object made of sound. The thrum of it purrs under his palm. "Maybe the day just turned over again."

"Did your day ever start this way?" She flips to another page. "You died. I died. Don't you remember the pain? The dissolution? The fade-out?"

Gun doesn't want to think about that. "Then what is this?"

She shrugs. "This is the thing that comes after the thing that came before."

"The hereafter?"

"It's funny that people call it the hereafter," she says to the papers. "It's after, sure, but it isn't here. Well, I mean, it isn't there. The after doesn't happen in the here that was there, so why do we call it that when we're still alive?" She turns a page. "All these places we imagine and put names to: heaven, hell, Valhalla, Hades . . ." She raises her head, looks around. "Bailiff," she calls.

A sweep of organ sound blooms from the floor beside her, minor chords and shivering notes in a rising scale that ascend into a human form. The waitress leans into this bailiff, starts quietly saying stuff, and from where he's standing, Gun can't make any of it out. He rolls his shoulder again. Maybe the hereafter works like they sometimes say, how you get to live your greatest dream. Just look at the waitress there with the bailiff, the way she holds up her chin and points to this and that in her stack of papers; she seems to grow more confident, more like a lawyer, with every murmur that comes out of her mouth muffled by the steady organ drone.

The bailiff never says anything, just snaps a nod at the end. The waitress says what looks like thank you and closes the folder. The bailiff melts back into the dissonant music of this place.

She turns back to Gun. "We have business to get to."

And yes, she's all business now. All lawyer, in her mannish slacks and tie, but he's not about to wind her up about it, not when he's finally, suddenly tumbled to this whole setup. The way this heaven could be about not only how she gets what she wants but how he gets what he wants too. And how they're in it together. He crosses to her table with the open briefcase and the little triangular folded card reading *Prosecution*. He leans in, talks quietly because even though there's no one but the two of them here, now, it feels like a solemn space that would want quiet. "Hey, whose trial is this? Because I think there's something you need to know."

She snaps the briefcase shut. "It's yours, Gun. I told you I'd give you a trial."

"Well, but," he says, "there's something I learned last night that—"

"Of course, but please, first we'd like you to have a seat."

Gun turns, and across the floor is the witness stand, its surface humming softly with organ chord. He moves toward it, steps up behind its partition where a chair waits. Next to the witness stand is the judge's bench, and at this added height he can see over the partition and into it, where the cat with the black coat and the one white ear sleeps curled on the judge's chair.

"Mr. Gun." The waitress lifts her voice toward him. "If I can have you come here."

She looks annoyed. He hasn't been called to the stand. He doesn't know what he's doing. He steps down from the witness box and crosses back to the waitress with the doe eyes and the big teeth standing by her table.

She says, "If you could please take a seat over there."

She's doing that hand-out, palm-up thing where your fingertips point where you want someone to go. It's the second table just opposite the center aisle. Gun feels dumb. He follows her direction. Goes and sits behind the second table and awaits instructions. This trial is too strange. A woman telling him what to do.

There's a whoosh, and the figure of the bailiff materializes again beside the waitress. They lean their heads together, and then she bobs a nod, and the bailiff shrinks away in a flurry of arpeggios.

The waitress with the doe eyes and the big teeth walks into the open space between the tables and the judge's bench, folder in hand. Stands center stage.

"May I please have the complainant for the prosecution enter the courtroom," she says.

Sound effect: crowd noise, then a quieting.

Sound effect: shoes walking across a polished stone floor, clop, clop, clop.

Two the True Blue steps into view. She's not wearing the pale peach cotton skirt and the white blouse with tiny eyelet flowers. She's dressed in black. For a moment she looks Gun in the face, expression blank in the way blank can say other things, can say things like rage, then seats herself behind the table for the prosecution.

Bees stir in Gun's stomach. There's one of those little folded cards on the table in front of him, and he turns it to read. *Defendant*.

Gun is up from his seat. "What is all this?"

"It's your trial, Gun," the waitress with the doe eyes and the big teeth says. "I told you I'd give you a trial."

"But not like this."

She points the corner of the folder at him. "I was as surprised as you when I saw what was in these notes. There were things you didn't tell me about the two weeks we shared." For a moment she looks down, then snaps her eyes back to his. Her voice is low and cold. "You weren't who I thought you were at all."

Heat pushes up from Gun's chest into his face. He swings his head round like he might find some other defendant entering the courtroom.

The waitress with the doe eyes and the big teeth is making that hand-out, palm-up gesture again toward the chair behind him.

He sits. There's a hot weakness in his knees.

She opens the folder, pulls out one slice of paper, closes the folder, and lays the page on top. She walks with it back to Gun's table and stops just opposite him, so close he has to crane his neck to look up at her. She projects her voice like there's an audience in the seats, a jury in the jury box, but she's looking right at him. "The victim was found in the sorting room of the newspaper office."

Gun's throat closes on its own like there's a little mousetrap in there.

"Cause of death was determined to be poison," she continues, "an apparent suicide."

"Yes, suicide," Gun blurts. "The guy was disgraced, he was depressed."

He jerks his head toward Miss Blue at the opposite table. She's not looking at him. She has her face pointed straight ahead, her jaw clenched and her lips pressed together.

"I am here today," the waitress says, "to prove that the victim, Three the Goatee, was murdered."

Sound effect: crowd noise punctured with mutters of surprise.

Gun squeezes his eyes shut. Tries to reach down into himself to rip himself away from the forward flow of time.

"And that he was murdered," the waitress says, "by the defendant, One the Gun."

Gun is on his feet again, leaning over the table at her, his voice cracking. "This is a joke. What about that drunken custodian? What about the preacher and the widow?"

The waitress's face doesn't lose the calm, lawyerly, businesslike blankness. "They'll have their day in court. This is yours."

He finds the air in his lungs. He tries to laugh. "None of this is real at all! Because if I'm dead, and you're dead, what's she doing here?" He points his thumb toward Miss Blue. "She's not dead."

"I just subpoenaed her," the waitress says.

Gun doesn't know what the hell that means. He swings toward Two the True Blue, who still won't look at him. "Miss Blue, this is all wrong, you have to know, I—" Then back to the waitress. "What kind of lawyer are you? You're not a lawyer. You're a waitress."

"I'm prepared to testify." It's the voice of Two the True Blue, sounding ragged but weirdly steady. "On the day in question"—her face still turned away from his—"when Three and I were leaving the office the defendant called him back and made a point of showing him the poison. And threatened to go to the college to see him. It was a setup to make it *look* like suicide."

He's starting to feel sweat under his arms. "Not true! I was trying to be neighborly—"

"You and I both know," says Miss Blue in stony profile, "there's no reason to put the poison under a microscope. It's all in the pharmacopeia book. And even if you wanted it tested, why do it at the college? You were threatening him. You were setting him up."

"No, you have it wrong."

Her face swivels to his. Her color is wan, and her eyes are ringed with red. "How could you do this to a man who was nothing but good? How could you do this to me?"

Gun looks away, rubbing the back of his neck. It occurs to him that no matter how petulant Three the Goatee used to get at Gun's shenanigans, what Miss Blue said is true: He was good. Gun pushes this away. The guy was a liar, he was lying to Miss Blue, he didn't deserve her. Gun says, "I didn't do anything to you, Miss Blue. I would never disrespect you."

"All you've *ever* done is disrespect me!"

The ragged blast of her voice rings in his ears and makes his scalp prickle. She's never shouted at him before.

"Disrespect me, trick me, be inappropriate toward me. And now you've murdered the man I loved."

Her shout trails into a kind of croak. Tears draw lines down her cheeks.

He can't look at her. He pivots to the waitress and sticks out his chin. "Prove it."

The waitress looks at him a moment, then turns away and steps to that center stage spot again. Turns back round to face him. She raises her voice. "I call the first witness."

The word *witness* seems to echo even though there are no real surfaces in this place, just the architectural hum of organ sound.

Gun's eyes twitch around. Who the hell could possibly be a witness?

Something catches the edge of his vision, a twinkle of light. Some strange sphere floating down from above.

A bubble.

Like the bubbles that used to lift off and away when each day would circle back on itself.

Opposite from before, this bubble grows as it descends. Size of a grape, size of a plum, size of an apple.

Along the shifting surface of color and gleam across the sphere he can make out, like it's some weird little convex film screen, the figure of himself, the figure of Two the True Blue—they're in the office, and she's reaching for the book on the high shelf, and now Gun's watching himself step behind her, move his foot behind hers. A quick trip, and she's in his arms.

"What the hell!" he shouts. "What does this have to do with anything?"

"It's disrespect," the waitress says. "Didn't you say you wanted me to prove disrespect?"

"She slipped pulling down a book," he says. "She said so herself."

"I call," the waitress says, "the second witness."

Another bubble, another small, shiny movie of Gun playing the tripping trick on Two the True Blue.

"I call," the waitress says, "the third witness."

Another bubble, and this time he's watching himself kiss Miss Blue.

"Oh, come on," Gun says. "You know she wanted it. She was always being so coy. She led me to believe that—"

"This really is who you've become, isn't it?" The waitress shakes her head at him. Her face at first looks judgy but shifts into sadness. She turns away. "I call," she says, "the fourth witness."

Another bubble, another bubble. None of them pop or float away, they just bob around, playing his sins on repeat.

"Kissing isn't murder," Gun says. "Tripping a girl into your arms isn't murder."

"It's motive," the waitress says.

Another bubble: Gun in Miss Blue's apartment, his hands clamped on her arms, her face exquisite with fear.

"But I didn't," Gun pleads, gripping the edge of the table. "I stopped myself."

And now the bubble he really doesn't want to see. The one that seals his fate. It floats right in front of his face. Gun at the newspaper office upending the packet of poison into Three the Goatee's teacup.

He jerks back and the chair falls over behind him. "This isn't a real hearing," he blurts. "You're not a real lawyer. I don't have a lawyer. I declare a mistrial."

The lawyer with the doe eyes and the big teeth puts the piece of paper back in her folder. "See, normally a defending attorney is a needful thing, but apparently here, things are a little quicker and easier." She sweeps the folder toward the cloud of bubbles hovering round him. "Because we know exactly what you did."

"You don't know my motivation. You don't know what's inside me."

"But you do know, Gun," she says. "You don't need a lawyer for that."

A bead of sweat runs down the side of Gun's face.

The bubbles are lifting away, floating higher, but they still hover.

"This is a trial of the heart," she says. "All you have to do is be innocent, and you go free."

Gun whips his head around. He's getting the hell out of here. He goes to move out from behind the table. Something trips him and he goes over. Clatters into the overturned chair. A length of chain is running between his ankles now. Shackles. He's on the floor looking up. Just past the table, over his head, the two women are standing and looking down. Their faces judge him from above. The bubbles bob and sparkle over their heads. He tries to push to standing but goes down again. And up on the table, looking down on him, the cat with the black coat and the one white ear licks her paw and then draws it over the top of her head.

One the Gun crawls into the aisle between the two tables, tries to grab Miss Blue's legs, but she steps out of reach.

Now she and the lawyer are standing shoulder to shoulder in that center stage spot at the middle of the courtroom. *Thump*, and the cat with the black coat and the one white ear is down from the table and crossing to them, sitting at their feet. The three of them stare back at Gun with the judge's bench looming behind.

One the Gun's heart pounds hard against his chest. He fumbles one hand up to the corner of each table, gets his feet under him, and lifts himself up on shaky legs. The bubbles hover above the women in that center stage spot like carnival balloons in a hawker's hand. The courtroom looks too vivid, somehow. Like there's extra light all around him. He's afraid he might faint but tries with everything he has to stand his ground and take it like a man. He pushes his chin out at the lawyer, like dignity, like disdain. "And what is my sentence, Miss . . ."

She purses a little smile at him, cocks her head. "Yeah," she says, "I actually do have a name. In all the time you knew me you never bothered to ask."

His stomach feels like he swallowed a handful of tacks. He puts on a defiant look. "Well?"

The space around him looks strangely shiny and opaline.

"It's Ten," she says. "If you care. Ten the When. Although I'm thinking of changing it to Ten the Begin Again."

Without thinking he says, "I want to begin again."

Ten the When smiles, taps the folder against her free hand. "Doesn't everyone."

The thudding in his chest. To his left and right the tables are gone. Behind him the benches are disappearing. Organ sound receding. Nothing is left but the judge's bench and the women and the cat and him. And that strange light is closing in around them. A wall of color and reflection is closing in around them.

It's a bubble.

For a second One the Gun's eyes tick down, and the black, black eyes of the cat with the black coat and the one white ear come up to meet his.

And then the bubble is enfolding him as it closes in, leaving the judge's bench, the other bubbles, the cat, Ten the When, and Two the True Blue outside. Holding him inside.

He lurches forward, expects to bust through the concave, iridescent wall, but he bounces off. Lands on what he first thinks is the floor, but it's warped—it's just more of the surface of the bubble.

The bubble that's still closing in. The figures of the cat and the women are growing faint outside.

"Wait," he says, "I'm not a villain! I'm . . ." He pushes it out. "I'm sorry."

When's voice sounds muffled, but he thinks he detects something in it, something different from the coldness she's been projecting. Like what she says has hope in it. Or urgency. "Any person can be redeemed if they can look at their own guilt and really, truly want to change."

"I do," he calls. "Really, truly."

But when he tries again to break through the wall, he bounces off. Lands on his back, his elbows crooked against the slick curve of the bubble floor.

"Do you?" she asks, not like she doesn't already know. "Really, truly?"

Panic is a fist pressing up into his diaphragm.

He tries to stand, slips, and goes down.

Scrambles up, his hands flashing out in all directions, but all they find is the slick surface, and he's down again.

Sweat soaks his shirt and runs down his back.

The bubble is close now. The air feels thick.

He drags in a breath.

He screams.

Shrill and piercing, whanging off the walls and back into his ears.

He's on hands and knees, and the breath is raking in and out of him.

The bubble has stopped shrinking. Maybe he could stand up to his full height, but he's not sure.

His ankles aren't chained, he realizes, but it doesn't really matter, does it?

This weird iridescent prison. He can't see the others anymore. What he sees all around him is his own reflection, multiplied like he's inside some ghoulish spherical fun house.

And he is not what he wants to see right now.

He raises his voice to ask it again, his throat hoarse, "What is my sentence?"

As if to ask again might change the outcome, but all that's left to answer is the length of time. The punishment is all around him. Gun to the left, Gun to the right. Everywhere he looks his own eyes look back.

Sound effect: the lawyer's voice, "As long as it takes."

Sound effect: the hammering of the gavel.

As the bubble takes him off and away, its inner surface all light, all reflection, all he's left with is himself.

ABOUT THE AUTHOR

Gigi Little is a book designer and the editor of the regional best-seller *City of Weird: 30 Otherworldly Portland Tales*. Her writing can be found in journals and anthologies including *Portland Noir*, *Spent*, and *Dispatches from Anarres*, and she's the art director of the award-winning picture book *A Tree of My Own*. She lives in Portland, Oregon, with her husband, fine artist Stephen O'Donnell.

ACKNOWLEGMENTS

IF I COULD LIVE ONE day over and over, I still wouldn't have enough time to list out all the people who've contributed to this book or to me as a writer.

Thank you, first and foremost, to Mom, Dad, Edina, Frank, and Lizehte, for doing all the best things families do, in all the best ways. Thank you also, Mom and Frank, for reading the book and giving your feedback. And to Heather, my first writing buddy, with whom I first started writing "books" at the age of, what, ten?

To my husband, Stephen, for his love and support, for his expertise in fashion history that ensured that my characters would be dressed correctly, and for his artist's eye that helped me immeasurably with the cover art.

To Steve Arndt, writer, poet, ambassador to the Portland writing community. I'm a part of it because of you.

To my mentor Tom Spanbauer, gentle genius and noble soul, who taught and guided and supported and lifted up so, so many writers. You were what a hero should be.

To Kathy McFerrin, without whom, among other things, I never would have met Steve, without whom I never would have met Tom and many of the people I'm thanking now.

To my two writing groups who read and critiqued and helped shape this book through the years. The Gong Show: Bradley K. Rosen, Doug Chase, Holly Goodman, Brian S. Ellis, Christy George, Shannon Brazil, Robin Carlisle, and Kirsten Nelson. And the Henry Writers: Steve Arndt, Kathleen Lane, Liz Scott, Laura Stanfill, Dian Greenwood, Sara Guest, and finally Robert Hill, who was the first person I gave the manuscript to in full, who would have been the first person to read it in full, had fate not intervened. I miss you, Robert.

To the Forest Avenue Press family, and in particular editor at large Liz Prato and copyeditor Gina Walter who probed my words and punctuation and facts and clues with the fabulous fastidiousness of a first-rate gumshoe.

To Christopher Alexander, who gave me my first diary, that started me writing at the age of eight (and to his mom, Jeni, who probably actually picked it out for him for my birthday). I'd travel through time to see him again.

To the many generous, wonderful people who consulted on, offered advice for, blurbed, helped promote, or otherwise supported this book and me, including David Ciminello, Mo Daviau, Lidia Yuknavitch, Mark Russell, Kevin Sampsell, Kurt Baumeister, Michelle Carroll, Tegan Tigani; the Dangerous Writers including Sage Ricci, Diane Ponti, Colin Farstad, Kevin Meyer, Matty Byloos, Krista Price, John Hinds, Adam Strong, Domi Shoemaker, Wes Griffin, Hobie Bender, Lucky George, Allison Frost, and Margaret Malone (and too many more to mention); Frances Lu Pai, Nui Wilson, Carl Lennertz, Susan DeFreitas, Kerry Cohen, Brian W. Parker, Josie A. Parker, Jenny

Forrester, Shawn Levy, Virginia and Matthew Brandabur of Moss Rock Retreat, Ken Jones, Mary Jo Schimelpfenig, Keith Mosman, Jeremy Garber, Tove Holmberg, Jill Owens Leigh, Cindy McGean, Joe Rogers, Cathy Camper, Amy Bullard, Alex Bullard, Abby Baylie-Little, Shena Kieval, Mara Kieval, Peg Kieval, David Lambert, Kallan Dana, Nicholas O'Dittle, Michael Keefe, Mary Desch, Kelley Baker, Jonathan Stanfill, Hadley Stanfill, and Trixie Stanfill.

And finally, and most of all, to Laura Stanfill. Publisher, editor, friend. Literary powerhouse, purveyor of joy, giver of so much. Thank you for making my book better and for being my dream publisher through and through.

WHO KILLED ONE THE GUN?

GIGI LITTLE

READERS' GUIDE

RADIO SHOWS

OLD-TIME RADIO, OR THE THEATER of the mind, as it was called, is a wonderful art form to explore. You can find recordings in many places, including radioarchives.com, otrr.org, oldtime.radio, and YouTube. For detective-specific shows, try the podcast *The Great Detectives of Old Time Radio*, which airs shows in chronological order and archives them on its website.

The below list is by no means exhaustive but is a selection of many of the radio shows that influenced me as I was writing this novel.

DETECTIVE SHOWS

The Adventures of Frank Race
The Adventures of Philip Marlowe
The Adventures of Sam Spade
Barrie Craig, Confidential Investigator
Broadway's My Beat
Candy Matson
Crime and Peter Chambers
Dangerous Assignment
The Falcon
Jeff Regan, Investigator
Johnny Madero, Pier 23
Let George Do It
The Lineup
The Man Called X
The New Adventures of Sherlock Holmes
Night Beat
Pat Novak, for Hire
Pete Kelly's Blues

Richard Diamond, Private Detective
Rocky Jordan
Rogue's Gallery
Yours Truly, Johnny Dollar

Some of the protagonists in this list are classic gumshoes and some are not, but all solve crimes. And although not technically a detective program, one of the most entertaining crime-related shows of radio's golden age is *The Lives of Harry Lime*.

SCIENCE FICTION AND SUSPENSE
2000 Plus
Dimension X
Escape
Exploring Tomorrow
Quiet, Please
Suspense
X Minus One

AS AN ADDENDUM, FILM NOIR was another obvious influence on this novel. And these few films in particular:
The Big Sleep
Double Indemnity
Murder, My Sweet
The Set-Up

BOOK CLUB QUESTIONS

1. If you could live one day over and over, what would you do?

2. Would you do something bad?

3. If you had a name like the characters in this novel, what would it be?

4. Do you think Granddad's philosophy is true? Can anyone be redeemed if they can look at their own guilt and really, truly want to change?

5. Do you think One the Gun, notwithstanding the time loop, was destined to become a villain? Why, through the course of the repeating days, did Gun become worse while When became better? How much of their change in character (growth or decline) came from the power and privilege inherent in the time loop, and how much came from something else?

6. Toward the end of the book, One the Gun comes to a conclusion that he believes solves the mystery of who killed Five. Do you think he got it right?

7. Nine the Divine's involvement is very much left open at the end of the book. Assuming One the Gun's final deductions about Five's murder are correct, do you think Nine the Divine knew about the murder? Do you think she was complicit? Why specifically, and in what frame of mind, did she leave the church?

8. Do you think Four the Door, despite his temper, was as innocent as he appeared to be? Did he know of his sister's involvement? Did he know who killed Five?

9. Do you think Eight the First Mate actually did fight and kill the man in the tavern?

10. The author plays with the tropes of classic characters of old-time radio and pulp fiction in the book. In what ways was Six the Kicks a classic femme fatale? In what ways was she not?

11. Is Seven the Heaven a commentary on religion or is he a flawed man?

12. Do you think *Who Killed One the Gun?* is a feminist novel? Why or why not?

13. How does the shift in One the Gun's identity comment on historical pieces of art (movies, radio shows, and books) and who gets to be the hero?